MW01134344

QUANTUM PREDATION

ARGONAUTS

BOOK FOUR

IRIDIUM

PUBLISHING
A DIVISION OF

HOOKE
PUBLICATIONS

BOOKS BY ISAAC HOOKE

Military Science Fiction

Argonauts

Bug Hunt
You Are Prey
Alien Empress
Quantum Predation

Alien War Trilogy

Hoplite
Zeus
Titan

The ATLAS Series

ATLAS
ATLAS 2
ATLAS 3

A Captain's Crucible Series

Flagship
Test of Mettle
Cradle of War
Planet Killer
Worlds at War

Science Fiction

The Forever Gate Series

The Dream
A Second Chance
The Mirror Breaks
They Have Wakened Death
I Have Seen Forever
Rebirth
Walls of Steel
The Pendulum Swings
The Last Stand

Thrillers

QUANTUM PREDATION

ARGONAUTS

BOOK FOUR

Isaac Hooke

Text copyright © Isaac Hooke 2017
Published March 2017. All rights reserved.

www.IsaacHooke.com

ISBN-13: 978-1-5208-8379-3
ISBN-10: 1-5208-8379-X

Cover design by Isaac Hooke
Cover image by Shookooboo

contents

*To my father, mother, brothers, and
most devoted fans.*

one

Numbers. A perversion of numbers.

Rade sat in his office aboard the *Argonaut*. He was reviewing the bookkeeping via his Implant, going over the entries Bax, the *Argonaut's* AI, had made over the past month. One of his rules was: always triple-check anything where money was involved. Always. It was very easy for a station's maintenance worker to purposely over bill. Or for an AI tasked with bookkeeping to siphon a small amount off the top each month for itself, for that matter. Even though Bax was the vessel's AI, Rade wouldn't put it past the sentient machine to do such a thing.

In fact, Rade had heard about the AI cores aboard a few merchant ships that had made quite a business for themselves by secretly bleeding away profits from the owners, making enough so that when they were sent to be decommissioned for spare parts, the AIs were able to buy their deeds of title back from the dump. The last time Rade had checked the ship registry, he had noticed at least twenty vessels registered to the AI cores that ran them, with human crew complements of zero.

Each entry in the books was linked to the corresponding digital receipt or invoice. When he confirmed that everything was correct, he ran a quick analysis on the current year's dataset. He perceived a noticeable uptick in expenses after each mission, marking the times he had brought the Marauder class vessel back to dry dock for repairs.

Very little of those repairs had anything to do with damage taken during the mission, but rather were due to upkeep and maintenance costs. That was one of the problems with purchasing an older ship for so cheap upfront: he had to pay higher maintenance costs on the backend. Given the extent of those costs, it was a good thing he had the backing of a wealthy client like Surus to pay for them. Then again, all of those costs were tax deductible. Combined with the amortization expenses applied to the *Argonaut* herself, and the interest expenses on the loan, he very rarely had to pay anything to the taxman. The banks were a different story altogether, of course. If he ever wanted to ruin his day, all he had to do was glance at the huge monthly debt service.

A perversion of numbers indeed.

A notification appeared in the lower right of his display. He was receiving an incoming call from Fret, his communications man.

Rade dismissed the books and accepted the call. A holographic image of Fret appeared before him. He was seated at his station on the bridge next door. His posture reflected that: his arms floated in the air before him as if resting on an invisible table.

While he might seem rather ordinary while sitting, when he stood, Fret was taller even than Rade. Unlike the other male members of the crew, however, there was no hint of any musculature underneath the fatigues he wore while on duty, as he was the leanest man aboard.

"Fret," Rade said.

"Boss, I'm receiving an incoming call request from Talan," Fret said. That was a nearby station the *Argonaut* was passing by while en route to a meeting Surus had arranged with another Green operating in the area. "Voice only. We're close enough to enable a realtime link."

"Source?"

"A man named Muto Batindo," Fret said. "He claims to be a representative of the Kenyan government. According to the station records, he's an employee of the Kenyan consulate aboard Talan."

"What the hell does he want?" Rade said, mostly to himself. "All right, tap him in."

Fret winked out and a moment later a voice came on the line. "Hello?"

"Hi," Rade said.

"This is Muto Batindo of the Kenyan consulate in Talan," the voice continued. "Am I speaking with Mr. Rade Galaal of Unlimited Universe Security Consulting?" The speaker had a distinctly Kenyan accent.

"You are," Rade said cautiously.

"I was browsing your InterGalNet presence," Batindo said. "Your credentials are very impressive."

"What can I do for you, Mr. Batindo?" Rade said.

"I hear you can offer assistance to people who find themselves in a bind," Batindo said.

"Depends on what you mean by a bind," Rade said. "But I'll help you out, so you don't incriminate yourself on an insecure channel. We're not mercenaries, despite whatever impression you may have had while browsing our InterGalNet presence. We don't accept just any mission. Assassinations, kidnappings, gun running, those sorts of things, they're not for us. If you're looking to have us perform anything of questionable legality, I suggest you disconnect now while you're ahead."

"Thank you for the warning, Mr. Rade Galaal," Batindo said.

"Very welcome." Rade waited for the guy to disconnect.

The man didn't.

"So, now that you've passed my initial client screening," Rade said. "I'm still waiting for you to tell me what it is my team can do for you."

"My government has lost contact with one of its outposts," Batindo said. "We have also not heard from two tax collection ships that were sent to the planet. You're the closest for-hire vessel with reasonable armaments in the area. I would like you to transport me to this outpost so I can check on its status."

"Name of the outpost?" Rade said. "And system?"

"The outpost is called Kitale," Batindo said. "It is located in the Nyiki system."

Rade checked the map. "That's on the outskirts of known space. A pioneer outpost."

"Correct," Batindo said.

Rade considered the job. The current system didn't get many traders. It could be weeks before Batindo was able to secure another ride. Yet Rade didn't want to completely take advantage of the man, since it was obvious Batindo was worried something bad had befallen the outpost. Rade didn't blame him: pioneer colonies had high failure rates. Natural disasters; political strife; alien invasions; these and more were par for the course when living on the outskirts of human territory.

"We can do this job for one hundred thousand, standard currency," Rade said.

"Please, Mr. Rade Galaal," Batindo said. "You price yourself out of my range. And I prefer digicoins."

"You can pay the equivalent of one hundred thousand standard currency in digicoins, if you wish," Rade said.

"You won't budge on that amount?" Batindo said.

"Look, we're not the cheapest you can hire," Rade said. "But we're the best. If you don't want to pay, you're welcome to hire the next ship that comes by. It costs a lot of money to operate a starship. We have propellant costs. Geronium expenses. Oxygen and food fees. Maintenance and upkeep. Then there are the mechs we have aboard, which we'll put to use if things get rough where we are headed. Deploying those mechs doesn't come cheap. We have to pay for the booster rockets for the return trip back into orbit, not to mention any repairs needed after the operation."

"How about fifty thousand?" Batindo said. "With a provision for another fifty if we have to use the mechs. I am hoping they won't be needed where we are going."

Rade pursed his lips. "Sixty-five thousand without the mechs. With a provision for another thirty-five if we use them."

Batindo hesitated.

"We're the only ship in the area..." Rade said.

"All right Mr. Galaal," Batindo said. "You drive a hard bargain. Sixty-five thousand it is. When can I expect your arrival?"

"I'll have my astrogator change course for Talan station shortly," Rade said. "We should be there in four hours."

"Thank you," Batindo said. "I will wait for you in

departure bay five aboard the station."

"I'll expect ten K deposited in my account before we arrive," Rade said. "I'm transmitting my account information now."

"It will be done," Batindo said.

Rade disconnected, then tapped in Shaw. "Take us to Talan."

"You got it," Shaw replied. "What's up?"

"We have a new client," Rade said.

"Ooo," Shaw said. "Finally something for us to do. Other than ferrying Surus randomly around the galaxy pursuing dead-end leads. Have you told our alien employer, yet, by the way?"

"No," Rade said.

Shaw paused. "She probably won't take it too well."

"Probably not," Rade said. "Talk to you later, babe."

He tapped out.

"Bax, tell Surus to come to my office at her convenience," Rade said.

"Will do," the *Argonaut's* AI replied.

Rade thrummed his fingers on the desk, his mind wandering as he waited. He thought of the other planets he had visited on the outskirts of known space during previous missions as a security consultant, and as a spec-ops soldier in the military. Because of his track record for finding himself in the wrong place at the wrong time, his first reaction when he heard about a frontier colony losing communications with the rest of the galaxy was to assume something bad had happened. It could be a simple communications failure, but with his luck, it was probably alien contact.

I always seem to find myself in the middle of an alien invasion. It's like the universe has a fetish for introducing me to unfriendly aliens.

He dismissed the thought as random paranoia wrought of too many days in deep space. He had been to his fair share of frontier colonies. In fact, he had been stationed on a few during his tour of duty, and on most he had never heard a peep from any aliens. Then again, there were the other times, the outlier scenarios...

His gut was telling him this was a bad idea. And yet his mind promised him it was fine.

Follow your gut.

Normally he would have, but there was the small matter of the sixty-five K the latest client had promised to pay. Besides, if the colonists really were in danger, and the *Argonaut* was the closest ship in the region, he had a moral duty to help in whatever way he could.

He dearly hoped it wouldn't be in the role of first responder.

Surus arrived a few minutes later. The Artificial was the epitome of beauty with her high cheekbones and flawless skin. She wore her long black hair in her customary pony tail, like Shaw. Her tight fatigues accentuated her perfect figure, and Rade had to remind himself that he already had a woman, one who he adored very much. Besides, it was silly to be attracted to what was essentially a robot. Still, tell that to his hindbrain.

"Hello, Rade," Surus said.

Rade nodded slowly. The Artificial was merely the host for the Green Phant that resided within, the alien entity that referred to itself as Surus.

"Sit down," Rade said.

She did.

He wondered how to broach the subject. Probably

best to dive right in.

"So," Rade said. "Apparently a pioneer outpost owned by the Kenyan government has failed to check in. I was contacted by the Kenyan consulate in Talan, and asked to investigate. I agreed."

Surus frowned. It looked strangely wrong on that normally serene face. "Why didn't you consult with me first?"

"Because it's my security company?" Rade said. "And my ship? It's not like you have anything else for the team to do at the moment. And you already agreed we could take on other clients when we weren't busy hunting Phants."

"But that's just it," Surus said. "We're currently hunting Phants."

"Really?" Rade said. "That's news to me. Where's our latest lead?"

"We don't have one," she admitted. "But I mean, we need to remain open in case news comes in from one of my eyes and ears."

"We haven't had anything to do for the past three months," Rade said. "You've been paying us to idle. Look, my men need something to do. Besides, it'll take three weeks, a month tops to detour to the outpost. You can't tell me you expect to receive news of a Phant over the next month?"

"It's possible I just might," Surus said. "You know we have to be ready to jump on the news when we do. We can't allow the trail to go stale. Phants can be very... evasive, to say the least. Especially when they realize they've been uncovered."

"Well, I'm going to have to overrule you on this one," Rade said. "Come on, aren't you the least bit curious why the colony lost contact?"

"Intergovernmental politics within sub-nations do

not interest me," Surus stated.

"So just because Kenya as a nation state is not a major galactic player, even though one of its outposts is potentially in danger, you consider them too small and unworthy of your attention, is that it?" Rade said.

"Something like that," Surus said.

"Well, they're offering six months pay for basically a month's work—a week and a half to fly there, and a week and a half back. I plan to distribute the money to the men as a bonus, on top of what you're already paying us."

Surus didn't answer for several moments. "It's probably a simple malfunction, you know: problems with the comm nodes stationed at the Slipstream."

"Probably," Rade said. "If so, then we've made an easy sixty-five K."

"That's only three months pay," Surus said. "You just told me six months."

"Yes, it'll be six if I can figure out a way to incorporate the Hoplites into the mission," Rade said.

"I see."

"I don't know why you're so upset," Rade told her. "What's the difference between drifting through a bunch of unrelated star systems for a month, and traveling somewhere with purpose for that month? There isn't any."

"The difference is simple," Surus said. "By accepting the contract, you've forced us to complete it, no matter how long it takes. Whereas if we were simply drifting between star systems, as you call it, we could drop what we were doing at a moment's notice to pursue a lead." She hesitated, then added: "And frankly, I don't want your team risking their lives if this proves to be more than a comm failure. Especially if it's some petty internal conflict between rebel factions.

9

I need you and your men to stay alive. We have far more important matters at stake, such as the protection of the whole galaxy. The security of some tiny, relatively unimportant nation matters little in comparison."

"Oh, we're going to stay alive, don't you worry on that account." Rade regarded her uncertainly. Then he nodded to himself. "I think I get what's going on. You're scared of losing control of my team. You're happy having us just drift back and forth aimlessly because it makes you feel like you're in control, and doing something."

"That's not it at all," Surus said. "I already told you it's because of the restraints on our freedom: it affects our ability to drop what we're doing and pursue any leads that come our way."

"Well, I'm going to hold you to the promise you made when we first signed you as a client," Rade said. "And that was: we were allowed to take on other jobs, at my discretion. That latter part is key. *My* discretion. Besides, maybe this incident is related to a Phant. You never know."

"Doubtful."

"And yet there's always a chance," Rade said. "Because we all know that Phants can easily hide within any machine, even the AI core of a starship." Hiding in AIs wasn't possible on all ships, of course. Most United Systems warships had had their AI cores shielded since the First Alien War; the *Argonaut* itself had a shielded core.

"Fine," Surus said. "Will you at least let me continue with my originally planned rendezvous?"

"With the Green in this system?" Rade asked.

"Yes, of course," Surus said.

"I can do that," Rade said. "After we pick up the

client from Talan, we'll swing past the asteroid we were tracking earlier. You can have your meeting, and then we'll reverse course to the Slipstream and continue toward the Kenyan colony."

"Thank you," Surus said.

"You weren't expecting this Green to give you any leads in person, were you?" Rade said.

"No," Surus said. "I planned it as more of a perfunctory meeting than anything else, mostly to confirm that the Phant is properly performing his duty."

"You've started to distrust the other Greens, haven't you?" Rade said. "After our last mission..."

"Yes," Surus said. "I was surprised by what Azen did. Injecting a retrovirus into a candidate for empress so that he could take control of her once she succeeded the throne. I have to keep close tabs on the other Greens in this sector. I'm not sure who I can trust anymore."

"Neither am I," Rade said pointedly.

"You can trust me," Surus said.

"Can I?"

She smiled for the first time since the meeting began. "If you can't trust me, then who can you trust?"

"My men," Rade said. "Shaw."

"We've been through three missions together," Surus said. "We fought together in the First Alien War."

"I know," Rade said. "But that doesn't mean I really know who you are. You keep to yourself in the quarters I assigned you. Harlequin visits with you the most, and even he tells me he feels he doesn't really know you. I'm not surprised he voted against continuing to have you as a client."

"I asked him about that," Surus said. "He told me

he didn't do it out of any mistrust of me, or my motives. He did it because he felt dropping me as a client would be safer for the crew, because of the nature of the missions I take you all on."

"Yes," Rade said. "Exactly. This is another reason why I need to accept this mission. We need something easy for once. A bit of a break for my men."

"I have already agreed to allow this," Surus said. "If you don't mind, I would like to return to my quarters."

Rade frowned. "Whether you agreed or not, I was going to take the mission. I told you: my company, my ship."

"Yes," Surus said. "I ask again, may I return to my quarters?"

"You may," Rade said.

With that she got up and left.

Rade stared at the hatch behind her.

He was starting to wonder if it was a bad idea to continue with her as a client. If she was going to be so intractable, forcing him to fight for every side mission, he wasn't sure she was worth the trouble.

All he had to do was remind himself of how important it was to hunt down those rogue Phants remaining in their region of space, and just how dangerous to humanity they really were.

He sighed.

She's going to be our client for many years to come, most likely. If we survive that long.

I'm just going to have to deal with it.

two

Half an hour out from Talan station Rade heard the familiar ding that told him money had been received in his account. He pulled up the bank interface on his Implant. It was the ten K deposit.

So far, so good.

Fret tapped in a few minutes later. "We're receiving the required orbital pattern from the station's Space Traffic Control. Looks like they want us to take up a position two kilometers from their port side, twenty degrees inclination."

"Relay the information to Shaw," Rade replied.

She would have to account for the planet's gravity while coming up with her orbital vector. Talan orbited a Venus type greenhouse world that the Asiatic Alliance was in the process of terraforming. Judging from the severe acid rain down there, it looked like they had a few more centuries to go.

"We've entered the specified orbital pattern," Tahoe reported in later from the bridge. Rade was still in his office, and had left his best friend and first officer in charge of the conn.

"Good," Rade said. "I want you to join Harlequin in a shuttle to pick up Batindo."

"You got it, boss," Tahoe said. "Any chance I can make a quick detour to the Nova Dynamics outlet while I'm there? I heard they have quite the collection of used combat robots. Maybe I can find us a bargain."

"Sorry, Tahoe," Rade said. "Surus is pissed enough about this whole operation as it is. Let's not try to further aggravate her. Besides, I haven't received confirmation of my combat robot license renewal yet this year. Even if you find a robot you like, they'll never let you buy a new one when they see our license has expired."

"We can use the license Surus has," Tahoe said.

"As I told you, the alien is regally pissed," Rade said. "Now isn't the time to go asking her any favors. Go to the station, pick up Batindo, and come straight back."

"All right," Tahoe said. "Don't need a pissed off alien on my case. It's times like this where I'm very glad I'm not the one interfacing with the client. It's probably not too different from dealing with a bossy lieutenant commander like in the old days, is it?"

"Not very, no," Rade said.

"The alien lieutenant commander from hell," Tahoe said.

"Sounds about right," Rade said. "Rade out."

He disconnected.

Harlequin and Tahoe took one of the Dragonfly shuttles to Talan station and returned in forty-five minutes with Batindo aboard.

Rade was waiting in the hangar bay airlock with Shaw to greet the client. Besides the fact that she was the biggest shareholder of the ship, having borrowed against the equity in her parents' farm to help finance the purchase, she was also his partner in life, and he wanted her there to meet this man he had taken on as a client. Her female intuition often sensed things about people that Rade did not.

When the hangar pressurized after the shuttle docked, Rade opened the inner hatch of the airlock and stepped inside with Shaw.

The ramp of the Dragonfly shuttle was folding open at that very moment. Tahoe stepped outside. The muscular Navajo cast his gaze throughout the bay, taking in everything around him. Even though this was a friendly ship, Tahoe's training would make it hard to let his guard down. Probably a good thing. His movements reminded Rade almost of a bear protecting its cub: tense, with a hint that he was ready to spring forward and attack at a moment's notice. If Rade had been the one retrieving the client, he probably would have behaved the same way.

Batindo came down shortly afterward. He couldn't have been more of Tahoe's opposite, both in terms of looks and body language. He had a round, dark face, and diminutive stature. Wattle underneath his chin shook as he walked. His stride was self-absorbed, almost imperious. He carried a walking staff in his right hand, taller than him, ending in a thick wooden globe. He wore what could best be described as a mix of traditional and modern Kenyan clothing: over a dress suit a long, red and black checkered blanket hung from his shoulders. Around his neck were three flashy golden chains where a tie should have been. His corncob-styled hair was dyed a bright red, matching the color of the blanket. His dress shoes seemed slightly sandal-like, in that there were cuts for his feet to "breathe."

Batindo seemed completely at ease, and yet he held his head high as he stepped into the hangar. Like he ranked above everyone on that vessel, and they were lucky he deigned to honor them with his presence.

His eyes swiveled toward Rade, but then immediately locked onto Shaw beside him, and remained there as the man walked forward. He tripped on the deck where two connecting panels formed a slight indention, forcing Tahoe to catch him.

"Release me you brute!" Batindo said.

When Tahoe did so, Batindo rubbed at the spot on his blanket where Tahoe had touched him. "You dirty my *shuka!*"

"Uh, okay," Tahoe said.

Batindo turned once more toward Rade and Shaw and smiled widely. "Mr. Rade Galaal?"

"That's what my public profile says…" Rade said.

Batindo nodded. He focused his attention entirely on Shaw once more.

"I was not aware that you had such beautiful servants," Batindo said.

"Batindo, this is Shaw Chopra," Rade said. "The astrogator of the *Argonaut*. And its biggest shareholder."

"My apologies!" Batindo said. "I was not expecting, well, let me just say, someone of your caliber. I assumed the crew was filled with mercenaries and other ex-military types, you understand."

He reached for Shaw's hand and she allowed him to take it. He began lifting it to his lips.

"I'm actually ex-military." Shaw smiled sweetly.

Batindo froze before he could kiss her hand. Then he looked up and smiled feebly. He released her hand as if he had been stung. It wasn't her words so much that had gotten to the man, Rade suspected, but her tone. Soft, yet subtly threatening.

"You have prepared quarters for me, I assume?" Batindo said.

Rade nodded. "Two of my men have given up their stateroom for you." That would be Lui and Harlequin, who had agreed to temporarily quarter in the cargo hold with Surus. "Tahoe will escort you."

"Thank you," Batindo said. "I am sure you have many stories to tell me. Of the days you spent in the military. Of the clients you've taken on since then. I look forward to hearing them all in the days to come."

Rade forced a smile. "For sure."

When Batindo was gone, Rade glanced at Shaw.

"I don't like him," she said.

"Should we keep him as a client?" Rade said.

Shaw shrugged. "Who am I to go against your decision? Let him stay. The boys could use some laughs. Besides, Kitale colony might actually be in danger."

"We could always go there on our own," Rade said. "To check up on the place, and leave him here."

"He could prove useful passing certain checkpoints on the way to the Kenyan outpost," Shaw said. "His diplomatic status will open some doors I'm sure. Or Gates, to be precise."

"All right," Rade said. "He stays."

Rade had the *Argonaut* fly to the asteroid it had been tracking before he received the call from Batindo, and Surus took a shuttle down to the surface, where she conducted her secretive meeting with the Green, who had arrived in a Marauder class ship similar to the *Argonaut*. She returned to the ship and then Rade gave the order to proceed toward Kitale.

The next week and a half of the journey proved relatively uneventful. Batindo did his best to boss around the crew, but failed miserably for the most part. At first Rade had given him free reign of the *Argonaut*, but when he started coming aboard the bridge unannounced, Rade posted a Centurion robot with strict instructions to bar his entry. So then Batindo would wander around to other parts of the ship, like engineering. TJ was on duty there, and didn't take kindly to the man, leaving him with a black eye.

When Rade called TJ to his office to discipline him—mostly at the insistence of Batindo—TJ told him the man had "blabbed his mouth off constantly, distracting me from the engine upgrades I was working on. I told him to leave, but he wouldn't shut up, boss. He left me no choice but to deck him a good one, so I could actually get some work done."

Rade decided he wasn't going to dock TJ any pay, because essentially the loyal crew member had done the right thing. And TJ could have severely injured the man—a black eye was nothing. Rade instead told TJ to report to Tahoe.

"Tell him I sent you," Rade told TJ. "And that he is to see to it that you perform a thousand push ups within the span of an hour."

From the way TJ's eyes glinted, Rade knew that TJ was looking forward to the impromptu PT, and in fact viewed it as a challenge.

Though Rade had assigned a Centurion with a chef program to his quarters, Batindo often invited himself to the wardroom and bothered the men while they ate. He seemed to love the sound of his own voice. When he had first boarded, he had told Rade he looked forward to hearing all of their stories. Well, it seemed Batindo had meant that he wanted to regale the crew with stories of *his* heroic adventures at the Kenyan consulate instead, the highlights of which included his sexual liaisons with the wife of the director of station security, and harboring Kenyans who had committed various crimes aboard the station.

It took five days to reach the Slipstream to the adjacent system, and another three to reach the Nyiki system, a time span that couldn't have passed too soon.

Rade was on the bridge when the *Argonaut* emerged from the jump Gate in the target system. He had his tactical display active in the upper right of his vision.

"Lui, tell me what we're looking at," Rade said.

"We're looking at a double binary star system," Lui said. The Asian American was in charge of the ops station. "We have a red subgiant and blue dwarf orbiting one another. And revolving around them are two more stars, about sixty million kilometers away, the same distance from our own sun to Mercury: a yellow main sequence, and a bright giant. Planets have formed around the four of them, the first starting a billion kilometers from the combined barycenter, and proceeding outward to five billion kilometers. There is an uncharted Slipstream on the far side of the system. No outgoing Gate. Like most pioneer outposts on the edge of known space, the system appears relatively dead. There isn't any mining activity on any of the asteroids or planetoids. Nor any ship traffic."

"Not very self-sufficient then, are they?" Rade commented.

"Suppose not," Lui replied. "Kitale colony resides on the closest planet to the double binary barycenter. I am detecting signs of habitation: what appear to be several colony domes grouped close together. They're all intact. Though, this is odd: there don't seem to be any defenses. Ordinarily for a colony like this you'd see a starship of some kind in orbit, or at least an orbital defense platform, or maybe some surface-to-air defenses. But there's nothing."

"What about the comm nodes linking them to the InterGalNet?" Rade asked. "Are they still active by the Gate?"

"The comm nodes are active, yes," Lui said. "And according to the pings, they've continued to pass in and out of the system, transferring data between this system and the rest of the galaxy. They definitely aren't the source of the communication failure. And as far as I can tell, the nodes are still sending and transmitting data to Kitale."

"Get Bender to help you spy on those packets," Rade said. "I want to know exactly what they're sending and receiving. "Meanwhile, Fret, send the station a standard hail."

"Will do," Fret said. "I should have an answer in three hours."

Rade had been ignoring a flashing notification in the lower right of his display. It was Batindo, attempting to tap in.

Rade finally picked up, voice only. "What is it?"

"The AI tells me we have arrived in Nyiki," Batindo said. "Is the colony still intact?"

"As far as we can tell, it is," Rade said. "Though there are no defenses of any kind. No ships, no orbital defense platforms."

"Hmm. Very odd," Batindo said. "According to the records, they had one defense platform. It should be in a geosynchronous orbit above the dome cluster."

"Well it's not there anymore," Rade said. "Communications are still active, apparently. The comm nodes are sending data to and from the colony."

"Have you hailed them?" Batindo asked.

"We have," Rade said. "My communicator tells me we should have a response in three hours."

"Don't count on it," Batindo said. "If they haven't replied before, why would they suddenly start now?"

"I don't know," Rade said. "You'd be surprised at the difference a ship in the neighborhood can make."

"We shall see," Batindo said. "In the interim, please set a course for Kitale. I expect we will have to pay a visit with the local governor and ask him in person why he isn't responding to official Kenyan government communication requests."

"I'll have my astrogator set a course," Rade said.

"Ah, your astrogator!" Batindo said. "Say hello to her for me, would you?"

"Sure thing," Rade said.

"And what about that other woman I have seen walking in the halls occasionally?" Batindo said. "When do I get to meet her? Whenever I attempt to speak with her, she always runs away and locks herself away in the cargo hold."

"That's probably for the best," Rade said.

"Why?" Batindo said.

"She doesn't like strangers," Rade said.

Batindo was silent for several seconds. "I've never met a woman who didn't like me."

"She's not a woman," Rade said.

"Ah," Batindo said. "One of those, is she? I don't mind."

"I'll only say this once, Batindo," Rade said. "For your own good, drop the matter. Forget about her. And don't try to talk to her again."

"I can't promise that I won't..." Batindo said.

"It's your life," Rade warned him. "I'll set a course for Kitale and let you know if anything new comes up."

Rade disconnected. It was late evening, so he retired to his quarters to relax with Shaw. She cooked him up a dish of chicken and rice.

"This is fantastic," Rade said, downing the food voraciously.

"Thank you," Shaw said. "Just doing my part to protect you from the atrocious food of the wardroom. Robots can't cook."

"Don't tell that to the rest of the crew," Rade said, finishing his plate.

"Here's something else I'm not telling the rest of the crew," Shaw said.

She dragged him to the hydro-recycle container in the head, and they showered together.

Some time later he found himself lying awake on his bunk. A bad dream had awakened him.

He went to the head, activated the noise canceler, and asked the *Argonaut's* AI: "Bax, any news? Did we get an answer from the colony yet?"

"There has been no answer from Kitale, no," Bax replied. "But Bender has some news."

"Is he still awake?" Rade asked.

"Yes," Bax said.

"Tap him in."

A moment later a hologram of the heavily muscled black man appeared in front of Rade.

"Hey Bender," Rade said. "I'm surprised you're still up."

"I keep late hours, bro," Bender said. "Getting in some quality sniping time."

"Oh yeah," Rade said. "What's that new VR game you and Bender have been playing?"

"Me and Bender?" Bender asked. "While it's true I've been known to play with myself, I don't usually do it in VR, if you catch my drift."

"Sorry, late night," Rade said. "I meant you and TJ."

"Mechs vs. Aliens IV," Bender said.

"Nice," Rade said. "I'll have to try that sometime. Listen, Bax said you had some news for me."

"I do," Bender said. "I finished my analysis of the packets passing back and forth between Kitale and the Gate comm nodes. It's just your standard InterGalNet traffic. Freetube videos, app downloads, messages sent between friends and family, the usual crap. Kitale colony seems to be just fine. I'm not sure why they're ignoring us."

"All right," Rade said. "Thanks." He disconnected.

There was nothing more they could do but continue toward the planet.

Rade glanced at his tactical display, and regarded the location of the outgoing Slipstream with suspicion. There was no Gate in front of it, meaning that the *Argonaut* wouldn't be able to pass through, but that didn't necessarily mean alien craft couldn't enter. He had seen alien ships traverse Slipstreams without Gates before. Specifically, Phant ships.

The next morning, after Rade had settled in on the bridge, Lui spoke up.

"This is odd," Lui said. "I'm detecting what looks like the wreckage of two Kenyan corvettes on the surface. Tanga class, according to Bax's analysis. There is also debris from what I'm guessing is an orbital defense platform on the same continent. I'm getting a ping from the black box associated with the defense platform. Looks like it went down a month ago."

"And the corvettes?" Rade asked.

"I'm not getting any ping from their black boxes," Lui said. "My guess is, either they were destroyed, or removed. But I'd say they probably went down at around the same time as the orbital defense platform."

"Bender, I don't suppose you can remotely hack

into that black box to find out what happened?" Rade said.

"No," Bender said. "The ping is mostly for retrieval purposes. There's no remote interface to the actual contents. You'll need to open up the box and remove the holographic storage chip if you want to get in."

"Too bad." Rade glanced at Lui once more. "Are you detecting any surface-to-space defenses on the planet yet? Or anything else that could have downed those corvettes?"

"Nope," Lui said. "The only thing that could have eliminated those corvettes is the orbital defense platform. And the warships apparently took it out at the same time."

"Are you seeing any signs of life in the cluster of habitation domes composing the colony?" Rade said.

"Yes, in fact," Lui said. "People are walking about, driving and flying vehicles, generally going about their lives. They're all fairly dark-skinned. Typical of Kenyans, I suppose. Data packets continue to transfer back and forth between the planet and the comm nodes near the Gate. They're piggybacking off the comm nodes built into the *Argonaut*, in fact, as per standard networking protocol."

Rade glanced at Fret. "And yet their government is not answering our hailing requests?"

"No," the communications man replied.

"The mystery deepens," Shaw said.

"Why don't we try contacting a citizen?" Rade said.

Fret shrugged. "It's worth a try. I can extract the recipient ID from one of the packets, and use it as the destination address for a message. Bax can handle the translation between English and Kenyan. What would you like me to say?"

Rade rubbed his chin. "Tell them who we are, and ask them if anything unusual is going on in Kitale. Ask them what happened to those ships."

Rade tapped in Batindo. According to the location data, the Kenyan was located in sickbay.

"Batindo, why are you in sickbay?" Rade asked.

"Err, I tried to talk to the strange woman you mentioned," Batindo replied.

"What happened?"

"Like you told me, she doesn't like strangers," Batindo said.

"What happened..." Rade pressed.

Batindo sighed. "I tried to touch her. An innocent touch, mind you! On the shoulder! She spun around and gave me a black eye. Your crew seems to dole them out with alarming regularity."

"Yes, they do that," Rade said.

"So I trust you weren't tapping in merely to check upon my health?" Batindo said.

"No." Rade updated him with the latest news regarding Kitale.

"The wreckage of two corvettes, you say?" Batindo asked.

"That's right," Rade said.

"That is very disturbing. It would seem we have discovered the fate of the two corvettes my government sent to the colony a few months ago. Tax compliance vessels."

"Kitale wasn't paying its taxes?" Rade said.

"Exactly so," Batindo said. "And apparently, they weren't too happy to see the tax collectors. It is sedition, then."

"Probably," Rade said. "Which means you might not get the welcome you were expecting."

"You will accompany me to the surface to

investigate?" Batindo asked.

"We'll do whatever you need us to do," Rade said. "We agreed to provide you with security services, and we will."

"Thank you," Batindo said.

Three hours later Fret reported in. He had received a response from the private citizen. "The recipient says everything is fine. He didn't answer my question about the crashed corvettes, however."

"Let's try another random recipient, same questions," Rade said.

During the final leg of the journey, Fret repeatedly sent different inquiries to inhabitants of the dome, but always everyone replied that all was well. And they either ducked the questions regarding the warships, or claimed not to know anything about them.

And so the *Argonaut* began its final approach to the planet while there were still many questions left unanswered.

three

P ut us in a geosynchronous orbit above the dome cluster," Rade said.

"Will do," Shaw replied.

"Fret, any response to our official communications yet?" Rade asked.

"No," Fret said. "But I've been in contact with more private citizens. They keep saying everything is fine down there."

"Lui, any change in the habitation domes?" Rade said.

"Not really," Lui said. "People still seem to be going about their daily lives. If anything, it almost seems a little *too* busy. As if they're trying to put on a show for us watchers in orbit, to make sure its perfectly clear that everything is A-okay."

Rade leaned forward in his chair, resting his arms on the station in front of him. "This is damn strange. Tahoe, what do you think?"

"I don't know what to believe," Tahoe said. "The citizens tell us everything is normal down there. And for all intents and purposes, everything *does* seem normal. But then you have the official channels refusing to answer our hails. Which leads me to believe that everything is *not* fine."

"It's almost like something a despotic government might orchestrate," Shaw said. "Hoping to get rid of us."

Rade thrummed his fingers on the station for a moment.

Tahoe extended his noise canceler around Rade. "You're planning an away mission."

Rade nodded. "I promised Batindo I'd escort him down."

"Maybe we should only take some of the crew," Tahoe said. "In case things sour down there."

"Probably a good idea," Rade said. "Except that if things do sour, we might need every last man."

"But if we're captured, wouldn't it be helpful if we had someone still on the ship to spring us?" Tahoe asked.

"I definitely agree," Rade said. "I do plan to leave a few combat robots aboard. They'll be in charge of any rescue."

"I'm not sure I trust some robot..."

"Robots are just as capable as anyone else," Rade said. "I consider them part of our brotherhood. Especially those we've fought alongside already."

Tahoe bowed his head, ceding the point.

It's just too bad that many of those robots that fought alongside us were destroyed in those past battles, their personalities restored from backups.

Rade glanced at Shaw. She was looking right at him.

A text message appeared from her. *You better not be planning to leave me behind.*

Rade smiled sadly at that. He sent her a text back. *I wouldn't dare.*

Rade sat straighter and dismissed Tahoe's noise canceler. "Lui, you're absolutely positive there are no surface-to-space defenses down there?"

Lui sighed, obviously becoming a little annoyed that Rade had asked so many times. "Unless they're running some new weapons tech we've never seen before, then no, they absolutely, positively have no surface-to-space defenses. One-hundred-percent guaranteed."

"Famous last words!" Bender quipped.

Rade nodded. "All right. I've made up my mind. We're going in. Tahoe, prepare two shuttles. We'll go down in separate fire teams as a precaution. I want five Argonauts per shuttle, and four Centurions."

Tahoe nodded. "It'll be like traveling overwatch, except in shuttles."

"Exactly," Rade said.

"So eight Centurions in total..." Manic said. "Half our inventory. That should leave enough combat robots aboard to defend the ship."

"That's right," Rade said. "More than enough, actually, considering how dead the system is."

"What about Hoplites?" Manic asked. "Can we bring them down?"

"Good luck getting them past the port authority," Lui said.

"He's right," Rade said. "And given that everything seems relatively normal down there, I can't justify the expense, as much as I'd like to charge Batindo for their deployment. If we do end up needing them, we can have Bax drop the mechs from orbit."

"Could be too late by then," Fret muttered.

"Bax, have Batindo meet us in the shuttle hangar bay," Rade said. "Have one of the Centurions help suit him up."

"Surus is coming?" Tahoe asked. "You said five Argonauts per shuttle. That makes ten of us in total. If you're counting her as an Argonaut."

"I didn't mean to count her as one, no," Rade said. "But I would assume she is coming. I can't force her, obviously, but I'll confirm with her on the way."

In the tight passageway outside the bridge, he did just that, tapping in Surus.

"We're escorting Batindo down to the surface to investigate," Rade said. "Do you want to come?"

"Mmm," Surus said.

"Is that a yes or a no?" Rade asked.

"I'll consider it."

"Fine," Rade said. "If you're not in the hangar bay in ten minutes, we're leaving without you."

He and the others proceeded to the bay and suited up. The robots were already waiting inside the cabins of the respective shuttles.

Rade took his place in the second shuttle, between Bender and Batindo. Rade was surprised to see Surus seated opposite him, already suited up.

"Quick change," Rade commented.

She nodded stiffly behind her faceplate.

So she's coming after all. She can bemoan the mission all she wants, but she's got cabin fever like the rest of us. Wants to see some action, no matter how small and inconsequential.

When everyone was aboard, the ramp closed.

Batindo was uncharacteristically silent next to Rade.

"First time making a drop?" Rade asked.

"No, of course not," Batindo said.

"Could have fooled me," Bender said. He switched to a private line that excluded Batindo. "This is going to be fun watching this bitch! Manic, you have a front row seat."

Next to Surus, Manic was seated across from Batindo, and facing the consular official.

"Mind if I hitch a ride on your cam, Manic?" Fret transmitted from the other shuttle.

"Go right ahead," Manic said. "I'm authorizing all of you now."

Rade smiled, shaking his head. He had no interest in watching Batindo sick up, so he switched to the external camera of the shuttle and watched as the hangar bay depressurized instead. Moments later the first shuttle departed.

"Take us out, Shaw," Rade said.

"Roger that," Shaw replied from the pilot's seat.

The shuttle lifted from the deck and accelerated into the zero gravity of the void. To the left, the planet swallowed the view. Shaw began decelerating, taking the vessel into free fall. And Rade thought his stomach was doing somersaults before...

After the flames of atmospheric entry subsided, Rade saw the greenish hued planet below. There weren't any oceans; the surface was covered in bleak, rusty-gray rocks. According to the scans, the planet had an atmosphere and magnetosphere, but was otherwise uninhabitable by humans. The sensors had picked up a few Forma pipes embedded near the equator—those were used to pipe gases locked away within the mantle into the air for terraforming purposes—but the project seemed to have been abandoned after only four pipes, either due to lack of funding, or the trapped gases proved far less abundant than originally believed.

The shuttle shook violently.

"It's going to get a little rough here on out," Shaw said.

"Look at that sissy bitch," Bender said over the private line.

Rade dismissed the external video feed and

couldn't help but glance at Batindo. The shuttle shook again. The man's eyes bulged in his head, and his faceplate became smeared with fresh vomit.

Rade checked Batindo's vitals, wanting to ensure the vomit hadn't clogged his oxygen vents. He seemed fine, other than a skyrocketing heart rate.

Rade remotely accessed the AI of Batindo's suit and had it apply a sedative. It didn't help, judging from the continual protrusion of the man's eyes.

Shaking, the shuttle made its way toward a cluster of geodesic domes that were linked together by metallic conduits running along the rocky surface of the planet. The overall effect, at least when viewed from above, was to give the domes the appearance of a giant molecular model.

"See that," Bender said. "That's the molecular model for butane down there."

"So that's what you snort," Manic said.

"Least I don't sniff glue like you," Bender said.

"Shaw, how does it look down there?" Rade asked.

"All clear," she replied. "The automated air traffic controller systems are guiding us in."

"I'm not sure if that's good or bad," Harlequin said over the comm. He was piloting the other shuttle.

"Probably good," Rade said.

"Unless they intend to take us prisoner," Fret commented over the comm.

"What, you really think they're going to take a consular official prisoner?" Manic said.

"Uh, yeah?" Fret said. "If the colony has declared independence, then this guy has no standing among them at all. And neither do we, I might add."

"Got my standing right here," Bender said, patting his rifle.

"Fret can't see what you did," Manic said. "He's in

the other shuttle."

"Let me guess, he patted his rifle?" Fret transmitted.

"Yeah," Manic said.

"How clichéd," Fret said.

"You're clichéd, bitch," Bender said. "Who even says that?"

A wide metal rim lined the bottom of the main geodesic dome. Several pairs of hangar doors were embedded within it.

One of those pairs opened and the lead shuttle containing Tahoe and the first fire team flew inside.

"Shaw, circle until we hear from Tahoe," Rade said.

Shaw turned away at the last moment and circled back as per his instructions.

"So," Tahoe said. "We got some other shuttles docked here with us, but otherwise it's clear. Port authority hasn't arrived yet. Should I tell them to shut the doors and proceed with pressurization?"

"No," Rade said. "We might as well come in, too. Take us there, Shaw."

She turned the shuttle around and steered toward the double doors, then touched down inside. The bay doors closed and atmosphere began to vent inside.

Surus sat up straighter in her seat. "There's a Phant here." She was transmitting on the private line that excluded Batindo.

"What, in the bay?" Bender said.

"No," Surus said. "Somewhere in the colony. Maybe the adjacent dome. The feeling is faint, at the moment. But there's definitely a Phant."

"Bet you're glad you came along after all," Bender said.

Surus nodded behind her faceplate, and fixed Rade

with a stare that seemed full of gratitude. "It was a good thing your boss convinced me."

"Yes, good for all of us," Rade said. "We would've been walking into a trap set by a Phant without even knowing it." He glanced at Lui. "Can you confirm the gravity levels?"

"They're a match to the readings I gave in orbit," Lui said. "We're at ninety-eight percent of Earth gravity."

"That's why I feel so light on my feet," Manic said.

"Feels the same to me," Harlequin transmitted form the other ship. "At least relative to the artificial gravity aboard the *Argonaut*. The tension on my servomotors is approximately—"

"I was joking," Manic interrupted. "Human sarcasm, Harlequin. You have to learn it if you ever hope to fit in with us."

"Ahh," Harlequin said. "I understand now. Let me try. My hands are so light, when I lift them, they feel like balloons!"

"Uh, leave the sarcasm to us humans, please," Fret said.

Bender was laughing. "Man, you robots are entertaining as hell. Please, don't say anything else Harley boy, you're killing me here."

Rade regarded the different external cameras to get a bead on the docking bay. He saw the other shuttles Tahoe had spoken of, various classes that resided within the designated landing zones, as indicated by the yellow circles and white crosshairs painted onto the deck and its rivets. About half of the parking spots were empty.

When the external atmosphere stabilized, a hatch irised open on the far side of the hangar. An enforcer robot emerged from the hallway beyond, escorted by two towering walker units. About the size of an average human being, the enforcer had a wide, thick body that looked like it was made of large blocks of steel, reminding Rade of an Inukshuk—a series of rocks piled into the shape of a man. The walkers that flanked it meanwhile were twice that height, about the size of Hoplites. They had two long, ostrich-like legs connected to T-shaped upper bodies. Beneath the twin overhangs of those Ts were laser turrets and missile launches. Essentially, gunships on legs.

"Love the customs folks," Manic said. "Always great to get a hero's welcome."

"Tahoe, have two of your robots exit calmly, weapons down," Rade said. "Leave the HS3s inside." HS3s were head-sized scouts that the team used to explore new environments. Sending the HS3s out now might be considered an act of aggression, prompting the walkers to shoot the scouts down.

"Roger that," Tahoe said. "Sending two Centurions outside, weapons down."

four

R ade glanced at his overhead map and saw Units A and B exit the first shuttle. He switched to Unit A's point of view. The robots kept their hands firmly at their sides, and purposely let the rifles hang from the straps on their shoulders.

"Tell them who we are," Rade instructed Unit A.

"Greetings," Unit A began, using the external speakers of its jumpsuit. By Rade's orders, all of the combat robots were wearing jumpsuits—that way they would have the same protection as the rest of the away team, in terms of Phant repelling capabilities. Admittedly, he hadn't known there would be a Phant on the surface before giving that order, and he had done it mostly to prevent any opponents from knowing which of them were humans and which were robots when targeting them through scopes. The robots had activated holographic images in their faceplates to appear as Kenyans, and updated their public profiles to give them Kenyan names and birthplaces.

"We are members of the security consulting company Unlimited Universe," Unit A continued. "We are here to ensure the safety of Muto Batindo, of the Kenyan Consulate of Talan, who seeks an audience with the Kitale governor."

"All of you, please exit for customs processing," the enforcer said.

"Customs processing," Tahoe said. "Why don't I like the sound of that."

The walker robots stepped forward, making room for two more walkers to enter from the hallway behind them.

"Please exit," the enforcer repeated. "Or we will drag you from the shuttles."

"We should go back," Batindo said.

"It's a bit late for that now," Rade said. "You're the one who wanted to come here, remember?"

"Yes, but I didn't expect this treatment!" Batindo said.

"Well what the hell did you expect then?" Rade said. "The red carpet to be rolled out and champagne and ladies waiting for you with their arms out? You're the one who told me sedition was likely in play here. That you suspected the governor shot down those tax collection ships."

"Yes but, I guess... I didn't think it through," Batindo said.

"You didn't think it through," Rade said flatly. He felt the anger rising inside him.

"For some reason I believed you could guarantee my safety," Batindo said. "But I realize I was wrong. Nothing can protect me from those robots."

"Listen, Batindo," Rade said. "We have two options at the moment. Either we fight our way out of here, or we surrender peacefully. The chances of surviving the latter are, well, probably close to a hundred percent. You might be arrested, but you will survive. As for fighting our way out of here, the chances are maybe, what... fifty-fifty?"

"Approximately twenty percent, by my calculations," Harlequin said. "We would have to fire the shuttle miniguns before lift-off and attempt to disable all of the robots. More walkers would likely emerge from the hallway to reinforce the ranks. And if we made it outside, other shuttles might launch from adjacent bays, and pursue."

"So you see, Batindo," Rade said. "The best option at this point is surrender. Besides, you don't know what the governor wants, yet. Maybe he'll let you go."

"You think the Phant is in possession of the governor?" Fret asked over a private line.

"That would be a good assumption," Surus said.

"Then we'll be putting ourselves straight into its hands," Manic said. "We'll be at its mercy. It'll execute us."

"I'm not so sure," Rade said. "If the Phant wanted us killed, it would have ordered those walkers to open fire already. What do you think, Surus?"

"It knows I'm here," Surus said. "It also knows I can't be killed by conventional means. It will want to lay low and analyze us, buying time until it comes up with a strategy."

"All right," Rade said. "Shaw, open her up. Let's set the game in motion."

The ramp went down.

"Everyone out, both shuttles," Rade said. "Weapons down."

The clamps restraining Rade telescoped open, and he stood up. Batindo arose beside him, but swayed. Rade caught him, and helped him down the ramp.

When they reached the deck, Batindo forced Rade away, and stumbled forward a few meters, before falling to his knees.

"Batindo, you all right?" Rade glanced at his vitals.

All green. In theory he was fine.

Batindo fumbled with his helmet latches.

"Don't—" Rade began.

Batindo ripped off his helmet and inhaled deeply of the air.

"Remove the helmet," Rade finished.

Batindo leaned forward and kissed the grime-covered deck rivets.

"Guess he wants to expose himself to contagions," Bender said.

"We'll use priv exclusively from now on," Rade said on the private line. "Batindo doesn't need to hear everything we say."

"There probably aren't contagions, you know," Lui said over the same comm band. "Given that this is a habitable dome, after all."

"You know my rules," Rade said. "Helmets remain on at all questionable outposts when we're on a mission."

"We've had liberty on some pretty questionable outposts and stations in coreward systems..." Fret said.

"True," Rade said. "But we weren't on missions then. Remember, these jumpsuits are shielded to protect against psi attacks. If the Phant Surus has detected is a Black, we don't need it controlling our minds. Helmets stay on."

"Don't forget the anti-Phant emitters we've since installed in the spine areas of the suits as well," Lui said.

"Yes," Tahoe said. "Though those will still work to physically repel Phants even if we take off our helmets."

Rade helped Batindo to his feet, and made him replace the helmet.

The eight Centurions—still displaying Kenyan

faces on their faceplates—led the way to the customs robots on the far side of the bay. The Argonauts followed.

"Who is in charge here?" the enforcer asked when the Centurions were five meters away.

Rade stepped forward and the Centurions parted to let him through. He had left his public profile unchanged, so that the customs officials would see he was CEO of Unlimited Universe.

"By order of the port authority," the robot said. "You must surrender your weapons."

Rade glanced at the menacing robots towering over him, then turned to look at the Argonauts behind the screen of Centurions. Surus fingered the Phant stun rifle she had slung over one shoulder.

"I definitely don't want to give up the stun weapon," Surus said over the private line.

Rade pursed his lips, then turned back to the enforcer.

"We'll leave the weapons in our shuttles," Rade said via his external speakers.

"No, leave them with us," the enforcer said.

"We leave them in the shuttle, or no deal," Rade said.

The enforcer remained motionless for several moments. Rade could almost feel those camera lenses it had for eyes boring into him; likely it was calculating how many Centurions and Argonauts the walker units could mow down before Rade's team returned fire. Indeed, Rade half expected the laser turrets in the walker units to rip into him at any moment.

But finally the enforcer spoke: "As you wish. You may stow your weapons in the shuttle."

Rade exhaled, then turned toward his men. "You heard the enforcer. Put the weapons back in the storage racks."

Surus regarded her Phant stun rifle wistfully.

"We'll come back for it," Rade told her as he walked back to the shuttle.

Surus hesitated. Then: "I will do as you say. This is your operation, and I trust your judgment."

"Thank you," Rade said. "Because at the moment, we're not entering this city with that weapon."

"Maybe she can hide it inside her jumpsuit somehow?" Fret asked.

"Good luck with that," Bender said. "The suit assemblies are way too tight."

"He's right, I can't," Surus said.

The Argonauts and Centurions entered their respective shuttles and placed their weapons in the provided racks.

"Units G and H, I want you to stay behind," Rade sent. "Take one shuttle each. Seal the ramps and don't let anyone touch our equipment. Especially that stun rifle."

"You got it, boss," Unit G returned.

Rade and the others returned to the customs officials.

"You have cleared customs," the enforcer said. The walker units stepped aside, revealing the hallway beyond. "Kitale colony welcomes you. You say you seek a meeting with the governor? I have relayed your request, and the governor has cleared his busy schedule to receive you. I have marked the location of his office on your overhead maps."

Rade received the map request. "Bender, clear the data."

A moment later Bender said: "It's safe. No viruses or Trojans are piggybacking on the packets."

Rade accepted the map marker data and saw the

waypoint appear on his overhead map. He already had the complete layout of Kitale displayed on that map, courtesy of Batindo.

"You are to proceed to the governor's office immediately," the enforcer said. "An escort will be waiting for you outside the terminal to ensure you arrive safely."

"To ensure we arrive safely?" TJ said over the private line. "Or to ensure we don't wander somewhere else, first?"

"You may remove your helmets at any time," the enforcer continued. "The air is breathable, of course. We follow all environmental regulations, and have the highest bacterial filtration standards in the region."

"We'd rather not," Rade said.

"Suit yourselves," the robot replied. It extended a hand toward the hallway, beckoning Rade and the others forward. Two more walker units awaited therein, but had stepped aside to allow the party members to pass.

"Centurions, lead the way," Rade instructed.

He and the others followed the Centurions into the hallway. A pair of double doors on the far side led into a relatively empty terminal. There were different travel kiosks, some of them manned by robots and Artificials, but otherwise no clientele. Rade did note several security cameras monitoring the premises.

"Anyone else find it odd that no one is buying any tickets out of here?" Fret said.

"Uh, bro, how can they buy tickets out?" Bender said. "When there are no ships to take them anywhere?"

"Good point," Fret said.

Outside the main exit to the terminal, four more walker-style mechs waited to escort them. Rade and the others exited, and took the stairs down to where the walkers resided. The machines towered over the party, their huge guns pointing down at them.

"Surrender your weapons immediately," one of the walkers said.

"Uh," Tahoe said.

Rade slowly lifted his hands. "We've already given up our weapons?" he said via his external speakers.

An automated cart weaved between the walkers, rolling forward.

"Surrender your weapons *now*," the walker said.

Rade glanced at his companions, then shrugged. "Guess we've been discovered."

He reached into the hidden compartment in his harness and retrieved the grenade he had stowed there and tossed it into the cart. The other Argonauts followed his lead.

"Happy?" Rade told the walker.

All of the turrets swiveled toward Shaw.

She smiled sheepishly past her faceplate, then reached behind and underneath her jetpack, retrieving a concealed blaster she had lodged there.

"Sneaky," Bender said.

Shaw tossed it into the cart.

The automated device rolled away.

The menacing walkers remained in position for several moments, keeping their turrets trained on the party, and then finally lowered their weapons and stepped back, revealing a dark-skinned man standing before the Argonauts.

Actually, not a man: according to the public profile Rade accessed via his Implant, the individual was an Artificial.

"I will escort you to the governor's office," the Artificial said.

"How did you know we wanted to go there?" Manic said.

"A hunch," the Artificial replied with a sly smile.

"See, Harlequin?" Manic transmitted as the Artificial led them down the street. "This thing understands sarcasm. So it's not beyond you AIs."

"I'm not sure it actually understood," Harlequin said. "Or merely pretended to. That's what I do, sometimes."

"Once a poser, always a poser," Bender said.

"Come on, don't be so hard on Harley," Manic said. "Bender means you're a poet. Once a poet, always a poet."

"It is all right, Manic," Harlequin said. "I know that Bender cares about me. He—"

"*What!*" Bender said. "Shut the hell up AI." His voice pitched upward a few octaves as he continued. "Bender cares about me. Bender loves me. Bender wants to caress me." He cleared his throat. "Uh, no, bitch. When we're done here, I'm going to invite you to the combat room and I'll show you how much I care about you."

Rade couldn't help but smile. He knew that if Harlequin were injured in any way, Bender would be the first to come to his aid. His oneupmanship was all act. That was one of the consequences of the intense training they had gone through to qualify for the MOTH brotherhood all those years ago. Competitiveness was rewarded, but some of the trainees unfortunately took it to the extreme, and it became a permanent part of their personalities. But throw them into the fires of battle, and teamwork, as well as the protection of one's brothers, overrode all.

"You know, if I didn't know better," Lui said. "I'd think Bender and Harlequin were lovers."

"I don't need this crap," Bender said. "I'm muting everyone save the boss. Good-bye."

The Kenyan Artificial led them into a pedestrian-friendly area, free of vehicles. Most of the buildings here were low-rise apartments, with retail areas on the first floors. The commercial properties seemed to mostly repeat every block, and usually contained at least one variant of grocery store, hair salon, clothing outlet, butcher, bakery, and a restaurant or cafe.

Kenyans walked the closely-packed streets, along with errand robots—human-shaped constructs of black and yellow polycarbonate. Some of the men wore red and black checkered blankets draped across their bodies, the same "shuka" Batindo had worn on their initial meeting. Many of the men also dyed their hair red, like Batindo. According to Rade's Implant, red traditionally signified power in their culture.

The fabric wraps seemed more common on the women, which proved far more colorful than their male counterparts. His Implant labeled those particular articles of clothing as "*kangas.*" From the necks of the women hung extensive, plate-like bead necklaces.

Both men and women wore sandals. Rade could have sworn the soles were lifted from rubber tires, given the tread patterns on them.

Delivery drones buzzed overhead, carrying various parcels to and from the retail shops. Otherwise, there were few aircraft above—the layout of the colony wasn't really all that conducive to air travel, given that the city was spread over eight separate geodesic domes. There was ample space for those drones, though.

The robots and drones ignored the party, save for perhaps cursory glances, but most of the people scowled at them as they passed.

"They seem real friendly," Manic commented.

"You'd give dirty looks to foreigners wearing jumpsuits in your environment, too," Fret said. "Especially when your air was safe to breath. It's almost kind of insulting that we have helmets on, like we think they're dirty."

"Sino-Koreans from Earth do that sort of thing all the time," Lui said. "Visit any SK colony, and you'll see Sino-Korean Earthers wearing surgical masks."

"My point exactly," Fret said. "The Earthers wear the masks because they consider the colony air impure somehow."

"You're all overlooking the obvious point," TJ said. "How would you feel if a bunch of obviously former military men surrounded by combat robots waltzed into the downtown core of your colony one day? Of course you'd give them hostile looks."

"I'd love to see what kind of looks these people would be giving us if we still had our rifles," Bender said.

"I thought you muted us all?" Lui said.

"No, just you," Bender said.

Rade noted the continual presence of security cameras, which were situated within protective glass domes atop the street lamps. Rade thought the inclusion of those lamps was somewhat superfluous, considering that the glow bars embedded in the geodesic dome could have provided light at all hours, but he supposed the city designers had opted for something more traditional. Besides, they needed an inconspicuous place for the cameras.

He momentarily activated his augmented reality pass through, which would allow virtual augmentations and advertisements to interact with his Implant.

Sure enough, he started seeing ads popping into

his vision, courtesy of the retail shops. He wasn't interested in getting a tattoo done, or picking up sausages that were the "cheapest in town," so he turned the pass through back off.

One particular restaurant had placed a real physical menu out front, in the form of a wooden sign resting on the pavement. He saw such items as Ugali. Wali wa Nazi. Lukuma Pusi. His Implant translated them, respectively, as: Cornmeal. Coconut rice. Green Kale.

"Mm hmm! Have a look at these mighty fine menu items," Bender said. "I wanna get me some Ugly. Or maybe some of the Wally Way Nutsy. Or how about that tasty Look At Ma Pussy. I bet Surus will like that."

"I bet I will, too," Surus said.

"I'll join you," Shaw said.

"Ooh!" Bender said. "I didn't know you two were into that. Can I watch?"

"Bender, are you hyper today?" Shaw asked.

"Is it that obvious?" Bender said. "I get this way when my weapons are taken away."

"Just stay calm, everyone," Rade said. "We'll deal with whatever comes our way."

"What if when we arrive, the Phant is nowhere to be found?" Tahoe said. "Pulling the strings from behind the scenes?"

"That's certainly a possibility," Rade said.

"We might have to give up Batindo to the governor, if so," Tahoe said. "Assuming the governor continues to play the sedition card."

"If it comes to it, we'll give up Batindo," Rade said. "But we'll return to spring him, of course. I never abandon a client. Especially when he hasn't yet paid in full."

They had all been using the private band, excluding Batindo, but as if on cue, the consular official spoke over the common channel. "How come you're all so quiet?"

"We're concentrating on the mission, bro," Lui replied over the same band.

five

Rade and the Argonauts followed the Kenyan Artificial to a subway station, and crowded into a relatively empty train that took them through a connecting tunnel to another dome. When they emerged from the destination station, they found themselves in an area where motor vehicles occasionally drove past.

"The Phant presence is stronger here," Surus said. "This is about as pronounced as the feeling will get. Our Phant is definitely in this dome somewhere."

"It's too bad you can't pinpoint the position with any greater accuracy," Lui said.

"I wish I could," Surus said. "Though I believe it's a safe assumption that we are being brought to the Phant, or one of its proxies."

The team kept strictly to the sidewalk. The buildings here were mid- to high-rise apartments and office buildings, though again retail sections abounded on the first floors. The vehicle traffic was moderate on the adjacent road, and tiny cars zipped to and fro.

"Look at these things," Bender said, apparently referring to the vehicles. "They're like go karts, like what Manic drives."

"I don't drive a tiny colony car," Manic said.

"Suuure you don't," Bender said.

"He doesn't," Fret said. "He has at least three sports cars. TJ, tell Bender."

"Bender knows already," TJ said.

"Sports cars are basically go karts," Bender said. "Besides, real men don't drive. They fly."

"No," Lui said. "Real men pilot mechs."

"Wooyah," Bender said. "You won't get any argument from me there."

The Artificial took them to a tall office building. The overhead map labeled it the "legislature." Four walker robots stood guard at the entrance, while more of the mechanical monstrosities patrolled the grounds.

"Well, if there's one thing to be said for this governor," Tahoe said. "It's that he likes his security tight."

"Just the way I like my pussy," Bender said.

"You mean ass," Manic quipped.

Inside, the team crowded into two elevators and emerged on the top floor.

Combat robots stood guard at the end of a hallway before a pair of double doors. These were Centurion Model 6As—easily identifiable by the characteristic elongated heads that looked like motorcycle helmets replete with dark visors in the fronts.

The Artificial led them to the door, and the party entered the office beyond. A robot receptionist sat behind a desk in front of a floor-to-ceiling window that offered a panoramic view of the city. Hallways branched off to the left and right, leading to more offices. One Centurion 6A stood guard in front of either hallway; plasma rifles hung threateningly from their shoulders.

"Plasma rifles!" Bender said. "Bitches got plasma rifles! Model AR-49s, by my reckoning. I'd give up whooping Harlequin's ass for a year to get my hands on one of those."

"Please, have a seat." The receptionist beckoned toward the four oversized chairs on one wall, which were capable of fitting their bulky jumpsuits. "The governor will see you shortly."

Manic took a seat immediately, as did Fret, Lui and TJ.

"Where the hell am I supposed to sit?" Bender said.

"The floor is always available," Manic said.

Bender leaped forward in a blur and ripped Manic from the chair. Then he sat down and folded his arms over his chest, wearing a defiant expression that seemed to be daring Manic to do something about what Bender had just done.

Manic stood up and brushed the lint from his jumpsuit. "I didn't want to sit anyway."

"Shaw," Lui held out his hand. "I saved this seat for you."

"Thank you," Shaw said. She took the seat. "At least one of you is a gentleman."

"What about me?" Batindo asked. "I am the client..."

"You can sit in my lap," Bender said, flashing his golden grille and tapping the thigh region of his leg assemblies.

Batindo shuddered and turned away.

A boxlike robot on treads emerged from a side hallway shortly thereafter.

"I can take three of you to see the governor," the robot said.

Batindo stepped forward, as did Rade and Surus.

"The rest of you, access my video feed and observe," Rade transmitted. "I've granted read privileges to all of you."

The robot rolled away down the hall, and Rade and his two companions followed. Offices lined the route; their doors were closed, and the viewing windows beside those doors were shuttered. The lights were off in most of them.

At the far end, another Centurion 6A stood guard in front of a thick wooden door. The entrance clicked open, and the boxlike escort robot beckoned for them to enter.

Rade found himself in a large room facing another floor-to-ceiling window. Behind a spartan desk sat a dark-skinned individual dressed in a spritely business suit. Though he didn't wear a shuka blanket, his hair was fashioned into corncobs and dyed red like Batindo's.

It was an Artificial, according to the public profile.

Four more Centurion 6As stood guard inside, at each of the corners of the room.

Rade gazed at the necks and bodies of the closest robots in turn. Rade saw no sign of any neon-colored condensation, which would have indicated Phant possession.

Rade walked past the desk to the floor-to-ceiling window. The closest combat robot turned its body fully toward Rade, following his movements. It seemed ready to attack.

Rade ignored the robot and glanced over his shoulder to get a good look at the back of the governor's neck. The collar of the suit sat relatively low, allowing a good view of the nape; there were no signs of Phant possession.

The governor craned his neck toward Rade uncertainly. "Amazing view, isn't it?"

"Yeah," Rade said. He looked at the two robots

that resided at the corners closest to the window, but also perceived nothing. Hiding in a 6A would have been the perfect place for the Phant: it could control the meeting without drawing too much attention to itself. But it seemed these robots were Phant-free.

Rade left the window. The combat robot that he had aggravated continued to watch him with its weapon slightly raised. It obviously didn't trust him.

Smart robot.

Rade returned to the front of the desk to stand beside Surus and Batindo. He met the eye of Surus and shook his head.

"I'm Governor Ganye," the Artificial said. "Please, have a seat."

Rade took one of the three oversized chairs, while Batindo and Surus took the other two.

"Aren't you uncomfortable in those helmets?" Ganye said

Batindo was the one who answered. "We're more comfortable in the regulated environments of our suits than you are, I'm sure. Especially after what you've done."

The governor raised an eyebrow, as if perplexed. "And what have I done, Muto Batindo?"

"Refused to respond to official dispatches from the Kenyan government, for one," Batindo said. "Given that your communication systems seem intact, this could easily be interpreted as an act of sedition."

"Please, let us not talk of sedition here," the governor said. "You are my guests, and I expect certain behaviors—"

"Guests?" Batindo interrupted, casting a glance at the armed Centurions. "Then why do I feel like a prisoner?"

"The combat robots are simply a security

precaution," Ganye said. "You have taken similar precautions with your own escort. I counted eight robots in your party, and ten mercenaries."

"They are not even armed," Batindo said.

"But they would be, if I hadn't disarmed them," Ganye said.

"By the way, we're not mercenaries," Rade clarified. "We're security consultants."

The governor ignored him, something Rade was definitely not accustomed to. "And it is true that we have not answered communication request from the Kenyan government, Mr. Batindo. While our communications systems seem intact, they are in fact not. While civilian communication bands with their weaker encryption protocols remain open, the systems we use to decrypt official government messages are offline. We have received dispatches from the Kenyan government, yes, but we have been unable to decode them."

"Even if that was true," Batindo said. "Why didn't you send us a message in clear text, or via civilian channels?"

Ganye paused. Then he tilted his head, as if receiving a message only he could hear. Then a smile crept onto his face.

"Boss!" Tahoe said. "A bunch of 6As just rushed the office foyer. We're surrounded... they're forcing us to our knees... binding our arm assemblies behind our backs."

Rade stood. "Why are you arresting my men?"

The 6As pointed their plasma rifles at Rade. He reluctantly raised his hands.

"We would have sent a message via civilian channels," Ganye said. "Except for one small problem. You see, we've revolted against the Kenyan government, and declared our independence."

"And you actually expected that if you didn't tell our government this, they would leave you alone?" Batindo asked.

"Oh, I knew they'd eventually investigate," the governor said. "But I wanted to drag out that day for as long as possible. Because if I told them this planet was ours, they would have sent warships to beat us into submission immediately. By remaining silent, at least I have given my colony time to build more combat robots. And time to hire mercenary warships."

"I see," Batindo said. "So you admit you caused the wreckage of the two tax collection ships whose wreckages we observed on the surface?"

"We ordered their demise, yes," the governor said. "We shot them down with our defense platform when they arrived a month ago. We salvaged the comm node and black box from the lead vessel, preventing your government from remotely accessing the data."

"So you were stalling for time the past month, is what you're saying?" Batindo asked.

"Yes," Ganye said. "Unfortunately, the corvettes managed to destroy our defense platform in the process. If that platform was still intact, I might have used it against you as well. Then again, perhaps not, since I could always use an extra mercenary ship."

"You won't get away with this," Batindo said.

"Won't I?" The red-haired governor tapped his lips. "I could have you executed, you know."

"You wouldn't," Batindo said.

"It is well within my power." Ganye smiled. "I have already killed their tax collectors, after all. And whether I add yet another Kenyan government official to the long list of dead will not affect my fate in any way. They will still send their warships."

Ganye glanced at Rade. "Did I mention I've hired several mercenary ships? They should be arriving in this system any time now. I don't suppose I can convince you and your merry band to switch sides?"

"Oh," Rade said. "So now you're interested in talking to me?"

Ganye shrugged slightly.

"As I already said, we're not mercenaries," Rade told the governor. "Our services aren't for sale to the highest bidder. And even if I wanted to get involved in galactic politics, our vessel is no match for the warships the Kenyan government will send to secure the colony. Nor will the ships of any of the mercenaries you've hired, either."

"In that you are mistaken," the governor said. "You might be surprised at some of the craft Russian mercenaries have in their possession."

A notification was flashing in the lower right of his display. It was a call from Bax in orbit.

Rade connected.

"Go ahead," Rade sent.

"We have some mercenary ships coming in from the Slipstream," Bax transmitted. "I've got classes of all kinds on the way here, ranging from Marauders to Destroyers."

"Destroyers?" Rade said. "You're sure they're mercenary and not Kenyan?"

"I don't think the Kenyans sport the Russian flag," Bax said. "Some of these vessels are obviously stolen. They're title information has been altered to hide their sales histories."

"All right, I want you to reposition," Rade said. "Move away from the colony and try to avoid contact with any of those ships."

"Understood," Bax replied.

Ganye was saying something to Batindo, and when he finished he glanced at Rade. "We've identified the frequencies used by the comm nodes of your shuttles." The governor smiled. "We have begun jamming operations. If you will not join our cause, I cannot allow you to send any further messages in or out. I've also disabled your InterGalNet access."

Rade frowned. Though he hadn't disconnected, the comm status indicator had turned dark. "Bax, do you read? Bax."

No answer came. He tried to tap in Bax once more. The *Argonaut's AI* didn't connect.

"Tahoe, you there?" Rade tried.

"I'm here," Tahoe replied.

Well, at least they still had local connections. That was something facilitated by the transmitters in their Implants, and boosted by the jumpsuits; but without access to the city's comm nodes, they wouldn't be able to reach the ship. And the jammer was apparently preventing them from reaching the comm nodes in their shuttles, as Ganye said, preventing them from getting the signal boost they needed to contact the *Argonaut* in absence of the InterGalNet.

The governor glanced between the two 6A units that resided in the corners of the room behind Rade. "Arrest them."

The forward combat robots trained their rifles on Rade and his companions as the other two left their posts to obey the governor's command.

Rade flinched as his arm assemblies were forced behind his back. He felt the gloves press into his skin where flexicuffs were applied.

"We're being arrested as well, Tahoe," Rade said.

"I've been watching your video feed..." Tahoe responded.

"Your shuttles are hereby impounded," Ganye said. "And their contents confiscated. You will instruct the combat robots you have deployed in your shuttles to surrender immediately. I'm opening a window in the jammer to allow you to communicate with those robots. Be very careful what you say."

Rade switched to the viewpoint of one of the Dragonflies. The feed was relatively good—he was able to piggyback on the open comm nodes distributed throughout the colony once more.

He saw that walker and enforcer units had surrounded both shuttles. While the Dragonflies might have had a slim chance of escape earlier, they had none now.

"Units G and H," Rade transmitted. "You are to stand down. I repeat: stand down. Submit yourself to the authorities for arrest. However, only give them guest privileges to the shuttle. I don't want them completely locking us out."

"Understood," Unit G sent.

The signal abruptly terminated, and Rade knew Ganye had applied the jammer in full force once again.

"Take them to Marakdom," the governor told the robots that had secured Rade and the others.

"What's Marakdom?" Rade asked.

"The highest security prison we have," Ganye said.

The robots forcibly led Rade and his companions outside. The three of them rejoined only some of the Argonauts and allied Centurions. Robot guards watched them from all sides.

"Where is everyone else?" Rade asked.

"We couldn't fit in the elevators anymore," Lui said. "Not with all the guards. So they're taking us down in groups."

Rade gazed at the distant hallway as he waited for

the elevators to arrive.

"There is still a possibility he hosts a Phant," Surus said.

"I didn't see any signs of possession," Rade replied.

"The neck condensation only appears if the Phant is in control of the AI core," Surus said. "It's entirely possible the Phant retreated deeper inside the chest case of the Artificial, perhaps reprogramming or blackmailing the unit to behave the way it did, first."

"If it reprogrammed the Artificial," Lui said. "Then why would it even bother remaining inside? It could have just as easily resided within one of the Model 6As in the room. Safer that way. That's what I would have done."

"We should have seen something in the neck region of the robots, then," Rade said. "I checked them all."

"Could be that it momentarily relinquished control of whatever robot it was possessing," Shaw said. "To evade that initial check. Like Surus suggested might have happened to the governor."

"Maybe," Rade replied. "TJ, see if you can figure out how to bypass their jamming frequency."

"It's an ID-based jammer," TJ said. "Meaning that they're adjusting it to match the frequencies of our Implants in realtime, using the unique IDs assigned to those Implants. So even if we change frequencies, they can reinstate the jam. Not the easiest thing in the world to bypass."

"I have faith in you," Rade said.

The elevator opened, and his turn to go down came.

The robots led Rade and the others from the building. A truck with a wide trailer attached to the rear was waiting just in front. Rade was carried up and chained to the truck bed with the others. Two of the 6As assumed guard positions in the truck bed, while another two sat in the passenger area of the automated cabin.

"Well, looks like I've attained my dream," Bender said. "I've always wanted to go to prison."

"Nothing to call home about," Lui said. "Food's terrible. Gym's terrible. The air reeks of sweat and balls. And your roommates all want to get cozy with your backside."

"Doesn't sound too different from bootcamp!" Bender quipped.

"We're not going to prison," Rade stated emphatically. "Not if I can help it."

six

S ince his hands were bound behind his back, and secured to the truck bed via the chains, Rade flipped open the cap on the surgical laser in his glove by touch. It was located in the index finger. Normally that laser was meant to affect repairs on the jumpsuits of injured comrades, but it doubled as a weak cutting instrument in a bind.

He switched to Tahoe's viewpoint. His friend was situated at the most optimal viewing angle behind Rade, allowing him to get a good view of the flexicuffs and the chains that bound him. Rade positioned his fingertip next to the chain and activated the laser, choosing its most intense frequency, and setting the depth to automatically increase as the metal melted. He fired in rapid pulses, and a small cloud of smoke erupted from the chain. Around him, other Argonauts were following his lead.

It took Rade about five minutes to cut through the chain and free himself from the truck bed entirely. Since Rade couldn't use the laser to saw away at his flexicuffs directly—the angle was too extreme—once he was free, he instead slightly repositioned his body so that his wrists were next to Bender, allowing the latter Argonaut to work at them. Rade tried to be subtle about it, well aware that the 6As in the truck bed were watching them. Indeed, his movements caught the attention of one of the robots. It must have realized he had moved farther than the restraining chain should have allowed, because the robot promptly stood up.

"You there," the 6A said. It tilted its rifle toward Rade.

Right at that moment Rade felt the pressure against his wrists diminish: Bender had cut through the flexicuffs with his own laser.

Freedom.

Before Rade could do anything, Tahoe jumped the robot from behind. Tahoe had had his back to Lui, who had obviously managed to free him as well.

The 6A toppled to the truck bed, its plasma weapon landing within Rade's reach.

Rade wrapped his gloves around the weapon and wrenched it free of the robot's grasp. He knew security features prevented it from being fired by anyone on his team, so he tossed it TJ's way as he clambered to his feet. He fired his jetpack, smashing into the other 6A that had spun about to bring its weapon to bear. He hit so hard that the two of them were flung right off the truck bed and into the incoming traffic lane.

Rade heard the honk of a semi and quickly activated his jetpack again; he heard a screech and saw black smoke fill the air as the self-driving system of the vehicle slammed on the brakes. The front end of the cab struck a glancing blow to his leg before he could get away, and he was sent spinning into the pavement and crashed into a fire hydrant. His impact broke the hydrant right off and the water geysered. Onlookers scrambled to move back.

Rade hardly felt the blows—the suit exoskeleton

had protected him from the worst of it. There were no punctures, either.

He hurried to his feet on the sidewalk and spun toward the street—the 6A had been run over by the semi, and lay in a twisted mess on the solar panels that composed the asphalt. The traffic had ground to a halt, so Rade dashed to the robot and retrieved the plasma rifle, then he jetted onto the roof of a nearby mid-rise apartment.

He raced to the edge of the flat roof—torch-on membrane, approximately ten years old, a part of his mind noted, thanks to the short gig as a general contractor he had worked shortly after leaving the military. Then he leaped across to the adjacent roof.

He continued forward in that way, leaping from roof to roof, trying to make his way toward the blue dots gathered in the bed of the truck that he was tracking on his overhead map. If the vehicle went too far, without access to the city's comm nodes Rade would lose them.

The truck was swerving, and Rade knew his men were vying to get control.

"TJ, I need you to hack the lockout mechanisms of these plasma rifles pronto," Rade sent.

"Working on it," TJ returned.

Rade heard a distant screech, followed by a crash. On the overhead map, the truck had stopped moving. It looked like it had plowed into a low-rise building.

Rade glanced at the vital signs of his team members. All green. Every allied combat robot was online as well.

Rade reached the edge of the building that bordered the street where the crash occurred and he dropped to the elevated rim to aim down. Through the scope, he tracked two walkers approaching the scene from the sidewalk of the nearby avenue, their feet thudding and clanging across the pavement. Bystanders quickly ran from their path.

Rade centered the targeting reticle over the center of mass of the first walker and squeezed the trigger. Nothing. Frustrated, Rade continued to track the tango, and tried again.

"TJ..." Rade sent.

"Got it," TJ replied.

The third time Rade squeezed, a beam of superheated ionized gas emerged from the muzzle.

The walker halted, a hole cleanly drilled through its torso section.

The second walker's upper body immediately swiveled toward Rade.

He ducked and rolled away.

Behind him, several rents tore through the elevated rim of the rooftop where he had been lurking as the walker's invisible lasers fired.

He heard the rising thuds as the robot raced across the street, apparently it was planning on jetting up to his position.

And then he heard a crash.

He glanced at the overhead map and saw that the walker's red dot was quickly moving northward. Tahoe's blue dot was just in front of it.

"Got it," Tahoe said. "Man, I've missed driving these."

"Argonauts, join me on the rooftop I'm highlighting." Rade marked a nearby building on the map. It was on the way to the subway station that would take them back to the first dome, and the hangar bay where their shuttles were stored. According to the map, that hangar bay was the only one in the entire colony. If they wanted to get out of here, they had to make it to that dome.

Rade got up and jetted toward the destination building. On the map, he saw the blue dots of his companions following close beside him. When he glanced to the left, he saw Lui and Bender leaping from building to building across the street from him, along with three allied Centurions. It looked like Lui and Bender had torn the minigun turrets off of one of the walkers.

"Who has Batindo?" Rade asked.

"That would be me." Shaw apparently had a vehicle, because her blue dot was quickly speeding along the map; Batindo's dot was beside hers. At her present speed, she would handily beat them to the building.

"Got a Perdix swarm," Lui said. "Coming in from the east."

Perdix swarms were popular defensive units employed by colonies. Basically, you took drones, added lightweight lasers to them, and sent them out in swarms to act as backups during emergency situations. Designed for military use, they were overkill for most civic disturbances, but now and again, when a bunch of ex-MOTHs were set loose in the geodesic dome of a colony for example, they could prove useful. Especially considering that none of the Argonauts were equipped with the expensive electronic warfare countermeasures that could disrupt the drones' navigation. Nor did they have their Hoplite mechs, whose anti-laser shields could have offset the incoming fire and provided the group with at least a fighting chance against the airborne swarms. As it was, all it would take was one laser hit to the center of mass of his jumpsuit, and Rade, or any of his companions, would be taken down.

He glanced at his overhead map. "I see them. Looks like we're going to have to hole up inside the building when we get there."

"You sure you'll make it before the drones arrive?" Shaw said. "I mean I know I can, but you'll be out in the open for the next minute or so, judging from my estimate."

"Not out in the open," Rade said. He leaped off the current apartment building, firing his jetpack to cushion his fall as he landed on the sidewalk below. A frightened mother lifted her child into her arms, then spun around and ran in the opposite direction.

Rade hugged the walls of the buildings as he proceeded forward, placing the structures between himself and the line of fire of the Perdix drones.

The buildings interfered with the signal between himself and his Argonauts somewhat, so that the blue dots representing his companions on the overhead map occasionally stuttered and froze. Even so, he saw that the other Argonauts who hadn't secured vehicles were doing the same as him: staying close to the building walls.

But speaking of vehicles...

Rade directed his local AI to point out those vehicles running unpatched and outdated software— basically, something he could hack with the rootkit built into his jumpsuit. He dashed out into the middle of the road, directly in front of one of the oncoming self-driving cars that the AI had highlighted. The vehicle's automated system took over and slammed on the brakes.

Rade went to the passenger window. "Open up!"

The frightened passenger simply stared at him, apparently too petrified to move.

Rade bashed the glass with his rifle, breaking it, but

the vehicle was one of the few self-drivers that had steering wheels, and the occupant took manual control and sped off before he could open the door. She wasn't a very good driver, however—most people weren't, due to society's reliance on autonomous cars—and she slammed into another vehicle in the oncoming lane. She would be fine, thanks to the air bag.

Rade repeated the action, and finally got someone to evacuate a compatible vehicle: an old, three-wheel motorcycle-car hybrid. Once inside he applied his rootkit, and assumed full control. There was no steering wheel; he interfaced with his Implant, and controlled the direction of travel via his gaze.

He glanced at the time in the lower right of his HUD and realized he had wasted a full forty seconds flagging down a vehicle, time that could have been used to close the distance with the destination building. Hopefully he would make up for it shortly.

He spun the vehicle around and accelerated. He was out of practice himself, and sideswiped one of the cars parked on the side of the road. He quickly got the hang of it however and sped down the street.

Ahead, a walker robot placed its massive body in his path.

Rade swerved to the side, then set the vehicle to autopilot; he leaned out the window and aimed his rifle at the walker. He fired.

Direct hit. The robot's guns descended immediately as it went offline.

Unfortunately, since he was speeding through a red light at the time, another vehicle slammed into his from the side.

Rade was thrown from the three-wheel hybrid; he instinctively fired his jetpack to cushion his fall. He landed rolling. Behind him, he heard more screeches as other vehicles joined the pile-up.

Still lying on the ground, he spun toward the crash site, not sure what to expect: when he saw only stunned civilians stumbling from the wreckages, he clambered to his feet.

But then beyond the pile up he spotted three enforcer robots dashing toward him.

Rade ducked, making his way to the edge of a crashed vehicle. He aimed his plasma rifle past it and took down one of the robots.

They got smart then and dove for cover. One enforcer ducked into an alleyway, the other behind a lamppost.

Rade pulled himself lower, hiding behind the side of the vehicle as the enforcer behind the lamppost opened fire. Holes were melted in the broken windshield above him, but the laser did not find him.

Rade flattened himself on the asphalt and aimed his rifle below the undercarriage of the vehicle. He spotted one of the enforcers leaning past the edge of the alleyway, and he fired, taking it down. The other broke cover and jetted upward, heading for the rooftops.

Rade scrambled upright and aimed over the broken hood of the vehicle; he caught the robot in his sights just as it landed on the roof, and he squeezed the trigger. The enforcer fell.

He heard the characteristic clang and thud of approaching walkers.

"Rade, where... you?" Shaw transmitted.

"Coming."

He repositioned himself on the far side of the pile-up, and was just starting to track the incoming walkers when the leading members of the Perdix vanguard buzzed past the rooftop above.

Rade pivoted immediately, jetting at full burn toward a nearby building. He crashed through the window.

It was a sit-in bakery of some kind, and clientele who had gathered to watch by the window scattered, taking cover behind the tables.

Two Perdix drones descended into view near the window.

Rade ducked.

Laser bore holes appeared in the far wall behind the counter. It was dangerous to fire in there like that with all those civilians—apparently the governor had given the order to take down the Argonauts at all costs, despite the risk of civilian casualties.

As the incoming fire persisted, Rade low-crawled past the tables to assume a position near the entrance. Then he opened the door a crack and aimed his rifle outside.

The two drones still lingered in front of the broken window, scanning the interior. Rade suppressed a grin as he released two quick shots, taking both out.

But he saw more drones swooping down from above and heading toward the bakery. On the street, more enforcers were also racing toward his position.

Rade withdrew from the entrance and rose to a crouch. Remaining low, he made his way past the counter to the baking area, where robot chefs were hiding behind tables covered in balls of dough. There were two ovens on the far wall, beneath a window. The back door was open a crack to allow cool air inside.

Rade hurried to that door and peeked out. Enforcer robots were setting up in sniper positions on the rooftops across the street. Meanwhile Perdix drones were swooping down from above. On the other side of the street he spotted a subway entrance leading underground. Rade noted the position of the subway, then he went to the ovens. They operated on natural gas. Good.

"Get to the front," Rade said. "Tell the civilians to get out."

The robot pastry chefs obeyed.

He leaned behind the ovens and broke the gas lines, allowing the fumes to fill the room.

Then he went to the back door and waited. He peered through the crack outside. Enforcer robots, armed with rifles, were closing on his position from the street, while drones lined up in a long row above, buzzing as they targeted different parts of the building.

Rade programmed his jetpack to take him into the subway entrance. When he judged that enough time had passed for the civilians to flee the bakery, he threw himself against the back door, aiming his plasma rifle in front of him.

"Now!" Rade instructed his AI as he hit the partially open door.

The jetpack fired, the flames causing the built-up gas to detonate. Rade was thrown outside, but his jetpack used the momentum to carry him toward his target. Around him, enforcers and drones were sent hurtling backward from the explosion. Rade attempted to fire at the rooftop snipers, but he was moving too fast to attain a viable shot.

He flinched as he felt a sudden pain near his shoulder, and another pain in his side.

"Warning, suit breached," the voice of his local AI said.

Then he was falling down the steps into the subway.

seven

R ade smashed into the concrete floor at the
base of the steps and rolled a short ways into
the concrete tunnel. He retracted his helmet
faceplate—with the breaches, pressure had fallen
drastically inside the jumpsuit, making it difficult to
breathe. He took a long inhale.

Guess I'm imbibing the city's air after all.

He scrambled to his feet and dashed into the
underground subway platform, where people had
taken shelter from the fighting behind pillars and back-
to-back benches. He fired at the platform screen doors
as he ran, creating holes in the translucent
polycarbonate from which cracks spidered outward.
He hurled himself at the damaged area, firing his
jetpack to increase his momentum.

The weakened platform screen shattered and he
fell through. He issued countering thrust from his
jetpack to cushion his landing. After touching down,
he sprinted into the subway tunnel; he liberally fired
his jetpack between steps to give himself a bounding
pace.

Pain continued to flare from his wounds. He
glanced down and saw blood oozing from a
perforation on the right side of his midsection. More

blood trickled from a hole near his left clavicle.

He glanced in the digital rear-view mirror—basically the feed from his aft camera piped into the upper central area of his vision—and saw enforcers leaping onto the tracks behind him. Perdix drones followed. Rade quickly rounded the bend before they could get a bead on him.

In two hundred meters he came upon a maintenance door in the side of the tunnel. He broke through and slammed it shut behind him. A ladder led to a grille—it wasn't locked, and opened onto the sidewalk.

He emerged slowly, wary of tangos. He saw the building that he had marked just ahead. He hadn't realized it before, but it was a hospital.

Good. Maybe I can get my injuries treated.

It was surrounded by enforcers, which currently had their backs to him. They had taken cover behind various police cars. Perdix drones, humming like angry buzzsaws, were making dive-bombing runs at the windows.

Rade glanced at his overhead map. His team had holed up within the building, rather than on the rooftop as per his previous instructions. Probably a good idea. Their blue dots on the map had low ping times—indicating a strong, good signal.

"We see you, boss," Lui transmitted.

"I'll be right there," Rade sent.

Rade surveyed the parked cars nearby and his AI pointed out one that was hackable. Rade went to it at a crouch and took control.

The Perdix drones had apparently spotted him, because some were swooping down toward his position. Rade floored it.

The tires flattened under the assault, and the hood

and windshield became riddled with bore holes, but the engine kept running so he maintained the acceleration.

He broke through the line of enforces, striking a glancing blow to one of the police cars, and jostled up the hospital steps until he crashed through the glass front doors. He struck a thin pillar that separated the next set of glass doors inside, ending the impromptu joyride.

He kicked out the windshield and rolled across the riddled hood, landing in front of the vehicle at a crouch. Glass shards from the inner doors crunched underfoot. The acrid scent of burned electronics assailed his nostrils. He heard footsteps and the buzz of drones, both quickly growing in volume from outside.

Shaw, Surus, and three of the Centurions were waiting on the far side of the open concourse, leaning past the edge of a staircase. They had stolen plasma rifles in hand.

"About time you decided to crash the party," Shaw said. "Come on!"

Rade hurried across the concourse.

Shaw and Surus opened fire, taking down his pursuers—a glance in the digital rear-view mirror told him that so far two Perdix drones had swooped inside, along with one enforcer. All three crashed into the ground as he watched.

He continued his mad dash.

When he reached his Argonauts, he ducked behind the railing of the staircase they had gathered upon.

Shaw glanced at his wounds. "Good choice of building."

"You're being sarcastic?" Rade said.

"Not at all," Shaw said between rifle bursts.

"Okay, maybe a bit. Get to the convalescence ward. We're making our stand there. I'm marking the location on the map."

"What about you?" Rade asked.

"We'll be right behind you," Shaw said. "Covering your bee-hind."

Rade took the stairs two steps at a time, though he was feeling fairly winded by that point. He glanced at his overhead map: a swath of mapped areas had been cut through the darkness of the interior, indicating where the other Argonauts had passed. The rest was black and unmapped, as the city data Batindo had given them hadn't included any building blueprints.

He reached the second floor, passing Unit C stationed near the edge of the open stairwell.

"Hurry," the combat robot said.

Rade heard windows breaking and the distant sound of metal feet clanging across the floor; he continued up to the next level. Shaw and the others were close behind him, with Unit C bringing up the rear.

At the third floor he and the others left behind the stairwell and dashed across the hall. Two more Centurions—Units D and E—lurked outside different rooms, their bodies flat against the walls that bordered the doors. As Rade and the others raced past, the robots directed their rifles inside those rooms, providing suppressive fire. Afterwards, the Centurions joined the group, following on drag.

Rade reached the infirmary. TJ and Harlequin were guarding the entrance and waved Rade inside.

"Boss, we've gone and done it this time, haven't we?" Harlequin said.

"You're sounding more like a human all the time," Rade said.

"I've had good teachers," Harlequin replied.

Rade dashed into the room. The air smelled sterile within, heavy with the cloying scent of antiseptic. The room contained eight hospital beds, most of which had been upturned, and the mattresses removed. Argonauts and combat robots had assumed positions beside each of the six windows on the far side. There were tiny holes drilled through the external-facing wall where lasers had penetrated. The team had piled much of the room's furniture, including at least two standalone cabinets, against that wall to provide cover, and propped mattresses over the windows themselves, buttressing them with smaller pieces of furniture such as night tables and visitor chairs. The ex-soldiers aimed their rifles through the cracks between the mattresses and the windows and fired at different targets outside.

The Argonauts with Rade took up positions near the entrance behind him after coming inside. He noticed that the entrance door was shot off its hinges.

Tahoe was lying on one of the intact hospital beds, being tended by a Weaver. Bender lay on another bed with bandages around his bicep, and his leg. Another Weaver was currently examining his toe. Both men were conscious. The legs of their beds had been lowered so that the mattresses sat close to the floor, next to their doffed jumpsuit pieces.

It appeared that his team had taken several doctors and patients hostage: the Kenyan civilians huddled in the middle of the room between the upturned beds. Most likely the hostage-taking had started out as unintentional—the civilians happened to be in the wrong place at the wrong time. Rade wasn't sure how easy it would be to let them go at the moment, given how trigger-happy the tangos in the hallway outside were likely to be.

Batindo cowered in his jumpsuit next to the civilians. He hadn't picked up a weapon for himself. Even if he had, he probably wouldn't have known how to use it.

Rade noticed that not all of the Centurions had been able to acquire rifles either, and these unarmed combat robots idled near the hostages, watching them.

Shaw rushed past Rade and righted one of the beds. She grabbed a spare mattress that was lying nearby and replaced it. "Lie here."

"I can still fight," Rade said.

"I'm sure you can," Shaw agreed. "But for how long? You won't do any of us any good if you topple over from low systolic pressure in ten minutes. Now lie here."

Rade obeyed, tossing his plasma rifle to one of the unarmed robots beforehand. The Centurion nodded in thanks, and took up a position near one of the windows.

Shaw adjusted the length of the bed "legs," lowering them so that the mattress sat as close to the floor as possible. Then she rolled a spare Weaver over to him.

"Take off that helmet," Shaw said.

Rade brought his hands to his helmet, but his fingers hesitated on the open latch.

Shaw raised an eyebrow. "You're already exposed to the atmosphere..."

"Yes, but my helmet might still be giving me some protection from psi attacks, even with the faceplate open," Rade said. "Tahoe, you've taken off yours. Are you sensing anything?"

"No," Tahoe said. "But that begs the question, if I was being bombarded by some sort of psi attack, would I even notice?"

"Probably not," Rade said.

He hesitated a moment longer, then opened the latch and removed his helmet. His head felt cold immediately—he realized his hair was damp with perspiration.

He set the helmet down on the floor beside him. Shaw helped him remove the upper portions of his jumpsuit assembly, then the Weaver set to work on his wounds. One of its telescoping limbs applied a sonic-injector to his shoulder and side regions, and the pain immediately numbed.

Shaw lovingly combed Rade's damp hair while the robot worked. "You're going to be all right."

Rade nodded distractedly. He felt slightly embarrassed by the public attention, though the only ones watching him were the hostages and unarmed combat robots. "Shouldn't you be fighting?"

"I gave up my rifle to one of the Centurions," Shaw said. "So there's nothing else I can do except be at your side, anyway. Which is how it should be."

He wanted to put his helmet back on and shut them all out, even Shaw, and have some quiet time for himself, but he couldn't. Not yet. He forced himself to remain present.

He glanced at the hostages. He thought of how the Perdix drones had fired at the crowded bakery.

"I'm not sure those hostages will prevent the enemy from firing rockets or lobbing grenades in here," he said.

"I'm not so sure either," Lui said from where he was ducked underneath one of the windows. Leaning against a mattress, he cradled one of the heavy turrets he had ripped from a walker unit. "But apparently, we have a VIP in our midst."

"A VIP?" Rade said.

"Batindo says one of these men is a cousin of the Kenyan king," Fret explained. He resided underneath another window, and held a stolen plasma rifle between the crack formed by the shielding mattress and the windowsill above him: he was obviously piping the rifle scope's viewpoint to his Implant, because he occasionally squeezed the trigger.

"Which one?" Rade asked.

Fret pointed out a small man in a white lab coat. According to the public profile on his embedded ID, he was a general practitioner. His name was Ran Kato.

"Batindo recognized his name," Fret continued. "He's convinced the governor won't bomb us, not while we hold him hostage. We had Kato transmit his hostage status on all available channels, and lo and behold, that caused the robots to let up their main attack. At least for the moment."

Rade nodded slowly. "If he really is a cousin of the king, Governor Ganye could use him as leverage when the Kenyan warships come."

"That would be the wisest and most prudent thing to do," TJ said. "But that assumes the man we're dealing with is wise and prudent."

"And not just a prude," Bender joked.

"Like you?" Manic said. "What did you do, bicep curl a porcupine?" He was positioned underneath the window beside Lui, his rifle shoved into the gap between mattress and sill. His eyes momentarily focused on this reality, rather than that of his rifle scope, and he nodded toward the bandage on Bender's bicep.

"Actually I didn't," Bender said. "And how would that make me a prude if I did, bitch? Bicep curl a porcupine. What kind of a moronic—"

"What did you do then?" Maniac's eyes defocused

once more, and he squeezed the trigger on his plasma rifle. "Scratch another drone."

"What did I do?" Bender said. "I was beating off while watching you during the firefight, and I flexed my bicep muscle too hard in my excitement, and the muscle exploded."

"Ah, I can see that," Manic said. "I have that effect."

"Yeah," Bender said, laughing. "When other men witness your manly endeavors, their muscles explode. You make my muscles come, Manic."

"I'm sure I do," Manic said. "Though that looks more like blood to me, not come."

"My muscles had a period because of you," Bender said.

"I don't think Bender's injured too badly," Harlequin said from his guard position by the door.

"I probably am," Bender said. "But these Weaver bitches have dosed me up with so many painkillers I feel higher than a monkey hanging from a giraffe's dick."

"Hey boss," Lui said. "Got something strange to report."

Still lying down, Rade turned slightly toward Lui, but flinched. He felt pain through the numbing in his side, and he wondered just what the hell the robot was doing to him. He didn't want to look, however. That might make him vomit, something he definitely hoped to avoid, especially in front of his men.

"Go ahead," Rade said.

"While we were on the run down there, I detected a quantum Slipstream signature emanating from the legislature building. Of the kind Phants use."

"What do you think our Phant was doing?" Rade asked.

"I'm not totally sure," Lui said. "But we've seen evidence that the Phants use quantum Slipstreams for communications purposes in the past."

"Surus?" Rade said.

"We do use them," Surus said. "Mostly for communications between automated systems in this reality, for example between a remote base and a Mothership. It circumvents the twenty minute requirement my species usually needs when communicating Phant to Phant in the supra-dimension, and the Slipstream nature allows the signals to travel great distances."

"You think our Phant is communicating with a Mothership?" Rade asked.

"It's possible," Surus said. "But as you know, the closest Mothership is six centuries away. More likely, in my opinion, is that it was communicating with some other alien race, closer to this section of the galaxy."

"How could another race even understand the signal?" Lui said. "And the message it contained?"

"A learning process would be required of course," Surus said. "To give you an analogy, it would be similar to communicating with a stranger via Morse code, when the stranger didn't understand the underlying code. It would also require a race with the technology to read the quantum signals in the first place, which would emerge from the Slipstream of the target system. Usually such a race would be late Tech Class III, or early Tech Class IV."

"So more advanced than us, you're saying?" Lui asked.

"There's a good chance, yes," Surus said. "At least in some technologies."

"All right, well, the nearest uncharted system is quite a ways distant," Rade said. "I don't think we have to worry about aliens crashing the party for the time being."

"Famous last words," Bender said.

"I should note that quantum Slipstreams can be detected in the same systems from which they were sent," Surus said. "They don't necessarily have to target a destination system via an existing Slipstream. And they can pass through planets, even suns. If a vessel of some kind were hiding nearby, the signal would reach them..."

"Well, we have more immediate concerns in case you hadn't noticed," Rade said. "I'm not going to worry about hidden aliens or other speculations at the moment. Keep targeting those tangos out there, team. Let's not allow them to get comfortable."

"Oh, I think we all intend to make life as miserable for them as possible," Fret said.

The Weaver finished with Rade shortly thereafter. It healed his wounds, leaving pink scars in place. It applied bandages to either section, saying: "Wear these for the next day. It will reduce the scarring."

Rade shrugged. He had never heard of wearing a bandage to reduce scarring before. He supposed different cultures employed slightly different technologies.

Rade donned his jumpsuit, as did Tahoe and Bender; he replaced his helmet for the head protection it provided, but retracted the faceplate so he was still breathing air from the external environment. He retrieved the suitrep kit from his left cargo pant pocket, and applied patches to the perforations in the fabric of the jumpsuit.

"Might as well open your faceplates," Rade instructed the team. "And conserve your internal oxygen supplies."

The Argonauts complied. Except for Bender, who promptly replaced the helmet he had removed for surgery, and shut the faceplate.

"To hell with that," Bender said. "I'd rather use up all my oxygen than risk exposing myself to a Phant psi attack."

"There's no guarantee we're facing a Black," Surus said. "In fact, we're probably not."

"I don't care," Bender said. "When you've all lost your minds, and you're running around naked and chanting mantras and smearing each other with your own feces, I'll be the one who brings you all back from the brink and tells you I told you so. Even though you wipe your feces on me, I'll do that for you."

"Huh? Where do you come up with this stuff?" Lui said.

"Oh yeah?" Manic countered. "Well, when *you've* exhausted your O2 supply, and the team is stranded out in deep space, forced to make a spacewalk from the ramp of our Dragonfly to the hull of the *Argonaut*, and you suddenly find yourself breathing void, I'll be the one who tells *you* I told you so. Besides, what's the big deal? You already removed your helmet."

"Yeah well, I put it back on. Maybe I'm just a contrarian, you know what I mean? Never been one to follow the herd. It's suited me well in the past." Bender turned toward Surus and flashed his golden grille. "By the way, you interested in dinner tonight, hot stuff?"

Surus frowned. "No."

Rade didn't retrieve his rifle to rejoin the defensive; he simply felt too groggy. He blamed it on a combination of the medication, his healing wounds, and the exhausting flight to the hospital.

So he sat on the floor near Batindo with Shaw.

Bender and Tahoe tried to guard the rear, but they soon gave their rifles back to the unarmed Centurions and joined him, taking their places between two upturned beds.

"Man, can't keep my eyes open," Bender said. "I'm really crashing after that medical high."

"Shaw, take back your rifle," Rade said. "You're in charge. Bender, Tahoe and I are going to rack out. Wake us if you need us. Tahoe, Bender, set your alarms for an hour."

Rade set the alarm in his Implant, then he closed his eyes and was out cold in moments.

eight

Rade awakened to the beeping of his Implant alarm. He dismissed it and sat up, tentatively peering past the edges of the upturned beds he had hidden behind.

Half the team members were still arrayed underneath the mattress-blocked windows, while the other half remained guarding the entrance to the room, their rifles aimed into the hallway outside. Some of the Centurions had crouched behind the upturned bed frames to cover the walls, floor and ceiling themselves with their weapons, as if expecting the enemy to break through at any time. Probably a good idea to watch those areas, considering that plasma rifles could drill through the unarmored walls relatively easily. Though more likely the tangos would detonate charges if they really wanted to break through.

"Shaw, sit-rep?" Rade asked.

"Since you've been under, it's been fairly quiet," Shaw said. "No major attacks... the governor's robots seem content to allow us to slowly pick them off. My guess is Batindo was correct about the VIP."

He glanced at Batindo. The man remained cowering beside him. Like the Argonauts, he had opened his faceplate, which made it easier to see his dyed hair. None of the other hostages had red hair like that, but they were just as frightened. From the way their expressions soured when they glanced at Batindo, he knew they disliked the man. Red was supposed to signify power. Courage. And that he was demonstrating the complete opposite, yet flaunted the hair, made them resentful. Either that, or they just hated him because he was teaming up with these obviously foreign hostage-takers.

Rade studied Ran Kato next. The so-called VIP seemed calmest of the hostages. Because of that alone, Rade could believe he was the king's cousin.

"Bax, do you read, over?" Rade tried.

"They're still jamming our Implants," Shaw said. "TJ hasn't been able to find a workaround."

Staying low, Rade retrieved his plasma rifle from one of the robots and then went to Shaw's side. She had assumed a guard position at the entrance to the room with Harlequin, TJ, Surus and two combat robots.

Rade felt far more alert than he had an hour ago. Bender joined him.

"Hey hotty with a botty," Bender told Surus.

She ignored him.

"Seriously, bro?" Manic said. "You really want to sleep with an alien? A *bug*."

"Why not?" Bender said. "If the bug looks like her..."

"What if you touch the condensation on her neck while you're doing your thing?" Manic said. "You'll be incinerated."

"I'm willing to take the risk," Bender said. "It'll be worth it. Come on, look... that's some fine quality ass right there."

Surus gave him a withering look. "If you don't

cease and desist immediately, I will employ my fist with extreme prejudice on your face."

Bender tilted his cheek toward her and rubbed it with two fingers. "Come on, go ahead. Come on baby. You turn me on."

"Surus, defend the opening," Rade said. "Bender, either shut up, or join the others by the window."

"Sorry boss," Bender said.

Rade glanced at his overhead map and saw eight frozen red dots distributed throughout the partially-mapped hallways and rooms beyond, representing enemy units. The fact they were frozen, with ever increasing ping times, told him that it had been quite a while since any of the Argonauts had sighted those units.

"So what are we looking at?" Rade asked.

TJ was the one who answered. "We got eight tangos holed up down the hall. Some of them in rooms. Some of them in side hallways. Haven't seen any of them in at least half an hour, though. They're definitely keeping a low profile."

Rade shrunk the map and returned his attention to the entrance in the real world; he slowly stood taller, aiming his plasma rifle over Shaw's head and into the hallway beyond. Everything was indeed quiet out there.

He continued scanning the area for about five minutes, then he pulled away to give Bender a go.

He sat down on the floor and leaned against the wall. He was tempted to shut his faceplate so that he could mute them all and cave out. But now wasn't the time.

I just had an hour's rest.

Strange how it didn't feel that way, though.

Rade retreated from the entrance and made his

way at a crouch to the windows. Lui had propped his heavy gun on the center windowsill, pressing it between the shielding mattress and the window frame. Rade noticed that there were quite a few laser and plasma bore holes in the mattress that he hadn't seen before.

Lui notice his gaze. "They're definitely holding back. They only return fire when we engage. It seems they don't want to harm the hostages."

Rade glanced once more at the overhead map to count the red dots distributed throughout the rooftops and windows of the building opposite the hospital. More of those dots were in the street below, taking cover behind the police vehicles.

"Did you ever think," Fret said, "that it's not the hostages they care about, but us? Maybe they want to capture us alive to torture us? Or maybe they even want to hold us hostage."

"Why would they hold us hostage?" Lui said. "Who would pay any money to see us released? Well, Surus I could see... her Green friends would come running with cash. But how about the rest of us? Who are we, other than a bunch of lowlife security consultants?"

"Hey, speak for yourself," Fret said. "I happen to think very highly of myself."

"Oh I know you do," Lui said.

"I'm well-connected, bro," Fret said. "And I can think of more than a few people who would be happy to pitch in and help with whatever price my hostage takers set."

"Well good for you," Lui said. "Glad you have such an extensive support network. Funny that I've never seen any of these people, though."

"Hey, I have a life outside of work, you know,"

Fret said. "What do you think I do in all my spare time? Chat with random chicks on the InterGalNet?"

"That's what I thought, yeah," Lui said with a slight laugh.

"Could be that it's not us they want to take alive," Tahoe said. "Nor even the King's cousin. But him." He nodded toward Batindo.

The Kenyan sensed his gaze and turned his frightened eyes on Tahoe.

"Got an enforcer walking into view," Harlequin said. "With hands raised, and holding a white flag." Harlequin was viewing the hallway outside the entrance via his scope.

"Don't fire," came a distance voice. "I am the hostage negotiator."

"A negotiator?" Rade made his way to the front of the room at a crouch.

He peered past, and saw the black- and blue-colored polycarbonate body of the enforcer. It was indeed waving a white flag.

"Let's see what it has to say," Rade told his Argonauts. He shouted: "Come forward!"

The enforcer slowly approached, the hum of its servomotors and the clang of its metallic feet echoing from the walls. It wasn't armed, as far as Rade could tell. But that didn't mean it was not deadly.

"That's close enough," Rade said when the robot was five meters from the door. "You're the hostage negotiator, you say?"

"I am," the enforcer replied. "What will it take to ensure the release of the hostages?"

"We want safe transport to the hangar bay," Rade said. "Once we've reached the shuttles, we'll release four hostages. The rest will come with us aboard the shuttles. Once we've safely left the city, without any sign of pursuers, we'll drop off the remaining hostages at a location outside the dome, and transmit the positions to you. They will be given jumpsuits to survive the hostile environment, of course."

"I need to see that the hostages are alive," the enforcer said. "I need proof of life."

"I can give you access to one of our video feeds," Rade said.

"No," the enforcer said. "Video feeds can be faked."

Rade nodded slowly. He had already changed his mind, anyway. He didn't want the enforcer to see the positions of his team members in case the enemy was planning a surprise assault.

"Tahoe, bring one of them forward," Rade said.

"I need to see Doctor Ran Kato," the enforcer clarified.

Rade smiled inside. The enforcer had just revealed that the doctor was indeed the one they wanted.

"Bring him, Tahoe," Rade said.

Tahoe appeared a moment later, gripping Kato firmly in one arm. Rade and the others cleared slightly from the entrance, giving the pair room.

"You have your proof," Rade said. "Tahoe?"

Tahoe led the man back inside.

"The other hostages have not been harmed?" the enforcer said.

"Your attacks haven't helped," Rade said. "But so far, no, they haven't been harmed."

"And Batindo is still alive?" the enforcer asked.

"Would you like to see him, too?" Rade said.

"That won't be necessary," the enforcer said. "I will take your message back to my chief for consideration. As a show of goodwill, would you release one of the hostages?"

"In this day and age of modern communications," Rade said. "There's no need to courier messages back and forth. You're in contact with your chief, as you call him, at this very moment. He's likely viewing your audio and video feeds at this very moment—he's heard everything I've said. I have no time for your stalling tactics. Confer with your chief right now and decide if you'll give us what we want."

"I will confer," the enforcer said. "But I ask again, as a show of goodwill, will you release one of the hostages?"

Rade was reluctant to do that, because then the hostage might reveal where his Argonauts were positioned throughout the room once again.

"No," Rade said. "Now get the hell out of here. Come back only when you're ready to give us our escort."

The enforcer moved in a blur. It leaped toward the door, firing its jetpack at the same time.

Shaw managed to get off a shot and hit it in the arm. But the robot was already breaking through their ranks.

It drew a blaster it had hidden in a holster on its back and opened fire.

A Centurion fell.

The Argonauts unleashed a hail of plasma beams at their foe and the enforcer dropped.

"Careful on the crossfire!" Tahoe shouted. The shoulder assembly of his jumpsuit was smoking. It looked like a glancing blow.

"Sorry," Bender said sheepishly. "Got excited there."

Rade stared at the smoldering wreckage, and then transferred his gaze to the fallen Centurion under his employ.

"Is Unit F's AI core salvageable?" Rade asked.

"No," Harlequin said. "The laser passed clean through the core."

Drop my guard for only an instant, and Argonauts die.

"Um, by the way," Lui said. "You all realize the enemy now knows all of our positions, right? Thanks to our smoldering friend here."

"Everyone, to the center of the room!" Rade said. "Cluster around the hostages and seal your faceplates!"

Rade retreated with those who were near the entrance, while the other Argonauts withdrew from the windows. He sealed his faceplate as he ran toward the upturned desks in the middle of the floor, and pressurized the suit to protect his ears from what he expected was coming.

Before he reached the center of the room, he was sent hurtling forward by an explosion behind him as a rocket struck the opening.

He landed near the hostages and spun onto his back to aim his rifle at the door while still lying down.

But then more explosions came—it seemed charges had been placed on the eastern wall, near the front and back of the room, strategically placed to avoid harming the hostages. Plasma rifle beams immediately shot inside, hitting the areas where the Argonauts had resided only moments before.

Rade rolled behind an upturned bed frame next to two hostages and aimed at the forward breach. Other Argonauts covered the rear breach, and still others the enlarged main entrance.

A few moments of quiet followed as the dust cleared.

When the tangos rushed inside, Rade and the others were ready.

Rade took down a 6A, followed by an enforcer.

Motion drew his gaze to the entrance, and he fired at one of two 6As that rushed inside. Several plasma beams battered those two, so that they convulsed in place for a moment before collapsing.

Rade heard the thuds and clangs of falling bodies behind him, and he knew other Argonauts were handling the tangos breaching the rear quarter.

A Perdix drone flew inside. He took it down. Another. Someone else got it. A 6A followed. Plasma beams riddled it.

Rade continued firing with the others until the onrush stopped. The tangos started to hide behind the edges of the breaches they had torn. Rade and the others simply aimed at those edges and burned holes through the walls and into the robots lurking beyond. Metal bodies toppled, landing in view, only to be riddle anew by the Argonaut's plasma beams. The enemy didn't dare fire through the walls at them in turn, not when there were hostage lives at stake.

Finally quiet descended. Rade zoomed in on the holes the Argonauts had made in the walls, but spotted no further tangos in the adjacent room and hallways.

"Seems they've pulled back," Lui said.

"They decided they've risked the hostages lives enough," Tahoe said.

"More like the tangos have risked their *own* lives enough," Lui commented.

"Units A, B, clear the adjacent room," Rade said.

The robots got up and proceeded through the breaches at a crouch.

"Clear," the robots said a moment later.

"Check the entrance of the room while you're in there," Rade said. "Get beads on any tangos lurking out there. Units C, D, do the same with the entrance to this room."

The four robots proceeded to the designated sections of both rooms.

Rade saw a red dot momentarily appear in the doorway of a room across the hall, and Unit C opened fire. The dot ducked into the room.

"Tangos have retreated entirely," Unit C said.

"All right," Rade said. "Let's use the furniture in the adjacent room to shore up our defenses, and plug these breaches."

nine

Rade and the others dragged the bed frames, mattresses, cabinets and other furniture from the adjacent room into the original, and then piled the objects into the breaches, along with the bodies of the terminated robots, so that all entrances to the room were completely blocked. The team salvaged the weapons from the fallen robots, so that none among the Argonauts, neither man nor machine, remained unarmed.

"Centurions," Rade commanded. "I want two of you each to cover those plugged holes. Shove your rifles into the cracks and keep watch. Take down anything you see moving in the hallway, or adjacent room."

"Understood," Unit A said.

"Bender, Tahoe, keep watch on the windows," Rade said.

"You got it," Bender said, moving to the mattresses there.

"Got two hostages injured," Shaw said. She was kneeling beside a man with blood smeared across his bare knee. "They were trying to hide their wounds from me."

The man spoke in Kenyan, and Rade's Implant

translated. "I don't want treatment. I'd rather you let me go."

"Just because you're injured doesn't mean we're more inclined to let you go," Rade told the man. "It doesn't work that way. Not when we have Weavers." He glanced at TJ. "Assuming any of the surgical robots are still intact?"

"It looks like two of them are, yes," TJ replied.

"Good," Rade said. "Carry them over this debris, and have them tend to the injured."

Rade checked the vitals of his teammates. Lui's status was yellow, as was Fret's.

"Lui and Fret, I want you to let the Weavers treat your wounds as well," Rade said.

"After the civilians," Lui said.

"Fine by me," Rade ordered. "Surus and Manic, help them get those jumpsuits off."

TJ carried the Weavers over the debris-covered floor and set them to work on the hostages. When the surgical robots were done with them, they concentrated on Lui and Fret next, who had stripped off their jumpsuits with the help of Surus and Manic.

Rade felt at home through it all. Giving orders in a time of crisis, he was made for that.

But as the crisis slowly passed, he felt a sudden void growing inside of himself. Like a part of him was evanescing. And all he wanted to do was activate his noise cancelers and mute the world.

Can't do that, not yet. Not when the enemy might attack at any moment.

He retreated to the center of the room. "Let's shore up our internal defenses a bit. Tahoe, help me rearrange these bed frames around the hostages. We'll use some of the new debris, too."

Other Argonauts joined in, and they created a

defensive bulwark around the center of the room to better shelter the hostages, and themselves.

Rade took his place in the middle of that bulwark, next to the hostages. Tahoe returned to his guard position by the mattress-covered windows.

Night had fallen by then, cloaking the room in darkness. Rade gave strict orders prohibiting anyone from using any lights—this included headlamps and weapon lights, both in the visual and infrared bands. They all switched to thermal vision mode—something their Implants allowed without the need for helmets. He kept activating the "friendlies" overlay mode of his Implant, which applied blue outlines to the indistinct thermal forms of the Argonauts scattered across his vision, and placed the appropriate callsigns above them.

Shaw was next to him. Rade had opened his faceplate by then, and he gazed at her in the dim light, wishing he could see more than the outline of her face, and the green hot spots created by the thermal vision.

"How are you holding up?" he asked softly.

"I'm holding," Shaw said.

He removed the glove from his right hand, and reached toward her open faceplate. He hesitated, then finally touched her cheek with the palm of his hand.

"What?" she said. She sounded miffed.

"Nothing." Rade retracted his hand and sighed; then he raised his noise canceler about her so that the others wouldn't hear. "I just wanted to assure myself it was you, and that you're really all right."

"I can hold up as well as the rest of you," Shaw said. "I have a jumpsuit. It's the great equalizer, remember?"

Rade smiled sadly, though he knew she couldn't see it. "The physical side I have no worry about, not while you're in that suit. It's the mental part that bothers me."

"You don't think I have the mental fortitude to handle this situation?" Shaw said.

"I know you do," Rade said. "But that doesn't mean I don't worry about you."

"In all your years in the military, you've never been in a situation quite like this, have you?" Shaw said.

"No," Rade said. "Though some situations have come close. We used to train for scenarios just like this back in the platoon. Staying up for days on end to snipe a single target. Defending our positions on a mountaintop for a week. Or Trial Week. I told you about Trial Week, didn't I?"

"Yes," Shaw said. "Five days of no sleep and constant, abusive PT, with various painful evolutions thrown into the mix. You've told me the hopelessness gets so bad all you want to do is quit. Trial Week: the point where MOTH trainees either break, or pass."

"Yes," Rade said. "All of us trained for this. And have had the experience to backup that training. Except you. Which is why I worry."

"Don't," she said. "While I might not have gotten the training, like you, I've had more than my fair share of experience. When I was trapped on a barren planet nine thousand lightyears from home, with little hope of ever returning, I quickly learned to be resilient. I've learned that there is always hope, even when things seem hopeless. And if there isn't any, then we make our own."

Rade felt her bare hand wrap around his—she had removed her glove. He squeezed his fingers around hers. "I love you more than anything in this moment."

"And I love you," Shaw said. She raised his hand, lifting it to her face, and pressed it hard against her cheek. "You made me believe in love."

"And you made me believe I was capable of loving," Rade said. He chuckled. "But let's leave it at that before we get too sappy."

She released his hand and he withdrew it, wondering if he had said the wrong thing.

Probably. He was a master when it came to combat and command, but dealing with Shaw, well, sometimes he could be a big oaf.

But then she tilted her upper body forward and leaned the front portion of her helmet against his. She just held that position, her face a few centimeters from his own. He felt her hot breath against his lips. It smelled minty, despite everything they had been through.

He wondered what his own breath smelled like. Probably terrible. Shaw didn't say anything, though.

Her arms reached under his jumpsuit and she pulled his body into hers. "I just want to hold you here for the rest of the night. You were right. It's a front. I feel like I'm on the verge of collapsing. I put on this brave face, pretending I'm a super strong, super brave person. But inside I'm afraid. I want to believe we'll make it out. I want to believe this will end well. But a part of me just can't accept that. The weak part."

"Don't say that," Rade told her. "I know it's not true. You just told me we make our own hope. After hearing something like that from you, I know there's not a weak bone in your body."

"But there is," Shaw said. "All of this is a big lie, a front for you and the men."

"Stop it," Rade said. "You survived all those months alone on that planet nine thousand lightyears from Earth. You had to be strong to endure that."

"Again you use that example," Shaw said.

"You used it," Rade said. "Not me."

"Yes," Shaw said. "But if I'm truly honest with myself, I wasn't alone on that planet. I had Queequeg. My beautiful pet. Queequeg. Who died for me. And I had Fang. I've never forgiven myself for what happened to either of them. If I'm so strong, why couldn't I save them?"

"You can't save everyone," Rade said. "Not even I can. You've seen it. Watched men die under my command."

She slid her helmet to his shoulder, and rested it there. She was weeping softly. "But you've always saved me."

"And you've saved me in turn," Rade said. "In more ways than you know."

He held her for several moments until she had calmed down. Then he said: "Let's leave it at: we're both strong, for the most part, but have moments of weakness."

"Yes," she said. He thought she was smiling, from the sound of her voice. "That works for me. When we're done here, I seriously want to take a month off from all the Argonauting, and just spend some solid Rade and Shaw time together. You know, the kid-making kind?"

"We've been falling out of practice a bit, haven't we?" Rade said.

"A little," Shaw said.

"I promise to remedy that when this is done," Rade said.

"Good," Shaw said.

He saw Tahoe approaching at a crouch in the dark, and he released her and repealed the noise canceler.

Tahoe ducked down behind the bed frame beside him. "You missed the drama."

"Did I?" Rade asked.

"Batindo was getting antsy," Tahoe explained. "He was convinced the governor was coming for him any moment. I had to sonic inject him with a tranquilizer I purloined from a Weaver. Calmed him down, for now. Seems to be sleeping."

"Good." Rade glanced at the window area, where he had posted Tahoe.

"Lui relieved me," Tahoe said. "He's all healed up now. Got the Weaver to inject a stimulant to counter the numbing agents."

Rade nodded after seeing Lui crouched there beside Bender. He checked Fret's vitals. He was in the green, too.

"How are the hostages?" Rade said.

"Weavers have taken care of them," Tahoe replied. "They're sleeping."

Rade nodded. "I'm going to have to schedule some rack-out time for the others, soon."

"Probably a good idea." Tahoe raised a noise canceler around himself and Rade.

"So, any idea how the hell we're going to get out of this one?" Tahoe said. "Seems like there's no way out."

Rade suppressed a sigh. He felt like he had just had this conversation with Shaw. But that was part of being a leader: he had to bolster up those who followed him, sometimes individually, sometimes as a group.

"I don't know, Tahoe..." Rade said. "But we'll find a way."

"Do you think the governor is going to agree to our demands?" Tahoe asked.

"Well, they must realize by now we're not giving up without a fight," Rade said. "So unless they're willing to kill all the hostages to take us down, they're going to have to."

"That's good, then," Tahoe said. "And we haven't even talked about how we're going to capture that Phant."

"One step at a time, my friend," Rade said.

Tahoe nodded, then repealed the noise canceler. He remained near Rade, but didn't say anything more.

Rade raised his own canceler around Tahoe.

"Do you ever regret having kids?" Rade said. "Considering how little you've seen them over the years?"

"Where did you get that impression?" Tahoe told him. "I've seen them a lot. When on deployments, I relied on the InterGalNet to send videos and messages back and forth. And between deployments, living the base life, I saw them every evening."

"I was actually referring to that latter case, the base life," Rade said. "Because I meant seeing them in person. And you can't tell me that videos and messages are the same thing as face to face contact."

"No, they're not," Tahoe admitted. "Which is why I try to get my family to visit whatever bases we're spending liberty at these days. But while I might regret not spending as much time with them as I could, I don't regret having kids per se. I truly love them. I feel... complete with them, like I'll live on even if I die. When they were younger, I was afraid of never watching them grow up. I didn't want them to lose their father. But now that they're older, I'm not as afraid of dying. Because like I said, I feel like I have a legacy to leave behind. And that's a precious feeling. Something no one can take away from me. So no, I don't regret having kids." He paused. "I take it Shaw has been getting on your case about having a few, has she?"

"Surprisingly, no," Rade said. "I told her I wasn't ready, and she respects that. I just can't see myself piloting the *Argonaut* around the galaxy with kids running around the hallways and getting in the way of hardened military men. It's just not the kind of atmosphere conducive to raising a kid. Plus, they're going to idolize some of the men, no doubt. What if my kids end up growing into little versions of Manic and Bender?"

"That wouldn't be so bad," Tahoe said. "Those two are some of the most heroic men I know."

"I mean how the two of them are always scuffling with each other," Rade said. "And not just verbally."

"They're just play fighting," Tahoe said.

"Really?" Rade said. "You call black eyes and broken arms play fighting..."

"It is, for ex-MOTHs," Tahoe said.

Rade sighed. "All right, well, you get what I'm talking about though?"

"My kids fight all the time," Tahoe said. "I think it builds character."

Rade chuckled. "Sounds like you're trying to edge them toward a career as MOTHs."

"Actually, I haven't done any edging whatsoever," Tahoe said. "But I think they're going to choose that path anyway. They're already hanging out with Skullcracker back on Earth. He's putting them through a training regime."

"Nice," Rade said. "I'm surprised you haven't tried to dissuade them."

"Hey, you're the dissuader!" Tahoe said.

"I'm surprised you remember," Rade said. That had been his occupation before he joined the military. A *Disuasivo*, or Dissuader. Basically a bodyguard. Not too far removed from being a security consultant.

"Anyway, back on point," Tahoe said. "Why would I dissuade them? Being a MOTH is one of the best things that ever happened to me. Sure, it's hard as hell, but I don't regret a minute of it, and I wouldn't change a thing. If my two boys want to be MOTHs, then so be it."

"What about the girl?" Rade asked.

"She has no interest in the military," Tahoe said. "She's happy to collect basic pay at the hands of the government, and write books."

"She writes books?" Rade said.

"Yeah, or she's trying to," Tahoe said. "Not much of a market for books these days. But hey, I figure, as long as she's doing what she loves, what does it matter?"

Rade nodded slowly. "The things we talk about when we're holed up in the middle of a hospital, under siege by killer robots, with the only thing preventing a crazed governor from killing us all is one of the king's cousins we lucked out in capturing."

"Yeah," Tahoe said. "It never ceases to amaze me, either."

Rade waited a few moments to confirm that Tahoe had nothing more to say, then he repealed the noise canceler. "Okay, Argonauts, it's time to rack out. Bender, Tahoe and I will keep watch, since we rested earlier. Everyone else, except Harlequin and Surus, I want you to rack out with the hostages."

"But I just injected a stimulant," Lui complained from his position near the window.

"When you close your eyes, I bet you'll fall asleep in under five seconds," Rade said.

Lui hesitated, then replied: "Probably right."

"Good, so swap positions with me," Rade said.

"Surus and Harlequin, you might as well join the rest of us at the windows."

He made his way over the debris to the window area with Tahoe, and took up the post vacated by Lui. He left the robots in position by the plugged breaches.

He forced his rifle into the crack between the mattress and the window, and switched to the viewpoint of the scope. He scanned the opposite buildings in the dark, and the streets below, searching for heat signatures. He checked the overhead map for the positions of the tangos that were spotted last, but saw nothing out there in the corresponding real life locations. He did occasionally catch glimpses of heat signatures, as enemy robots repositioned, but they were never in the open long enough for him to pick off any of them.

"Surus, are you still detecting the Phant?" Rade asked.

"Yes," she said from her position two windows down from him. "He hasn't left this particular dome, if that's what you're asking. The strength of his presence has remained a constant."

"Why do you always call them 'he,' as if they're men," Bender said. "That seems kind of sexist, doesn't it? Associating the evil of Phants with us men. Like we're responsible for all the ills of the world."

"I call them 'he' because when I think of our prey, I am reminded of you," Surus said.

"*Me?*" Bender said. "What the hell? Like I'm an evil glowing mist intent on the destruction of humankind or something."

"I am reminded of something I can easily squash," Surus clarified.

"Ah," Bender said. "You're lucky you're our client, or I'd have to smack you up for that comment.

Course, I wouldn't want to mess up that pretty face of yours."

"Your weak blows would cause no damage to my face, I assure you," Surus said.

"Okay Bender, ease off the client please," Rade said. "Concentrate on the tangos out there."

"Sorry boss," Bender said. A moment later: "Sorry, Surus."

She made no response.

"See, I knew she wouldn't answer," Bender said.

"I didn't notice Rade answering, either," Surus said.

"He doesn't have to," Bender said. "Because he's the boss."

"As your client, technically I am your 'boss,' too," Surus said.

"Nope," Bender said.

The night passed without incident. The sleepers relieved Rade and the others after three hours to complete the watch, and Rade gladly took his turn in racking out.

ten

R ade awoke in the predawn hours as the glow bars embedded in the geodesic dome began to emit a deep red in simulation of a sunrise.

"Sit-rep?" Rade said, edging his way toward the blocked windows.

TJ glanced back from his position beside a furniture pile under one of the windows. "Nothing has changed since last night. It's dead out there. The whole area is still cordoned off by the police. Robot snipers lurk on the rooftops, and inside windows."

Rade accessed the feed from TJ's scope and surveyed the opposite building. He saw bore marks in the walls surrounding the windows where the Argonauts had attempted to hit whatever was hiding on the other side, but otherwise, there were no tangos.

He dismissed the feed, and saw similar holes in the walls and furniture next to the window. If the police wanted to, they could unleash a continuous barrage that would eat right through those barriers. But then they'd risk the hostages.

Those Kenyans are the only thing keeping us alive right now.

He glanced at the Centurions that had kept their positions at the breaches throughout the night. "Any movement in the hallway or adjacent rooms? Or signs they're sending up another hostage negotiator?"

"No," Unit A replied. "It is also 'dead' inside the building."

Rade exhaled. It looked like it was going to be another long day. He checked his meal replacement levels. Unless they could find some food in the hospital, they would have to start rationing soon.

"Maybe we should surrender?" Fret said.

"You really want to spend the rest of your days rotting away in a prison cell on some colony world?" Manic said.

"But at least we'll live to see another day," Fret said. "Once we're in prison, we can escape, and—"

"Escape, bro?" TJ said. "You know how secure colony prisons are these days? There's no 'escape.' Not from a place like this. You serve your forty year sentence, and you go home."

"Forty years?" Manic said. "That's lenient. After what we've done, our sentence will be a least double that."

"You would want to go to prison," Bender told Fret. "You're all ready to open up your ass, ain't ya? Come here... I'll knock out your teeth so you can give better blow jobs. Do you a favor."

"So that's what happened to your teeth," Fret said. "I always wondered about that gold grille you wear. But seriously, you and TJ are the best hackers we have. I'm sure one of you could find a way to break us out—"

"No," TJ said. "The first thing they'll do when we're incarcerated is short out our Implants. Then give us access-limited aReal goggles to wear instead. There is no way to escape the sandbox of those goggles. We won't be able to connect with anything."

"Speak for yourself, bitch," Bender said. "There's always a way. Never met a pair of goggles I couldn't privilege escalate."

"Yeah well, tell you what," TJ said. "How about you surrender, and meanwhile the rest of us will make our way to the shuttles. We'll leave a Dragonfly behind for you so that when you're released for good behavior in forty years you can take it into orbit and head home."

"If they arrest me, I'll free myself and take a Dragonfly into orbit long before you reach the shuttles," Bender said. "I guarantee you. I got skills, baby. Skills with a z."

"Look who wants to go to prison now," Manic said. "Maybe we should be knocking out *your* teeth, Bender. Or is that grille removable? I bet it is, you BJ master you."

"Hey, I just noticed," Fret said. "TJ rhymes with BJ."

"What are you trying to say?" TJ said, his voice dangerously soft.

"I do believe the bitch known as Fret wants to give you a BJ," Bender said. "You know, getting in some practice for the days to come."

"Guys!" Lui stiffened. "I'm reading increasing toxicity levels. They're piping gas in here!"

"Faceplates shut, Argonauts!" Rade said.

The glass portions of the helmets closed across the squad. The hostages didn't have faceplates, and in seconds they collapsed, succumbing to the invisible gas.

"What's going on!" Batindo said. He had shut his faceplate like the others.

"Figure it out," Rade said.

Next, from a small vent on the wall, thick white

mist began to flood the room.

"I'm getting troop movements in the hallways," Unit E reported from its position near the blocked entrance.

"Fire at will," Rade said. "Take down as many of them as you can."

"Retreat from the windows," Rade instructed his Argonauts. "Deploy behind the upturned bed frames next to the hostages. Robots, remain in position. Don't let anything get into the hallway, or the adjacent room."

As the Argonauts took their places in the center of the room, each of them crouching beside a hostage, Fret said: "We're using the hostages as human shields?"

"Essentially," Lui said.

Unit E collapsed at the entrance. A laser bore hole had passed clean through its head.

The white gas continued to pour into the room from the vent, becoming so thick that soon Rade couldn't discern his own hand in front of him.

Rade tried LIDAR, but the expected three-dimensional wireframe didn't appear.

"The gas is diffusing the LIDAR," Lui said.

"The fog is drifting past the breaches," Unit D said. "Visual and LIDAR-based targeting is useless."

"Switch to echolocation," Rade said. He did so, and soft squawking sounds emitted from his helmet. Promptly a white wireframe representation of his surroundings appeared, revealing the area the same way the LIDAR would have. It wasn't as detailed, though: it was like taking a high polygon computer-generated scene and reducing the polygon count so that the individual features lumped together. The low polygon count made his glove appear like a mitten, for example, in the way that it joined the individual fingers into a solid mass.

The helmets around him emitted similar soft chirps at different frequencies so as not to interfere with one another. Strictly speaking, only one of them needed to activate echolocation, because their Implants allowed them to share the resultant data; but it was always good to have them all operating for redundancy purposes.

"Echolocation won't work at these breaches," Unit D said. "Unless you want us to clear the blocking debris?"

"The enemy units know echolocation won't penetrate the debris," Lui said. "That's why they're flooding the rooms with gas."

"Centurions, retreat from the breaches," Rade said. "Join us in the center of the room."

Rade and the others waited for the attack to come. Several quiet moments passed. He heard the patter of steel feet in the adjacent room. Then a soft thud.

"Prepare for breaching explosion," Rade said.

It came soon enough. The loud bang momentarily disrupted the echolocation stream, whiting out his view. A moment later the three-dimensional wireframe overlay returned, in time to represent two humanoid intruders making their way into the room at a crouch from the side wall.

"Fire." Rade aimed his targeting reticle over the center of mass of one of the tangos and squeezed the trigger.

He heard a tumbling sound, like that of a grenade bouncing across the floor over the debris.

"Echobang!" Tahoe shouted.

A loud squawking erupted from just beyond the shield of upturned bed frames, randomly cycling through several frequencies and pitches to play havoc with their echolocation stream.

"Bender, coordinate with the AIs of our jumpsuits!" Rade said. "Set our squawk boxes to cycle through the sound frequencies, and freeze on the clean hits!"

"Roger that!" Bender said.

The chirps from the noise generators rapidly crescendoed around him. Whenever one of them got a hit on a "clean" frequency—one that allowed for proper digital reconstruction—the data would automatically transmit to them all, providing a glimpse of the room before the echobang squawker ruined it once again. By having Bender "freeze" those clean hits, the digital representation of the mist-filled room would seem to update in intervals, redrawing when the next data hit came in.

The enemy would use a similar tactic, though since they were linked to the echobang, their echolocation generators could counter in realtime to provide a constant live representation, giving the tangos a slight advantage.

Rade momentarily received an updated picture of the room. It refreshed in random intervals ranging from five hundred milliseconds to two full seconds thereafter.

The room appeared empty between several updates. He thought he heard a soft chirp intermixed among those of his men—enemy echolocation. The sounds seemed to come from all directions at once.

And then the display updated: two robot shapes appeared, halfway across the room.

Rade and the others fired immediately before the positional data became too outdated.

He heard clangs over the squawking of the

echobang; the shapes didn't move, of course, but in the next update the robots had vanished from view.

Two more tangos down.

"Unit D, see if you can find that echobang!" Rade sent.

Another tango appeared in the next update. Once again Rade and the others fired, eliminating it.

The echobang abruptly ceased chirping.

Rade's vision once more began to update in realtime; he left the helmet coordination in place, however, should the enemy try that tactic once again.

He scanned the room, waiting for another enemy to step into the fog.

That was when he noticed movement on the floor nearby, about a meter in front of his upturned bed frame. It looked like... a rifle swiveling into position?

"They're crawling on the floor!" Rade sent.

The low-resolution of the echolocation polygons had allowed the crawling robots to blend-in almost entirely with the floor. Rade and the others directed their rifles downward and fired at will, razing the floor in front of their makeshift bulwark.

The mist began to clear. The receding clang of steel feet in the next room told him the enemy was retreating.

"We've staved off another volley," Lui said. The relief was obvious in his voice.

"You think they'll give us safe passage to the shuttles now?" Fret asked.

"I doubt it," Rade said. "They'll be back again, soon, to try some other underhanded tactic I'm sure. But what they don't understand is that we're well acquainted with their methods, since we've used them ourselves many times... for every tactic they have, we have a countermeasure."

The mist had cleared enough by then that Rade could dismiss his echolocation and revert to the visual band. He saw that the explosion had cleared one of the wall breaches.

"Centurions," Rade said. "Secure that opening."

Rade waited for the robots to move into place.

"It's clear," Unit C said.

"All right, Units A and B, stand guard while the rest rebuild that breach," Rade said. "Unit D, assume a watch position near the entrance. Harlequin, check if Unit E can be salvaged. Argonauts, gather the weapons from the fallen. Lui, Tahoe, resume watch positions by the windows. Shaw, Surus, check on the status of the hostages. See if you can revive them. Maybe with some sort of stimulants the Weavers can provide."

Some of the Argonauts left their positions behind the bed frames to salvage the rifles from the terminated robots, and slung them over their shoulders.

Shaw and Surus examined the unconscious hostages, who were still breathing, then went to a nearby Weaver they had sheltered behind an upturned closet, and returned with a sonic injector. They moved from hostage to hostage, applying the injector to the arm region, waking them in turn. In moments all of the hostages were awake.

"This is really strange," Lui said from the position he had taken underneath a debris-covered window. "The police are all retreating. And fast. Like they're afraid the governor has decided to bomb the hospital or something."

"Time to get the hell out of here?" Fret said.

"Wait," Tahoe said. He lingered beneath another window, his rifle wedged in between the mattress and the sill. "I don't think they're planning on bombing the building. Something else is happening. Look past the buildings, into the sky beyond the geodesic dome. There's a strange black cloud."

Rade switched to the viewpoint of Tahoe's scope and saw the cloud he was talking about.

"Looks almost like the kind of cloud you'd see forming around a meteor during atmospheric reentry under certain atmospheres," Lui said. "Or maybe a large vessel."

"Looks like a hairy muff to me," Bender said.

The glass tiles composing the geodesic dome began to shake visibly. A clattering sound suffused the inner environment of the colony, seeming to come from every direction at once.

"Sonic booms are assailing the dome from the outside... shaking the glass tiles," Lui said. "Whatever that object is, it's big."

Distant screams were heard in the streets below.

An air raid siren sounded.

"Do you hear that?" Fret said. "That's the sound of a colony about to fall."

Sharply defined edges began to take shape near the outskirts of the cloud as the object within decelerated.

"That's no meteor," Tahoe said.

eleven

I n moments the cloud coverage subsided entirely, revealing an elongated diamond shape. It was colored molten red, perhaps from the heat of reentry. From the bulging portion near the middle, several tines protruded in a ray-like fashion. The clattering of the dome's glass had ceased, but the air raid siren persisted.

Above the ship, a massive formation of green clouds was forming, with the tips spiraling off into the higher atmosphere.

"Uh, what the hell is going on above the ship?" Tahoe said.

"Looks like a storm," Fret said.

"That's no storm," Lui said. "That's the planet's atmosphere. They're siphoning it away."

"What?" Tahoe said. "Impossible."

"Let's not throw out alarmist theories," Manic said. "You'll scare the children."

As Rade watched, the storm became even larger.

"I'm telling you, they're sucking away the planet's atmosphere," Lui said.

Rade switched back to his own viewpoint.

"Well, at least we know who our Phant was calling with the quantum Slipstreams," Manic said.

"Just goes to show you," Bender said. "Phants are so afraid of us, they have to call in their alien buddies. And those aliens in turn are so scared shitless of us, they have to suck the whole planet's atmosphere away before they feel safe enough to engage!"

"Or maybe they just operate better in the void," Lui said.

Shaw stepped over the debris to stand beside Rade, then she peered past the mattress that blocked a nearby window.

"Careful," Rade told her.

"I want to see it with my own eyes," she said, shoving her rifle past the mattress. "Or my own scope, anyway..." She was quiet a moment. "Incredible. So here we are, present at the forefront of an alien invasion."

"It's always been my dream," Manic said.

"Mine too." Bender stuffed his rifle into a bore hole on the exterior wall. He'd given up his minigun turret for the smaller weapon—the turret was simply too unwieldy, especially for the close quarters fighting that had followed.

Once he was in place, Bender seemed to address the aliens: "Nice ship you got there, bitches. Now give me some bugs to shoot!"

"We're all going to die," Batindo said.

"No," Bender said. "Just you."

"Now would be a good time to make our way back to the shuttles," Lui said.

"What about them?" Tahoe nodded toward the hostages.

"We let them go, obviously," Manic said.

"You're free to go," Rade told the hostages.

The men and women got up.

"Not you," Rade told the VIP, Ran Kato. "You

stay. We need an insurance policy in case Governor Ganye isn't done with us."

"Then I stay, too," one of the women said. She was dressed in a nurse's scrubs.

"That's completely fine with me," Rade said.

The remaining hostages hurried to the most recent breach; the robots had only just finished piling the debris into it, and stepped aside to allow the Kenyans through. The men and women frantically tore down the blocking furniture and in moments they were away.

"Centurions, track them through the cracks in the breaches," Rade said. "I want to know if anyone is waiting to receive them out there."

A moment later Unit A said: "There's no one. The hallway remains clear."

Rade switched once more to Tahoe's scope, which Tahoe had kept directed toward the alien vessel. The hull had darkened from red to black, perhaps having cooled after reentry. He saw dark streaks emerge from the tines protruding from the middle of the ship.

"Tahoe, can you track one of those streaks and zoom in?" Rade asked.

"On it," Tahoe replied. The display shifted to follow one of the streaks, and then the magnification increased: it appeared to be a dark pod of some sort.

"Who wants to bet that those are troop shuttles?" Manic asked.

"Lui, can you compute a trajectory?" Rade asked.

"Already have," Lui said. "Those things are headed straight for the geodesic domes composing the colony."

The air raid siren stopped just in time for Rade to hear several loud thudding sounds, joined by the noise of breaking glass. Via Tahoe's scope, he saw shards raining down from above. Dark pods followed, crashing out of view behind the buildings.

"Tahoe, see if you can get me a bead on one of those pods," Rade said.

Tahoe swept the streets below. "They all landed past other buildings."

"All right, then point your scope upward, toward the roof of the geodesic dome," Rade said.

Tahoe did so. Rade saw several punctures in the glass where the pods had impacted. Too many.

"I'm guessing the dome repair drones aren't going to be able to fix those in time..." Fret said.

"It's getting windy out there," Tahoe said.

Rade could hear the now raging wind, intermixed with screams. The holes in the dome whistled terribly as the air was sucked out.

"Shit!" Rade said. His faceplate was still sealed from the earlier attack, as were the faceplates of the other Argonauts, protecting them from the decompression that was in progress. But it wasn't the Argonauts he was worried about.

He glanced toward Kato and the nurse. "Does this hospital have auto-seal capabilities?" That was a safety feature that activated when a dome was breached to prevent loss of life.

"Not this one, no," Kato said. "But there is a storage compartment on the floor below where we keep emergency environmental suits."

He returned his attention to his Argonauts. "We have to get these civilians to those jumpsuits before the oxygen is completely sucked out of the dome. Lui, how long do we have?"

"I'd say about ten minutes, less if more of those pods break through," Lui said.

"All right, Kato, lead the way," Rade said.

Kato and the nurse hurried through the breach the

previous hostages had cleared, and into the adjacent room. The combat robots followed, with the Argonauts on drag. They kept their weapons at the ready.

The hallways were completely deserted. They passed a few fallen robots that the party had taken down during the siege, but otherwise there was nothing out there. The different hospital rooms had been completely evacuated.

They clambered down the stairs to the second floor and found the storage closet Kato had mentioned. The two Kenyans stripped down and put on the thermal undergarments required by the environmental suits, and with the help of the Argonauts they donned the various assemblies in record time. In moments they were completely suited up, and their helmets sealed.

"Give me access to your vital feeds," Rade commanded.

The two obeyed, and their green status indicators appeared on his HUD along with those of his fellow Argonauts.

Rade glanced at a doorway adjacent to the closet. It opened up into a room with windows. He motioned the Argonauts to assume a defensive position at the entrance to that room.

When everyone was in place, Rade said: "Units A and B, go to the closest window. Stay low... do what you can to stay out of view from any observers outside."

The robots obeyed. Rade switched to Unit A's video feed as it peered out into the street below. The wind seemed to be dying down: tree branches stopped waving, and flags hung limply.

"Told you they were sucking away the planet's

atmosphere," Lui said. "Notice how none of the external gases came rushing in here? We're operating in the void."

"Not that it really matters either way," Shaw said. "The atmosphere was just as poisonous as the void."

"It matters," Lui said. "Because it affects any future terraforming the Kenyans may have had planned for this planet. As in, it's going to take a lot more work to terraform going forward."

"Maybe that's what the aliens want," Shaw said. "To prevent us from colonizing this planet."

"Or it could be what I said earlier, that they operate better in the void," Lui told her.

"We have no idea what they want," Tahoe said. "Any guesses we make are pure conjecture at the moment."

"Unit A, scan the rooftops and windows," Rade said.

Unit A zoomed in and ran its camera across the requested areas. They seemed clear of tangos.

"Redirect your vision toward the dome," Rade instructed the unit.

The view shifted as the robot glanced toward the top of the environment. Dome Drones had clambered to the perforations and were in the process of repairing them. Those drones were directly connected to the metal framework composing the geodesic dome, which they used like a rail system. The robots had thick cylindrical bodies—essentially serving as kilns—with pincer-like hands that redirected the molten glass from the internal ovens into replacement material to fill the breaches. They were basically big 3D-printers.

As Rade watched, the drones began to drop from the dome one by one, crashing soundlessly into the street below.

"What—?"

"They're being shot down by some new friends," Tahoe said. "Look at Unit B's feed."

"I found one of the pods," Unit B said.

Rade switched to the secondary feed that Unit B was returning.

The Unit had focused on a pod that had crashed about three blocks away, judging from the zoom level. The upper part of the ovule pod protruded from the asphalt; cracks had formed in the surface of the road all around it.

As Rade watched, a spider-like creature emerged from the top of the pod and clambered down onto the street. Unit B zoomed out slightly, revealing more of them casually spreading out from the pod. Maybe ten in total. They carried what looked like large tracking turrets on their backs. Those turrets occasionally flashed—obviously firing some sort of laser. Tiny holes appeared in buildings where the weapons struck... that, or Dome Drones fell.

"Giant spiders carrying lasers!" Bender said excitedly. "Frickin' giant spiders!" He began to hum. "Bugs bugs bugidy bugs."

Rade glanced at the overhead map and saw Bender's blue dot headed into the room.

"Stop!" Rade said. He dismissed the video feed and reverted to his own vision.

Bender halted halfway to the window. He had raised his rifle, and obviously intended to pick off some of the creatures with the weapon. He glanced over his shoulder with a questioning expression on his face.

"I don't want you drawing undue attention," Rade said. "We're not equipped to fight at the moment. Without the shields and armor of the Hoplites, we don't stand a chance. Not in jumpsuits."

Bender sighed. "Yes, boss." He lowered his rifle and retreated to the hallway once more.

"What should we call these things?" Fret said.

"Let's call them Benders," Manic said with a grin.

"Har," Bender said. "More like, Bender's Target Practice."

Rade switched his viewpoint to Unit B to observe the aliens more. One of them stepped over a vehicle, leaving large dents in the metal.

"Fender Benders," TJ said.

"What the *eff?*" Bender said. "What's with the 'let's name aliens after Bender' crap today?"

"Alien spiders works for me," Shaw said. "Keep it simple."

Rade dismissed the video feed. Since neither Unit A nor B had been shot down, Rade carefully made his way inside the room and approached the edge of the window where the robots crouched. He signaled his other Argonauts to do likewise.

He peered down into the street below. So far, none of the aliens had reached the area. He zoomed in on the rooftops, double checking that no snipers were waiting to take them down.

"Look at that high-rise apartment," Tahoe said.

Rade switched to Tahoe's feed, and saw that he had zoomed in on a high rise about six blocks to the south. The spider-like aliens were clambering up the walls. They sometimes paused beside the windows to smash them, and pulled struggling humans out; occasionally those humans wore jumpsuits, many times not. Since the unsuited individuals were obviously still alive at that point, it meant the building had inner seals that had activated to preserve pressure in lieu of the breached dome.

Some men in jumpsuits fired down from the rooftops at the creatures. Robots joined them. 6As and walkers. The creatures fired back with the turrets on their backs, but some of the aliens were hit by the incoming laser or plasma fire and released the building, plunging to their deaths.

"That's reassuring," Fret said. "They can die."

"Of course the bugs can die!" Bender said. "And die they will." He petted his rifle.

As Rade watched, one of the creatures scaling the building completely disappeared.

"Did you see that?" Fret said. "Where the hell did it go?"

"Check out the rooftop," Tahoe said.

It seemed the spider had reappeared on the rooftop, where it was causing mayhem among the defenders.

A bright blue sphere appeared as Rade watched, and when it vanished another spider remained in its place. The bug reached down with its mandibles and tore an unready unit in half.

"Quantum Predation," Lui said.

"Huh?" Bender said.

"Two meanings. First: they're picking the humans off one by one. Predation in small, discrete quantities. Quanta. Second: see those jumping units? Blinking in and out of existence, teleporting behind the tangos to split them apart from the rear? They've got to be doing that via quantum Slipstreams."

"Quantum Predation," Bender said in understanding. "That should be the title of your foodie book. Quantum Predation: Devouring the West Coast, One Buffet at a Time, by Lui Pimplepocks."

"Pimplepocks?" Lui said.

"That's your pen name," Bender said. "Every

writer needs a pen name."

"But why Pimplepocks?" Lui used to have pockmarks from severe acne, and he had rejuvenation treatments done to fix that up. But inside, he probably still felt like he had those pocks, something that Bender was obviously more than happy to take advantage of.

"Because, it endears you to the reader," Bender said. "Pimplepocks makes you sound like someone relatable. Someone the Everyman can go to for advice. 'That Pimplepocks sure knows how to write a good yarn about buffets.' Besides, it's a better pen name than Pussy Gonzales..."

"How can all of you be so calm at a time like this!" Batindo said. "And making jokes. *Jokes!* The colony is falling to aliens! We're surrounded! People are dying out there! And it's like none of you care!"

"Bro," Lui said. "If I had a digicoin for all the times I've been surrounded by aliens intent on ripping me apart, I'd be a rich man."

"We care," Rade told Batindo. "We just deal with it in different ways."

"I can tell you right now," Surus added, addressing Batindo and the other two Kenyans. "The safest place on the colony is in this room, with these men. And with me."

Rade glanced at Kato and the nurse.

"You're free by the way," Rade told them. "You can go whenever you want."

Kato exchanged a glance with the nurse. "I think we'll stay for the time being. If you don't mind."

"We mind," Fret said. He turned toward Rade. "They won't be able to keep up. Not in those environmental suits."

"If it comes to it, they can hitch a ride on our

jumpsuits easily enough," Rade said. He turned toward Kato. "You may stay."

Kato inclined his head behind his faceplate. "Thank you."

"Bax, do you read?" Rade tried.

The *Argonaut's* AI didn't answer. The governor was still jamming the signal, apparently.

"TJ, any news on bypassing that jamming frequency?" Rade said.

"I'm working on it," TJ said.

Rade glanced at the street. "Okay, it's still clear so far, we might—"

Movement caught his eye. Looking up, he saw several more streaks falling toward the dome. Moments later many more pods tore inside. Rade noticed that the massive alien ship had gotten much closer than the last time he'd glanced upward.

One of the pods crashed into the street directly below the hospital. Once more the upper half protruded from the asphalt. A panel folded open near the top and the creatures began to unload.

"This situation is quickly turning from bad to really bad," Shaw said.

twelve

G et away from the windows," Rade ordered.

The Argonauts and robots complied.

"Well, we obviously won't be able to reach the shuttles now," Rade said. "At least not by conventional means. We're going to have to make our way to one of the subway stations, I think, especially considering that the Dragonflies aren't even docked in our current dome. We'll have to take the tunnels to the next dome, and make our way to the hangar, either through the subway system, or maybe the sewer system... as long as we stay out of sight. Unless there are shuttles docked in this dome we can use?" He glanced at Kato.

The doctor shook his head. "All docking with Kitale is handled by Geodesic Dome A. We'll have to go there, like you say."

"Well that makes for a poorly designed colony," Lui said. "Isn't it against fire code to require everyone to switch domes in the case of an emergency?"

"We don't have such stringent codes here," Kato said.

"Well, it doesn't surprise me," Lui said. "Considering how bright your governor is."

"Sarcasm!" Harlequin said. "I understand!"

"Woopty-do, Harley boy," Bender said. "Kudos to you for being less of an imbecile. Now turn around so I can give you your reward: a boot in the ass!"

Rade caught a glimpse of an alien forelimb as something crawled past the window.

"Vacate the room!" Rade and the others hurried from the hospital room.

"Something just shattered the window," Tahoe said from the drag position.

"This way, Argonauts!" Rade led the group to the staircase, taking it to the concourse.

In front of the glass doors leading outside, an alien spider lurked.

It spotted Rade and the others and broke through the glass.

Bender was already down on one knee and opening fire.

"Eat some plasma, bug bitch!" Bender said.

The alien collapsed; it slid across the polished floor, its momentum carrying it a short way across the concourse. Black mist spewed from what was obviously a wound in its thorax.

"How come aliens are always able to survive the void without wearing jumpsuits?" Manic said. "Where's the fairness in that?"

"These could be bioengineered," Harlequin said. "Designed to withstand vacuum conditions."

"Enough talking," Rade said. "Run!"

More of the creatures had lined up outside and were starting to come in. Their turrets were firing. Unit E dropped, its body riddled with bore holes.

A blue sphere appeared in front of the party. Rade was already firing his plasma weapon into it as the alien emerged.

The materializing spider collapsed in a heap in

front of him.

Rade swerved to bash in a side door, which led to an alternate stairwell.

The Argonauts followed him inside.

"Kato, is there another way out of the building?" Rade asked when everyone was inside the stairwell.

"The hospital connects directly to the subway system," Kato replied. "There is a stairwell in the eastern quarter that leads to it. I can take you there."

Kato led them up the stairs to the second floor.

"Wait!" Rade said. "Unit D, check it."

Unit D opened the door a crack, and peered past. "They're out there."

"Next floor!" Rade said.

The group proceeded upward.

As he ran, Rade glanced into the gap the stairs formed in the center of the stairwell, and saw that one of the creatures was trying to stuff its large body inside the first floor opening.

"Hurry!" Rade said.

The team reached the third floor and Rade said: "Continue to the fourth!"

At the fourth and final floor Rade had Unit D peer past the stairwell door. "Clear, so far."

"Lead the way, Centurions," Rade commanded.

The four remaining Centurions hurried into the hall and the Argonauts followed. Tahoe and Bender brought up the rear.

"Hunting these bugs isn't so much fun anymore, is it Bender?" Fret said.

"Speak for yourself!" Bender said. "I'm having the time of my life bitch!"

The group made its way toward the eastern wall. Unfortunately there was a floor-to-ceiling window there, and a spider clambered into view.

The alien saw them, and pointed its turret toward the glass.

Rade dropped to one knee as he ran, and slid forward a meter on the polished floor as he aimed. He squeezed the trigger, and the stricken spider released the window, dropping from view. In its wake remained the small bore hole Rade had carved into the glass.

The party continued down the hall.

"Blue sphere behind!" Tahoe shouted.

Rade spun about in time to see Tahoe and Bender shooting down the spider that had teleported there. It collapsed near them, its thorax seeming to smoke as its blood evaporated into the atmosphereless environment.

As the team advanced another spider clambered into view beyond the floor-to-ceiling window. Before the Argonauts could open fire the alien promptly dematerialized.

Rade spun about and, as he predicted, the creature appeared in the hallway behind the Argonauts inside a fading blue sphere. He wasn't the only one who had guessed the alien's intent, and the spider fell beneath the barrage of plasma fire.

"Do you think all of them can teleport?" Manic said as they continued forward.

"I believe only certain units have that ability," Harlequin said. "Otherwise, all of the aliens we saw emerging from that pod would be teleporting here to attack us."

Rade reached the stairwell and had Lui and Fret guard the nearby window while the robots kicked in the door.

"Clear!" Unit A said.

"Lead the way!" Rade ordered.

The team filed inside and proceeded down the

stairs.

They descended to the third floor without issue, but at the second floor the door smashed open unexpectedly, and long hooked legs reached inside, tripping Shaw. Those limbs began to drag her into the hallway...

Rade and the others unleashed hell immediately, some targeting the base of those appendages, others the legs themselves. The creature released Shaw, its appendages falling limp.

Bender raced to the door and fired several more bursts until he was satisfied the alien was truly down.

"Don't touch our astrogator, bitch!" Bender said.

"Bender, let's go!" Rade sent.

The team reached the first floor, and continued past the door to the basement.

"Units A, B," Rade beckoned toward the basement door.

The first Unit opened the door a crack, while the second peered inside. Then they both moved into the hallway beyond, Unit A going high, Unit B going low.

"Clear!" Unit A said.

The Argonauts proceeded into the basement. To the left was a long hallway, with doors leading to storage closets and rooms on either side. To the right, a pair of double doors.

"Go right," Kato said.

The robots opened the double doors and moved inside.

"Clear!" Unit A said.

Rade and the others passed the doors, finding themselves inside a concrete-walled pedway system. HLED lights provided illumination. Not emergency lights, Rade noted, but standard lighting. That meant the attack had yet to cripple the power grid. That was good, in that they wouldn't have to manually pry open any airlocks they found. But that also meant they'd have to hack through whatever security protocols were installed in those airlocks before the hatches would cede.

"This joins up with the subway," Kato promised.

"Can you transmit any subway maps you have stored in your embedded ID to me?" Rade asked Kato. "And any other building blueprints you have?"

"Done," Kato said.

Rade accepted the transfer request. His overhead map updated and he saw that the pedway did indeed connect with the subway system shortly.

The robots cleared an intersection, and the group approached a bend beyond. The Centurions went first, sweeping it, and then the remaining Argonauts rounded. Above the passageway digital signage displayed text in both Swahili and English. It read: "Zhana Station Stop."

"We're here," Kato said.

"Wait," Tahoe said. "What if the subway platform is crawling with aliens?"

"If it is," Rade said, "then we retreat to one of the other branches, find another building, and hole up until the attack abates. They can't do this forever. Every organic-based species we've met has had to rest."

"Sure," Tahoe said. "But some need less rest than others."

Rade signaled the Centurions forward.

Crouching, the robots slowly advanced to the edge of the passageway and halted to scan the platform beyond. Rade switched to Unit A's viewpoint. There were a few benches and seating areas between pillars, but otherwise the platform seemed empty.

Movement drew Unit A's gaze to the far side of the platform, where the dark shapes of spiders were scampering down the escalators from a surface entrance.

"Get back!" Rade said.

The robots retreated into the pedway, and Rade quickly led the whole team away.

"Do you think the aliens saw the Centurions?" Tahoe said.

"We'll know shortly," Rade said.

Nothing teleported in front of them, so Rade assumed the creatures had not.

"According to this map," Rade said as he ran. "If we take a right at the intersection behind us, the pedway leads to a financial services building."

"Hmm," TJ said. "I'm guessing a financial building will have full-blown auto-seals, complete with air locks."

"And probably blast shields to prevent against terrorist attacks," Lui said. "Might be tricky getting past the airlocks."

"TJ, we're going to need you to be at your hacking best," Rade said.

The group approached the intersection that led to the financial building.

Rade had the Centurions clear both sides, then the rest of the team hurried into the rightmost passage.

Before he took the turn, Rade spotted motion coming from the direction of the hospital: moving shadows danced along the wall, cast by the overhead lights around the bend.

The aliens were approaching from that side as well.

"Double time, people," Rade said.

The group proceeded deeper into the concrete corridor, climbing steps to a vaulted entrance. An airlock had sealed over it.

"TJ..." Rade said.

"Almost got it," TJ said.

"Defensive formation," Rade said, and the group formed up in a half circle around TJ, Batindo, and the other two Kenyans.

Rade saw the dim shadows of the aliens growing on both walls of the corridor behind them as the spiders approached from both sides of the intersection.

"If they spot us, and realize we're entering this building..." Tahoe said.

"Got it," TJ said. The airlock opened silently. It was expansive enough to fit the entire squad.

"Go go go!" Rade said.

The Argonauts rushed inside.

"Seal it!" Rade ordered.

The hatch began to shut. Before it sealed completely, Rade caught a glimpse of an alien forelimb coming into view at the end of the corridor. But before he saw any more the door shut.

White mist vented inside. The atmosphere was pressurizing.

The inner hatch opened a moment later, revealing a carpeted basement foyer. It was a rather small area, with two elevators beside an escalator.

"Let's take the escalator," Rade said. He didn't want to risk the power going out while they were in the elevator. "Units A, B, clear it."

As soon as the lead robot set foot on the escalator, the belt-driven staircase activated and began carrying the Centurion upward.

Rade waited for the robot to reach the top. He switched to its viewpoint.

He saw what looked like a bank, with ATM kiosks

near what must have once been the front door—an airlock hatch had sealed over it. Those kiosks didn't dispense actual physical currency, of course, and existed mostly to provide safety deposit box services to clientele. Robot tellers were situated behind glass walls nearby, ready to offer assistance to any customers.

"AIs," Bender said, sounding disgusted.

Beside the bank was a concourse leading to the rest of the building. Metal blast shields had lowered over the windows, so that no external light reached the area: HLEDs provided the illumination.

"Seems clear, at first glance," Unit A said.

"Check behind the teller areas," Rade said. "Don't break the glass, just peer past them... ask the tellers if they've seen anything."

Unit A leaped onto the counter in front of one of the tellers, and aimed his rifle down.

The teller lifted its metal arms as if surrendering. "There is no gold in the vault."

"We're not here for gold," Unit A said. "You must have accessed the external cameras by now. You know an alien invasion is in progress."

"Yes," the faceless teller replied.

"Have any of the aliens come inside?" Unit A asked.

"There was a breach on the fourth floor," the teller answered. "The security forces were dispatched. So far, they haven't found anything."

"And with our appearance, you've recalled those security forces, haven't you?" Unit A said.

"Yes," the teller said.

Units A and B continued along the counter, aiming their guns down into the area beyond where the tellers resided behind the glass. They swept their scopes over the back offices, but spotted no one else. Any human employees would have been evacuated a day ago, during the hospital siege, since according to the map the building was located just across the street from the hospital.

"Seems clear," Unit A said. "Though I'm sure you heard, the tellers have recalled the security forces. We can expect resistance at some point."

"Up." Rade told his men, and took the escalator. "If we encounter aliens, we have to take them down fast, before they can alert the horde. We have to assume they have squad-based communications similar to our own, especially considering the heat they're packing."

When he reached the bank, Rade turned toward the concourse that led deeper into the building.

"Units C and D, clear the concourse," Rade said.

The requested units moved forward. Rade spotted elevators on the far side of the area, next to a cafe whose security door was closed and locked. There was an open staircase that led to the second floor; beyond the railing of the upper walkway, he saw a couple of other shops and offices whose security doors were sealed.

The robots returned a moment later. "Clear."

"That looks like a stairwell door," Shaw said. "Up there, past the second floor walkway." A highlight appeared on Rade's vision, indicating the area. "Assuming you want to take the stairs..."

"I do," Rade said. "Centurions, clear the second floor walkway."

When the robots did so, the Argonauts climbed the open staircase and joined them.

A series of huge flower pots lined the glass railing. Round sections protruded outward from the main walkway over the concourse, imparting a balcony effect. Thick, decorative pillars climbed from floor to ceiling in those sections.

"Damn, it's eerie in here with those blast shields sealing the windows," Manic said. "And those security grilles over all the offices and shops. I feel like a mall rat sneaking around the mall after closing hours or something."

"Reminds you of your delinquent youth, does it?" Bender said.

As the team approached the stairwell Shaw had indicated, the door abruptly burst open. Two enforcer robots emerged, one moving high, the other low. Their rifles were raised.

"Down!" Rade said.

thirteen

The team ducked behind whatever cover they could find, including the series of huge flower pots that lined the walkway, and the pillars.

Bore holes appeared in the flower pot Rade had chosen to hide behind as plasma beams from the enforcers tore past.

"Mine!" Bender said.

Rade aimed over the edge of the flower pot; he noticed Fret nearby, hiding inside an alcove where a security door covered a restaurant.

Fret fired twice and the two enforcers dropped.

"Bitch!" Bender said. "I said they were mine!"

Bender emerged at a run from behind a nearby pillar and leaped onto Fret; Bender began gyrating his midsection rapidly, dry humping Fret from behind.

Fret shook him away. "Off damn it!"

"Don't take my shot next time!" Bender said.

"Calm down!" Rade kept his scope aimed at the stairwell in case more robots emerged. "You know it doesn't work that way, Bender. You can't call dibs on a target. If someone has a shot they have to take it, or risk allowing the tango to escape."

Bender sighed. "Yeah I know. Sorry boss. Just wanted to give him a hard time. Make him my bitch, you know?"

"You'll get your chance," Rade said.

"What, to make him my bitch?" Bender asked hopefully.

"No," Rade said. "To take down some bugs."

"Tell you what, I'm going to make him my bitch and squash some bugs, too," Bender said. "Damn, those aliens make me hyper. I need to kill or hump something. Surus, want to hang out in an empty office for a bit?"

"No," she said.

"Seems our criminal status is still set by the governor," Lui said.

"Great," Fret said. "We have all the city's security personnel after us, *and* aliens."

"I think these enforcers just thought we were bank robbers," TJ said.

Tahoe approached the fallen robots, keeping his rifle pointed at the stairwell door. He kicked one of the lifeless bodies. "These definitely look like the security personnel our teller friend summoned. They're not city."

"Doesn't matter," Fret said. "I have no doubt that any future Kitale robots we encounter will have orders to kill us on sight. They hold us in the same high regard as the aliens."

"I'll have to agree with that assessment," Rade said.

"At least the bitches recognize how deadly we are," Bender said.

"You like that, don't you?" Fret said. "A whole city trying to kill us, aliens and all."

Bender grinned, baring that golden grille. "You know me too well."

"Units A and B, clear the stairwell," Rade said.

The Units rushed past Fret and Tahoe and kicked open the door. They dashed inside: Unit A went high, B low. Several seconds later Unit A returned: "Clear up to the third floor!"

"Inside!" Rade said. "Units A and B, secure the stairwell to the fourth floor."

Rade and the others entered.

"TJ, see if you can lock the door behind us," Rade sent.

TJ paused beside the door. "Got it. Locked."

"How quick will you be able to unlock it again?" Rade asked. "In case we have to make a hasty retreat?"

"I already escalated my privileges," TJ said. "Won't need to run the rootkit again. The same is true for all the stairwell doors. They're running the same subsystem."

"Clear to the fourth floor," Unit A sent.

"Good," Rade said. "Continue to the fifth floor, Units. Meanwhile, Argonauts, to the third floor."

The Argonauts halted at the third floor. Batindo tripped along the way, and Rade helped him up, worried that the man had taken a hit at some point but had remained quiet. Rade checked his vitals: they were green.

"You all right?" Rade asked the client.

"Fine," Batindo said. "Just a little winded. It's been a long road from the wild savannas where I was born to this fallen colony."

"It's been a long road for all of us," Rade said. He glanced at TJ. "Lock the third floor door."

"Done," TJ said.

They proceeded to the fourth floor, and Rade also had TJ lock the door there.

"The teller said there was a breach on this floor..." Shaw sent.

"Yes," Rade said. "Which is exactly why I want to lock this door especially. If there's a breach, we're staying far away from the fourth floor, and any potential aliens that might be inside. We continue climbing until we find a clear floor, and then hole up until nightfall."

At the door to the seventh floor, Rade decided the group had traveled far enough. He sent the robots in to sweep the level.

Switching to Unit A's viewpoint, Rade saw the robots enter a small hallway. Elevators resided next to the stairwell. An unlocked door led to a washroom. Empty.

The robots reached a locked door at the end of the hall.

"Clear," Unit A sent.

"Inside!" Rade ordered.

The Argonauts gathered in the hallway, and TJ locked the stairwell.

The group assumed defensive positions in front of the locked door while TJ got to work. In moments he had it open.

Unit A peered inside. "It's an airlock." The robot opened the door all the way, revealing an alcove with an inner hatch a meter inside.

"Told you," TJ said. "This is a financial services building. They're going to go all-out with the safety features... airlocks every floor."

"Units A, B, go," Rade said.

The two units entered. Rade switched to Unit A's viewpoint, as usual. The outer hatch resealed, the airlock pressurized, and the inner hatch opened. The robots stepped inside.

"Looks like the aliens were here," Unit A said.

Cubicle walls were torn down and desks upturned.

"This is how I imagine Bender's house must look," Unit B said.

"*What!*" Bender said. "Goddamn AIs."

"Focus, Unit B," Rade said. "The aliens could still be present."

"I'm well aware of that," Unit B said. "I thought the joke would calm your nerves."

"Noted," Rade said. He realized he would have cut one of his own Argonauts more slack than the robots. Still, he thought of how much it had cost to buy those robots, which made him expect absolute professionalism from them.

"If the aliens did this, how did they get in?" Manic said. "All the blast shields are lowered, blocking the windows."

Unit A ran its gaze along the metal blast shields that covered the floor-to-ceiling windows. The robot focused on one particular shield that had been torn inward. It looked like it had been partially shot, and the spiders had forced their way inside the rest of the way.

"Apparently blast shields can't hold them out," Fret said.

"Not surprising, considering the weaponry they're equipped with," Shaw said. "And that these are merely standard-grade blast shields. Though what I'm wondering is: why would they need to bore through if they could simply teleport inside?"

"Could be what Harlequin mentioned: not all of the aliens have the quantum devices," Tahoe said. "That, or their destinations need to be in sight for them to teleport."

"Why would the destinations need to be visible?" Shaw asked.

"Just conjecture," Tahoe said. "But it could be

they need to calculate the destination coordinates... I'm guessing the devices work similar to the Acceptor teleporters the Phants use, which means there can't be anything obscuring the target coordinates or the devices won't work. And if they can't actually *see* those target coordinates, they'd have a hard time finding a spot in empty space, you know what I mean?"

"Assuming they can actually 'see' in the traditional sense of the word," Lui said.

"All right, looks like we're not going to hide out on this floor after all," Rade said. "I do want to take a look out that breached window, however, so you're going to have to sweep the office area, Centurions. But before you do, Unit A, please have a look at the rear of the inner hatch. Can you see signs of an attempt to force the exit?"

Unit A turned around. "I'll have to seal the hatch before I can tell you that."

"Do it," Rade said.

The robot closed the inner hatch. The video feed momentarily pixelated, but then returned. The hatch was closed. It appeared to be in perfect condition, without a single dent on it.

"I believe the aliens didn't realize there was an exit here," Unit A said. "Either that, or something distracted them and caused them to flee in a hurry."

"Probably when they discovered us in the hospital earlier..." Manic said.

"Okay," Rade said. "Reopen the inner hatch, in case you need to get out of there in a hurry. And then proceed to clear the office area. Give the breach a wide berth until you finish. And then if it seems safe, approach the breach and get a look at the city outside."

"Roger that," Unit A said.

The two split up and explored the different offices

and cubicles. They discovered no one, not man, robot, or alien. Then they slowly approached the breach on the far side of the room. Bright light from the glow bars embedded in the geodesic dome poured in from outside, evoking a deceptively cheery atmosphere.

Unit A signaled Unit B to stay back, and approached by itself. The robot kept its rifle held at the ready and aimed through the breach.

The city slowly came into view. Beyond the punctured dome, the massive alien ship dominated, a black diamond of doom that ate up most of the sky, towering to the heavens. It had finally come to a halt, having assumed a position next to the current geodesic dome, where the legislature resided.

Below, the streets teemed with aliens. Gone were the brightly-dressed Kenyans and buzzing drones, replaced by black spiders roaming in interminable silence. He occasional saw a flash of blue as aliens teleported through the horde, usually to avoid traffic snafus formed by the press of bodies.

Rade saw fallen combat robots and Perdix drones in their midst, along with dismembered human bodies. There was never any blood visible upon the human corpses—it had all evaporated away. The spiders trampled the robot wreckages underfoot, but avoided the fallen humans if at all possible: it was obvious they considered the bodies disgusting.

He spotted one alien dead among the fallen, lying on its back, legs folded over its thorax in a death pose. Two spiders dragged the crimped body away, heading toward the massive mothership.

Rade picked out a couple of spiders clambering across the exterior of a nearby building, which told Rade there were probably still more of them exploring the surface of the current office tower as well.

While most of the buildings only had a few aliens clinging to their glass and steel walls, one particular apartment complex a few streets down literally swarmed with the aliens. Some of them occasionally broke through the windows to draw out humans and split them in half. Many were extremely young, no more than five to ten years old. Mercifully, most of those the spiders grabbed were dead already, as the victims lacked jumpsuits.

Rade dreaded what would happen if the aliens realized more fresh meat was lying in wait inside the financial building.

"You're awfully quiet, Bender," Manic commented.

In response, Bender's heavy breathing merely echoed over the comm.

"I thought you'd be excited," Manic continued. "I'm disappointed in you, Bender. You've changed."

Bender ignored him. Clearly, he was disturbed by what he was seeing. Finally: "Those goddamn bitches. What they're doing to those apartment residents is inexcusable. I want to kill them all, I swear I do. If I ever get Juggernaut back, I'm going on a rampage. These bugs are going to rue the day they ever set foot in my colony."

"Your colony now, is it?" Fret said.

"Damn right," Bender said.

"What we're seeing isn't much different than what we observed earlier," Lui said. "Why are you getting all riled up only now?"

"No, it *is* different," Bender said. "Those are kids out there. The last building we saw was an office building. This is an apartment. *And there are kids.*"

The group watched the feed in quiet for some moments. Rade felt his own anger rising, and he didn't blame Bender for wanting to kill every last one of those bugs.

"Guess we won't be taking the subway to the adjacent dome," Tahoe said. "Look at the connecting tunnel. Unit B's feed."

Rade switched to Unit B's camera. The robot had approached after Unit A confirmed it was safe, and had zoomed in on the edge of the dome, which was visible from the current vantage. Beyond it, the conduit connecting the current geodesic dome to the next had been completely destroyed. Hundreds of spiders lurked between the domes, apparently standing guard.

Rade sighed. "I suppose not."

At that point, he wasn't quite sure how they were getting off the planet.

"I've been accessing Unit A's radiometry information," Lui said. "The Centurion has a clear view of the neighborhood..."

"And?" Rade said.

"I think I've found the source of the jamming signal produced by this dome," Lui continued. "I've pinpointed it to a transmission tower eight blocks to the south. Unit A, would you mind turning toward the center of the dome? I'm marking the location on the map."

Rade glanced at the overhead map and saw the waypoint appear. He switched back to Unit A's viewpoint; the robot had zoomed in on the designated tower. Rade could see various antennae and transmitters residing near the top.

"We'll never get there, not through those streets," Tahoe said.

"You are talking about the central communications tower?" Kato said.

"Send him the location," Rade told Lui.

Kato must have received it, because he said: "There is a subway stop not far from there."

Rade studied the surrounding area on the map, and noticed the subway entrance indicated as a point of interest. "We might just have a way after all, Tahoe. We wait until evening when the dome darkens, or until most of the aliens rest—"

"Assuming they rest," Fret interrupted.

"Yes," Rade said. "And then we take the subway tunnels until we reach that area. Then we surface, disable the jamming device, and restore communications with the *Argonaut*. Once we do that, you know what comes next, right?"

"Hoplites," Lui said.

"And my backup stun rifle," Surus added.

Rade dismissed Unit A's feed to view the world through his own eyes.

"What about the Phant trap?" Rade said, referring to the storage tank that could constrain a Phant. "We could have the Hoplites carry it down."

"Mmm, I'll just keep stunning the host until we return to the ship," Surus said. "Seems easier that way."

"Assuming that there is a host," Fret interrupted.

"Someone's negative today," TJ said.

"If there isn't a host," Surus said. "We'll find one." She glanced at Harlequin.

"I'm not being a host!" Harlequin said. "Choose Unit A!"

"Hey, why me?" Unit A said.

"Stop," Rade said. "There will be a host when we find our prey. Probably Governor Ganye. But Surus, won't continually stunning the Phant be hard on the Artificial?"

She shrugged inside her jumpsuit. "You did it to my host before, and she survived. Though Emilia didn't enjoy it, I admit."

"You'll have to give up control of your Hoplite to the AI if you want to keep stunning the host..." Rade said. He envisioned her sharing the cockpit with the Artificial, which would prevent her from using the inner actuators to control the mech.

"I have no problems doing so," Surus said. "I have a feeling we'll need to keep the weapon mounts of all of our Hoplites free. Leave the holding tank aboard the *Argonaut*."

"Okay then, when the time comes, I will," Rade said.

"Hey, I got a question for Surus," Bender said.

"I won't go out with you," Surus told him, preempting the question.

"No, that's not what I was going to ask," Bender said. "Close, though. My inquiry is in regards to the stun rifle. Or related to it, anyway. See, during the First Alien War, when you Greens teamed up with us, you gave us access to particle weapons that could 'snip' Phants from this universe, making them lose permanent contact with this reality. Whatever happened to that? Why do we have to go through this drawn out process of capturing Phants and throwing them into stars?"

"For one thing, those weapons require access to power sources your technology cannot provide," Surus said. "They were built into the golden mechs we temporarily supplied you with, if you'll recall."

"Then supply us with those golden mechs again," Bender said. "Or just patent up some new shit like you've done before."

"I think what she's saying is: she doesn't want to

give that technology to humanity," Lui explained.

"Well, yes," Surus said. "But there's something else. The weapons technology was never perfected. It turned out that some of the Phants could in fact return to this universe after we 'snipped' them, as you call it. The technique wasn't foolproof. That's another reason there are so many Phants still free in this region of space. Vanquished entities would reappear years later, ready to cause havoc. Throwing them into stars is the best way to get rid of them at the moment."

"Ah, too bad," Bender said.

"Centurions," Rade said. "Retreat from the breach and return to the airlock."

When the robots arrived, the Argonauts vacated the level and proceeded to the next floor.

The eighth level hallway was laid out almost exactly the same as the floor below: a few elevators next to a washroom door, beside a locked airlock. The sign above the airlock read, in Swahili: "Brightwood Insurance Inc."

"TJ, open the outer hatch," Rade ordered.

TJ remained where he was, working remotely. Rade knew he would simply piggyback on the Implants of those who were closer if the signal proved too weak.

"Why is this one taking so long?" Manic said. "When you got through the stairwell doors so fast?"

"All the airlocks are running on different subsystems," TJ said. "It's a security precaution." He paused. "Fret, you looking over my shoulder?"

"If it's bothering you, I can disconnect," Fret said.

"No, that's fine," TJ said. "Just not used to anyone being interested in this sort of thing."

"Looks like you're running a command shell of some kind," Fret said.

"That's right," TJ said. "It's the only way to work."

Fret chuckled. "In movies, to represent hacking they always show someone doing a command line directory listing. 'Hey look, I just did an *ls -alrt* and I'm getting access to the bank's financial systems!' Leet leet leet."

"That's stupid kids for you these days," Bender said. "You merely pull up a command line interface, and the bitches automatically assume you're a hacker."

"But in the case of you and TJ, you actually are," Fret said.

"Yeah but that's not my point," Bender said. "Because like you said, mind-typing in a command shell isn't hacking. That's like me saying I'm a sex master because I'm a good kisser. Though I guess in my case that's true as well. Hear that, Surus?"

She ignored him.

A moment later TJ announced: "I'm in."

fourteen

Rade had the robots repeat the sweeping process—TJ opened and closed the hatches that sealed the airlock, and the Centurions moved in to clear the space.

Switching between the feeds, Rade saw the blast shields remained entirely intact on the current level, covering all the floor to ceiling windows. There were no breaches in the metal.

The Units spread out after securing the perimeter, and mapped the interior office space: cubicles; offices; a kitchen; a conference room.

The Centurions completed their sweep and confirmed it was clear.

"By the way, I found a water cooler in the kitchen," Unit A said. "Along with some energy bars in a cupboard. And a vending machine."

"Ooo, vending machine," Bender said. "Time for my junk food fix. You bitches can have the energy bars. I get the chicken chips."

"All right, looks like we have a place to hole up," Rade said. "Tahoe, take us in."

The airlock could only fit four at a time, so Tahoe divided the squad into appropriate groups, and they entered in phases, opening and closing the inner and outer hatches in turn so that the airlock could properly pressurize.

When everyone was inside, Rade had Lui perform an extensive atmospheric scan.

"Definitely breathable," Lui said. "With no sign of any contagions."

Rade nodded.

"Do we risk opening our faceplates to conserve oxygen?" Tahoe said. "There haven't been any psi attacks so far..."

"Surus, are you still able to sense the Phant?" Rade asked.

"It's still in the dome," Surus said. "For the time being. But I have no idea how far away. It could be lurking in the coffee pot in the kitchen for all we know."

"But given such a small electronic device, the evidence of Phant possession would be obvious," Harlequin said. "We'd see condensation at least, and—"

"I was being slightly sarcastic," Surus said. "My point is, it could be anywhere."

"Oh," Harlequin replied.

"Did you notice, she called the Phant 'it' now?" Bender said. "I got through to her earlier after all."

"I meant 'he,' of course," Surus said.

Bender mouthed "bitch" behind his faceplate.

"I'm going to authorize open faceplates," Rade said. "But set your local AIs to automatically seal the helmets at the first sign of decompression. If one of those spiders decides to breach the blast shield, you'll need something with the speed of an AI to act. I'm definitely not going to allow anyone to remove their helmets entirely. Harlequin, teach the Kenyans how to program the AIs."

"We know how to do it," Kato said, the indignation obvious in his tone. "You think just because we're Kenyan, we're incapable?"

"No," Rade said. "Because you're civilians. Harlequin, make sure they do it right."

"Will do," Harlequin said.

"You're civilians, too," Kato pressed.

Rade pursed his lips. "We stopped thinking of ourselves as civilians a long time ago." He turned toward TJ. "Lock the inner hatch behind us."

"Done," TJ replied.

Rade issued instructions to his local AI to seal the faceplate if the pressure dropped by more than ten kilopascals within a span of nanoseconds. Then he opened the translucent composite.

The others presumably issued the same commands to their AIs and repealed their faceplates in turn.

"Now where's this damn kitchen?" Bender said. "I'm famished."

"Woe betide anyone who gets between Bender and his food," Tahoe said.

"Damn right," Bender said.

The Centurions guided the party toward the kitchen. The atmosphere in the office space was as moody as the rest of the building, with the cubicles lit only by the overhead HLEDs and all external light blocked by the blast shields.

When they reached the kitchen, Rade found himself in a room with a fridge, some cupboards, a coffee table, lounge chairs, and a countertop containing a sink, coffee maker, food reheater, and snack 3D printer—the vending machine. Several snack items lay behind the glass separator, already premade.

Bender made a beeline to the vending machine.

"All right, chicken chips time baby." He paused,

looking past the glass. "*What!* They don't have chicken chips! Damn it."

Manic joined him and peered through the glass. "Turkey jerky is just as good."

"Oh yeah, of course you'd like the turkey jerky," Bender said. "That's what you do all day on the *Argonaut* after all."

"Hey, got to pass the time somehow," Manic said. "If I don't jerk my turkey, who will? You?"

TJ joined them. "I got this. Vending machines are my specialty."

"Your specialty?" Bender said. "Man, I trained you! Fine, go ahead then, bro. There's nothing I want in there anyway."

"Fridge is empty," Manic announced.

TJ held his gloved hand over the vending machine, covering the area normally responsible for interfacing with an embedded ID and deducting funds.

"You trained him?" Tahoe asked Bender.

"Yeah, when we first graduated into the MOTH brotherhood," Bender replied. "And joined the Teams, the two of us hung out in the common area on base all the time. By ourselves, mind you... the platoon hadn't accepted us yet. You know, the whole newbie-caterpillars-haven't-proved-themselves-so-let's-haze-and-ostracize-them deal. The bitches.

"Anyway, we had a bit of free time in the evenings, when they weren't hazing us. There was a particular vending machine in the common room that pissed off most of the platoon because of the crazy high prices. Three digicoins for a bag of Liqits? I mean come on. I'll pay three digicoins for a bag of tits maybe, but not Liqits."

"Remind me what a Liqit is again?" Fret said.

"Bitch?" Bender said. "Mints?"

"Oh yeah," Fret said.

"So, TJ and I thought we could gain some brownie points by hacking into the vending machine," Bender continued. "We hoped it would give us at least a modicum of respect, and help tide over the platoon until we could make it to our first combat deployment. We were wrong, of course, and still got hazed for months afterwards, but that's beside the point. Anyway, with our advanced hacker skills, we thought breaking into something as simple as a vending machine should be a piece of cake. It wasn't. It took about three weeks, with me basically sharing everything I found out about the machine with TJ, and—"

"I shared what I discovered with you, too, bro," TJ said. "In case you forgot."

"Yeah, well, the solution turned out to be a buffer overrun," Bender said. "When you flooded the food selector interface with a particular bit sequence, you could reset the machine and boot into admin mode, at which point you could change all the prices. So what we did is flipped the price of everything from positive to negative, and added a zero to all the numbers. So basically the machine *paid us* when we ordered something from it. And big bucks, at that.

"The other platoon members loved us, of course. Or pretended to, at least for the five minutes it took them to empty the contents of the vending machine, exhausting the raw 3D-printing supplies to boot. The vendor restocked it two weeks later, and the platoon emptied it out within the hour. The vendor must have been surprised at how popular that particular machine on that particular base was.

"The vendor finally realized what was going on when they did their reconciliation at the end of the month. The vendor informed the base commander, and TJ and I had to pay back all the money from our salaries, even though the other platoon members had taken the majority of the items. Though our lieutenant commander gave us a firm chewing out, I believe he secretly admired us for it. Chief Bourbonjack certainly did, though he didn't show it at the time. Ah, the good old days."

"Unlocked," TJ said. "I set the price of everything to zero."

"Why didn't you set it to negative?" Bender said.

"Bro, I've developed morals since then," TJ said.

"Ha!" Bender said, pressing a bunch of buttons at the same time and filling the bottom up with different junk food items. "Morals? You're still a thief."

"Call me Robin Hood," TJ said. He scooped up the items from the bottom of the vending machine and distributed the packets to the team. There were ordinary potato chips, energy bars, and two types of jerky—turkey and ostrich. And of course candy bars, gum and mints.

"That was a good story," Fret said, taking a bite out of a candy bar. "But so far this mission we've only seen any actual hacking ability from TJ. Are you sure you haven't lost your touch?"

"Don't need to prove nothin'," Bender said. "You've seen what I can do many times. And let's be honest: I've built robots with more brains than you."

"You mean sex robots?" Fret said.

Bender shrugged inside his jumpsuit.

Fret turned toward TJ. "So what was your hacker alias back in the day?"

"You don't want to know," TJ said, munching on some jerky.

"Come on, I do," Fret said.

"The Italian Rapscallion."

"*The Italian Rapscallion?*" Bender said. He broke into laughter. "Oh man, that's the stupidest alias I ever heard."

TJ smiled, seeming indulgent. "Yeah, pretend this is the first time you've heard it."

"Oh I'm sure I've heard it, but it was so stupid my mind erased it," Bender said.

"Yeah, and maybe you should tell them yours?" TJ said.

"The Pussywillow," Bender said.

Manic exploded with laughter. So much so, that the bag of potato chips he was holding flew from his arms.

"You gonna be okay, bro?" Bender said.

"The Pussywillow!" Manic said, coming up for air. "And he says your alias was stupid, TJ. The Pussywillow! He actually called himself the *Pussywillow?*"

"It sounded good to me at the time..." Bender said. "You know, cause I got so much pussy in my university days... basically wallowing in it."

"Yeah man you're so cool, you got lots of pussy," Fret said. "What else did you get, chlamydia? Herpes?"

"The words of a jealous hater," Bender said. "You know there are cures for those, right? Bet you wish you got as much pussy as I did... I'd enter a bar and women would basically come up to me and pull down their panties. Wallowing in pussy. Ah, those were the days. Anyway, I couldn't call myself the Pussywallow now, could I? That would have been bragging too much. So I went with willow."

"Pussywillow!" Manic was rolling on the ground, seeming unable to breath from all his hoarse laughter.

"You know he's never going to let you live that

down, right?" Fret said. "Actually, none of us will. Run for your lives! The dreaded Pussywillow has joined the chat room!"

"Ah shut up, bitch," Bender said. He went to sit beside Tahoe, who pretended he wasn't interested in the conversation. "Some days I wonder why I bother to watch their backs. I should just let the aliens devour them. They take a perfectly good alias and ruin it. I was a frickin' awesome Pussywillow."

"I'm sure you were." Tahoe patted Bender on the shoulder.

"Yeah," Bender said. "At least someone appreciates the effort I put into the name."

"Not really," Tahoe said. It sounded like he was holding back a laugh himself.

"Argonauts," Rade said, finishing an energy bar he had found in one of the cupboards. "Tighten the range of your Implants and jumpsuit comm nodes. I don't want any of our signals passing outside this kitchen."

He decreased his own range, then pulled up the signal spectrum histogram on his HUD and watched as it halved in size, indicating the reduction he had asked for.

"I'm setting my alarm for five hours from now," Rade continued. "Which coincides with the time of the dome's simulated nightfall. Rest until then. Centurions, you're on watch. Guard the two entrances to this room."

"Do you want us to patrol the perimeter of the entire office?" Unit A asked.

"No," Rade said. "If the spiders come, I want to hide, not fight. Remember, we don't want to alert the swarm that we're here."

"So the Centurions are on watch," Lui said. "But what about the rest of us?"

"Those of you that feel like racking out, do so," Rade said.

It was too early for Rade to rack out himself. He didn't feel sleepy at all. Nor did he entirely feel like caving out. His mind was completely in the present moment. Active, alert, wary of an attack. How could he relax when he was in the middle of a colony that was falling to alien invaders?

Rade sat next to Shaw, who was seated close to Batindo, Kato and the nurse.

"Earlier, you mentioned something about a long road from the wild savannas where you were born to here," Shaw was telling Batindo. "I take it you were born on Earth?"

"Yes," Batindo said. "I'm an Earther. But ever since I was a child, I'd always dreamed of making my way into space. When I graduated university, I took the first space-based job available to me: a diplomat posting on the moon. From there, I worked myself into a consular position, and was transferred to Talan Station. Been there every since."

"Was Talon Station everything you dreamed of?" Shaw asked.

"No," Batindo said. "I wanted to explore the stars. It seemed so romantic to me. Instead I was stuck on that station. I can't tell you how excited I was to journey with you. But now I've realized I may have been over-romanticizing it. Traveling the stars isn't as enjoyable as I thought. In fact, it's downright terrifying."

"Space can be a terrible place," Rade agreed. "But it can also be... eye-opening. Whenever I journey to a new system, I can't help but feel a sense of wonder. I ask myself how these planets got here. Who inhabits them, if they're colonized. What kind of native species we might find, if the planets host alien life. And in a system like this, when I see an uncharted Slipstream that has no Gate built in front of it, I wonder, what resides on the other side of that Slipstream? Are there aliens? And if so, are they friendly, or are they hostile?"

"Well, in this case we've learned they are the latter," Tahoe said.

"Not so fast," Lui said. "This Phant may have convinced them we were aggressors in some way. Told them we were colonizing this planet as a stepping stone to conquering the neighboring system."

"Or maybe the Phant offered them a weapon, in exchange for assistance," Surus said. "The Phant would have sensed me when I arrived. He would have known I was hunting him. And he became desperate, wanting a way out."

"Why not just wait until the mercenary vessels arrived?" Lui said. "Then the Phant could have taken a shuttle to one of their ships, and escaped."

"Perhaps the Phant decided he did not have time," Surus said. "The mercenaries were still a few days away. Meanwhile, these aliens were apparently hiding closer at hand. Behind one of the four stars, maybe, confirming my theory that the Phant was in contact with these aliens for some time. When I arrived, the Phant may have panicked, and told the aliens they needed to accelerate their plans if they wanted to get their hands on whatever he offered."

The conversation slowly fizzled out, and the team rested. It only took about twenty minutes before the premade contents of the vending machine had been eaten—Bender had the machine 3D-print several more items, but he soon depleted the internal stock of raw foodstuffs. When you had a team of men as muscular as the Argonauts, appetites were not small. Rade decided he would make further stops on the different floors below to raid the kitchens, in lieu of rationing the meal replacements installed within their jumpsuits.

Three hours passed without any disturbances.

And then something happened.

fifteen

R ade had joined the robots by the door to observe the office area, paying particular attention to the blast shields. He had placed one of the kitchen chairs near the entrance and sat in it, keeping most of his body behind the door frame. He had modified the arm assemblies of his suit to act as makeshift bipods and arm rests, essentially hardening the exoskeleton so he could fully lean on it with the weight of his arms and not exhaust the muscles. He held his rifle out in front of him, and slowly pivoted his torso from left to right as he scanned the office beyond.

The Argonauts remained quiet behind him, resting and keeping to themselves, saving their energy for when it would be needed. Tahoe had joined the robots guarding the opposite entrance.

Rade found it strangely easy to focus, which he attributed to his years of training. He preferred watch duty to idling on the floor and waiting for the designated night time to come: at least it felt like he was doing something. And he still felt no desire to cave out. A good sign.

All was silent out there. It seemed the enemy was going to overlook them after all.

And then he heard a soft banging coming from his right.

Rade spun his rifle in that direction, toward the blast shield covering the floor-to-ceiling windows.

"Units A, B—" Rade began, but before he could finish he heard a woosh, and his faceplate slammed shut. His body was drawn forward so that he fell out of the chair; he disabled his locked exoskeleton so that he could catch himself before he hit the floor.

"The office area has depressurized," Unit A said.

Rade was lying on the floor half outside the kitchen, staring into the open area where the cubicles resided. He spun his head to the right, toward the cone of artificial sunlight that now shone into the office building. The blast shield on the far wall was riddled with a diagonal line of touching bore holes, and a spider was forcing open the resultant gash and crawling inside.

It hadn't seen Rade yet, he didn't think. He hastily shoved himself back into the kitchen.

"Got a spider!" he said over the comm.

He glanced at the vital signs of the others—all green, including the civilians. The AIs had shut the faceplates in time.

The robots remained in position by the kitchen door, just out of the alien's view. That wouldn't last for long.

Rade glanced at the ceiling; it was composed of a grid of flat metal supports with square panels set in between them.

"Those panels are removable..." Rade said.

"Think the metal framework can support our weight?" Tahoe asked.

"It's going to have to," Rade said. "Argonauts, follow my lead!"

Rade leaped onto the countertop beside the fridge—with a helping hand from his jetpack—and then reached up to dislodge the panel directly above him. He pushed it inward, and then slid the panel from view, revealing a dark hole that contained various PVC conduits and pipes.

Rade grasped the flat metal supports and, hoping that they would hold his weight, he pulled himself up. The supports bent slightly, but held.

"Send up the civilians next," Rade ordered.

The environmental suits didn't have jetpacks, so once the Kenyans attained the countertop, Rade reached down to help them up in turn. As the Kenyans moved into the inner crawlspace of the ceiling with him, he told them: "Try to stay on top of the metal grid. I'm not sure the panels by themselves will support your weight."

The Argonauts and combat robots scrambled into the claustrophobic confines after them, forcing Rade and the Kenyans to worm ever deeper into the dark crawlspace to make room.

As Rade advanced, he kept expecting the aliens to race into the kitchen at any moment and begin executing his brothers. So far that hadn't happened. But tell that to his racing heart.

Rade obeyed his own advice, sticking to the metal bars illuminated by his headlamp. The panels below were crowded against each other, and didn't shift much when he placed his weight along their edges. The conduits overhead occasionally caught at his bulky jetpack, and he had to halt and reach up to unsnag himself.

When everyone had gathered into the ceiling crawlspace, Tahoe, the last one up, replaced the original panel Rade had dislodged. Tahoe left the panel open a tiny crack, allowing him a view of half of the kitchen and one of the entrances. Rade knew, because he had tapped into Tahoe's video; he minimized that feed, placing it in the upper right of his vision.

"Headlamps off," Rade said. "Disable Implants and jumpsuit comm nodes as well. I want complete radio silence. No signals of any kind. Turn them on again when I reactivate my headlamp, or the alien attacks. Whichever comes first. Meanwhile, sit tight, and leave the panels where they are."

The confines became pitch black as headlamps deactivated throughout the squad. Rade disabled the adhoc networking functions of his Implant and jumpsuit, and Tahoe's feed vanished. Rade had already instructed the Argonauts to reduce the signal output to restrict the comm range to the kitchen, but now he was cutting out the team's EM emissions entirely. It was possible the aliens couldn't detect human comm signals, but he wasn't going to bet his life, nor the lives of his team members, on it.

Rade selected a panel half a meter in front of him and opened it a crack, partially revealing the kitchen below. He slowly lifted his rifle forward, braced his elbows on one of the metal supports, and aimed the scope through the crack. He had a good view of the entrance on the far side of the room, opposite the doorway Tahoe watched.

The tense moments passed. In the adjacent room, he caught sight of the spider as it plowed through the cubicle separators, upturning desks along the way. Its behavior almost seemed angry, but Rade knew it was a mistake to assign human emotions to the alien. What he called angry may have been the creature's natural state.

And then the alien, apparently growing weary with

its wanton destruction of the external office space, turned its attention on the kitchen. It literally ran right up to the opening, as if noticing it for the first time, and then plunged its thick head inside. It placed its forelimbs onto the left and right sides of the entrance like fingers and pulled its large body through.

Rade was reminded of something he had seen in his youth: a long-legged tarantula, emerging sideways from its slit of a nest in the desert sand, an image that had stayed with him for all of his life.

Rade hadn't expected the alien to fit that doorway, but it seemed able to compress its body to a high degree, and as it emerged into the kitchen he involuntarily shuddered. He noted that it didn't carry the usual weapon turrets strapped to its abdomen like the others of its kind; he supposed it was a scout unit of some kind, not meant to engage with targets except at absolute close range. If it had in fact come there with a turret, it was possible it had shucked it off somewhere in the office, so that it could squeeze through the smaller entrances, like the current doorway.

The spider twisted itself so that its sideways body was once more flat on the floor. Now that he had a chance to study it up close, Rade saw that while it didn't carry a weapon turret, it was in fact porting some sort of tank on its thorax region. He guessed the alien used that for respiration, or teleportation. Maybe both.

Long, thick black hairs covered the rest of its body, including the five pairs of segmented legs. The hairs became sharp spurs near the feet of those legs, forming claws or gripping extensions of sorts. Small devices were attached to the knee areas, and connected by a thin wire that formed a threaded circle around the creature. Rade guessed it was the alien equivalent of a strength-enhancing exoskeleton.

The head and thorax seemed fused into a single unit, attached to that round abdomen. The mandibles were made of four crushing organs, large blade-like protrusions from the head that had the ability to fold and unfold like a deadly blossom; the mandibles opened and closed very slowly as he watched. Several small dots on the head might have been eyes, or ears.

The creature remained still, its thorax rising and falling out of sync with the blossoming mandibles, as if breathing the atmosphere provided by the portable tank.

Rade kept his rifle aimed at its center of mass. He was ready to fire. He didn't want to fight here. Didn't want to potentially reveal their position and bring down the whole swarm on them. But if he had to...

The alien vaulted forward in a sudden spurt, rending the coffee table in two and making Rade start. He tracked the spider with his scope, watching it leap onto the fridge and tear the container to the ground. The vending machine was the next object of its wrath, which suffered a similar fate. The absolute silence of the whole thing imbued an eerie, almost surreal quality to the scene.

The alien moved noiselessly over the broken glass and steel, probing with two thick forelimbs that appeared to serve the dual purpose of feelers and limbs. It slowly edged forward, making its way toward the opposite exit. It would be coming into the view of Tahoe's scope soon, if it hadn't already.

As the spider continued advancing, for a moment Rade thought it was done with its sweep of the room.

But then it paused and retreated two steps to the far wall, where the table had been.

It stabbed upward in a blur, striking the ceiling panels and startling Rade anew. It tore through, pulling down a humanoid figure. Rade feared it was one of his own at first, but he realized the newcomer wasn't wearing a jumpsuit, but rather a business suit. His exposed skin had turned deep black, the limbs frozen in place.

It was some stranger who had been hiding there in the ceiling all that time. Someone Rade and the others hadn't noticed, who had died when the office depressurized.

Rade had almost reactivated his Implant when he believed it was one of their own the alien was attacking, and was relieved he had not. Hopefully Tahoe hadn't either. Judging from the alien's behavior, it seemed likely his friend had maintained radio silence. Maybe Tahoe couldn't even see what was happening. If so, he was lucky.

The alien stabbed its long legs into the corpse, then buried its folded mandibles into the chest until they protruded from the dead man's back. Those mandibles blossomed open, splitting the body in two. Red mist evaporated into the air.

The alien dove onto the upper portion of the body, those jaws moving back and forth slightly as if chewing, and then it violently spat out the material. It seemed angry, and proceeded to dismember the body into a gory pulp with its legs.

When nothing recognizable remained of the man, the alien departed.

Rade waited a full half hour before turning on his headlamp, signaling the others to reactivate the networking components of their Implants. He rebooted his own network, careful to limit the range to the kitchen.

"Why the hell didn't we realize that guy was hiding in here?" Tahoe said.

Apparently he had seen the incident after all.

"What guy?" Manic asked. Besides Rade and Tahoe, no one else would have been peering through the roof panels.

"Switch to my viewpoint," Tahoe said. "And you'll see."

"Ugh, that's disgusting," Fret said.

"Considering where he dropped from," Lui said. "He had to have crawled past a bunch of PVC pipes, which would have blocked him from view, at least from up here. Look at how dense the conduits are to the left of us."

"How did the alien know he was there?" Manic said.

"Must have smelled him," Lui said. "When you die in the void, your skin molecules are going to flake off."

"But why the hell did it have to do that to him?" Fret said. "Dismembering him like that."

"Guess it wanted to make sure the man was dead," Harlequin said.

"I could swear it took a taste before acting up," Tahoe said. "It sampled the man, then spat him out. That's when it really got riled up. It's like it got mad that he wasn't edible."

"Of course we're not edible," Lui said. "I'm not sure why it even bothered to try. Our lipids and proteins are probably poisonous to the thing."

"Maybe it hopes that if it keeps trying, someday it might be able to eat one of us?" Manic said.

"Don't think they're that dumb," Bender said. "More likely it was looking for someone. Or something."

"What do you mean, some*thing*?" Manic asked.

"Who normally hides inside a host?" Bender said.

"What, you're saying it's looking for a Phant?" Manic asked.

"Not a Phant," Bender said. "But our Phant. Surus."

"It's possible that our enemy has tasked the aliens with finding me," Surus agreed. "That only means we'll have to be all the more cautious going forward."

"All right, Tahoe, you'll have to move out of the way," Rade said. "I want Units A and B to confirm that the floor is clear."

Tahoe lowered himself onto the countertop below to allow the designated robots to get down. Once the units were in the kitchen, he clambered back into the crawlspace and replaced the panel, leaving it open a crack for himself.

Rade switched to Unit A's point of view as it explored the ruined level. He was reminded of the sights he had seen on the previous floor, what with all the crushed cubicles and office equipment. The Centurions kept their distance from the large gap that had been torn into the blast shield.

After a few minutes Unit A reported: "It appears the alien has departed."

sixteen

U nit A, approach the breach," Rade ordered. "I want to see if anything has changed in the city."

The designated robot carefully maneuvered closer to the hole in the blast shield, until it had a view outside. The swarm seemed to have dispersed somewhat, as the streets immediately below were less clogged by the aliens. The surrounding buildings had very few creatures clambering over the exterior surfaces.

"Still fairly nasty out there," Shaw said.

"Return to the kitchen," Rade instructed the robots. "And climb back up to the crawlspace. We'll stay here until dark."

The robots returned to the cramped crawlspace and waited with the rest of the team for the next two hours. It wasn't all that comfortable, being cooped up in that claustrophobic area, but Rade and the others managed. During the downtime, Rade shared the video he had taken of the alien's incursion into the kitchen for all the team to see.

When his alarm went off, Rade ordered the robots down to clear the level once more. After their sweep, Rade had Unit A approach the breach. The glow bars in the geodesic dome had deactivated, casting the city in darkness.

"Unit A, switch to night vision mode," Rade sent.

The robot obeyed, and the scene shifted in hue so that green color tones dominated. The streets had emptied, at least for the most part. The occasional spiders patrolled in pairs. Unit A detected more of the aliens lurking on the tops of some buildings, likely snipers scanning the avenues for any overlooked survivors who might attempt to flee.

The street lamps provided dim cones of green light. Again, Rade wondered at the strangeness of the city design; why create lamps when the glow bars could have lit the night? But then he remembered all the street lamps had cameras embedded underneath.

"TJ, if we got close enough to the street lamps, do you think you'd be able to hack into the cameras they contain?" Rade asked.

"I could hack in from here if we didn't have that damn jamming to deal with," TJ said.

Rade considered for a moment. "I suppose those cameras aren't all that useful to us at the moment anyway, considering we're planning on taking the subway system to the transmission tower, and avoiding the streets for the most part."

"What if the aliens have decided to use the subway system as their personal dormitory?" Shaw said.

"I think most of them have probably returned to their ship," Lui said. "Either that, or they've probably deployed special housing outside the domes to accommodate their particular atmospheric requirements. It can't be comfortable to operate in the void for hours on end. Those aliens we see out there? We're looking at the second duty shift."

"Units A and B, return to the kitchen," Rade sent.

"Everyone else, let's get down."

"Can we just remove the roof panels and leap down directly?" Manic asked.

"No," Rade said. "I want this hiding place left intact, in case we need it again."

And so the Argonauts began to worm backwards through the crawlspace and lower themselves down to the countertop in turn.

While they did so, Fret said: "I'm wondering something. You say they're operating in the void, Lui. You mean with suits, right?"

"I didn't see any evidence they were wearing environmental suits of any kind, no," Lui said.

"How do you know they don't have skintight jumpsuits of some kind?" Fret insisted.

"I suppose it's possible," Lui said. "But you watched the video Rade shared, right? And I'm sure you made your own of our earlier encounter. You saw the individual hairs on their legs, right?"

"A jumpsuit could enclose individual hairs," Fret said. "There are watertight coatings the military has come up with that you can spray over a porcupine, sheathing the individual quills in a thin polymer. I don't see why that couldn't be expanded a few tech levels to create a completely skintight jumpsuit, something flexible these spiders could literally spray over their bodies to protect them from the void. Maybe filled with an insulating layer that would provide the necessary pressure."

"Again, I suppose it's possible," Lui said. "These are aliens, after all, operating alien technology. But we've encountered a few resilient species in the past that were capable of withstanding the void."

"Yes, but those were bioengineered," Fret said. "The Phants notwithstanding, of course."

"And who's to say our current aliens weren't bioengineered?" Lui said. "For all we know, the Phant we're tracking created these aliens!"

"I doubt it," Tahoe said. "The Phant wouldn't have had time. That ship you saw in orbit would have taken centuries to build. And the Phants only arrived in our space fifteen years ago."

"You win," Lui said.

Rade lowered the civilians to the countertop and then followed them down, so that all of the Argonauts were in the kitchen.

"Kato," Rade said. "I've marked off what looks like the best route through the subway tunnels to our destination. I want you to have a look and tell me if you have any suggestions."

Rade transmitted the route to Kato, and the man accepted.

"Looks fine," Kato said a moment later. "That route will bring us closest to the transmission tower."

"Good," Rade said. "Centurions, lead the way. Take us to the airlock."

The combat robots led the squad to the main entrance, and Rade had TJ unlock and open the inner hatch, which the alien had left untouched. There was still atmosphere beyond the outer hallway, and Rade, remembering the unknown civilian who had died while hiding in the ceiling panels, decided not to compromise that atmosphere by opening both the inner and outer hatches at the same time.

He sent the Centurions through first to sweep the outer hallway in front of the elevators. When the robots reported it as clear, he had his Argonauts pass through the airlock in groups of four, opening and closing the hatches behind them.

When everyone was through, the group proceeded

into the stairwell and down toward the basement. They were spread out in a long line along the stairs, with the robots in the lead. Rade made a further stop on the fifth floor—which was still pressurized—to pilfer the kitchen. The vending machine there had chicken chips, much to Bender's delight, and the group ate until sated. They filled their harnesses with all the bags of chicken chips they could 3D-print and continued on their way.

They reached the second floor entrance and remained in the stairwell while the robots went forward into the walkway that overlooked the concourse. The Centurions fanned out, with two taking the stairs to the first floor, and confirmed that the area was clear.

Rade and the others emerged and proceeded down to the concourse. They took up defensive positions at the bank entrance, and Rade once more sent the Centurions forward.

The robots swept the bank, taking the escalators down to the carpeted basement foyer where the airlock led to the pedway. The group followed.

Rade halted inside the bank. He stared up at the security cameras.

"TJ, you said you could hack into the security cameras?" Rade asked.

"I could," TJ said. "But I'm not sure what use that would be. These ones belong to the bank. They're on a private subsystem, not linked to the colony's."

"Ah," Rade said. "So wait until we find some colony cameras, you're saying."

"Pretty much."

At the final airlock, once more Rade ordered the Centurions to enter first.

The robots did so, emerging into the pedway

beyond,

"Got some cameras here," Unit A reported. "These might be of interest to you, TJ."

"They probably will," TJ agreed.

"Secure that intersection," Rade ordered, gazing at his overhead map.

The robots approached the T intersection at the far end of the passageway, and carefully pied either side.

"Clear," the Centurions said.

Rade and the others passed through the expansive airlock, and then Rade set TJ to hacking into the camera system.

"Done," TJ said several minutes later. "These are definitely city-owned. I'm programming cameras along the route to transmit the locations of any lurking aliens. As long as we're within fifty meters of a colony camera, we should all receive the latest updates."

Fresh red dots appeared on Rade's overhead map, as shared via TJ's Implant. Larger blue circles surrounded those dots.

"The blue circles denote the range limits of the cameras," TJ said. "You'll see that there are a lot of spots not covered. Those include cameras that have malfunctioned, probably because the aliens attacked them, and also large swathes in the subway tunnels where there aren't any cameras."

Rade nodded slowly. "This should be good enough."

According to the data, there were two aliens standing guard on the main platform of the station stop ahead. And in the actual subway tunnel next to it, another two moved down the route, their red dots freezing in place as they passed out of view of the camera nearby.

"We're going to have to take out those two alien guards," Rade said. "And the other two in the tunnel. According to the map, we should be able to close to within twenty meters of the first two without being spotted, given the angle of the adjoining pedway passage and the current location of the aliens. Bender and Tahoe, I want you on point. You'll be in charge of taking those two out."

Bender flashed Rade the happiest grin in the world.

The group proceeded into the T intersection and made their way down the concrete passageway on the left toward the arched opening labeled "Zhana Station Stop."

Rade signaled the stop, and Tahoe and Bender slowly continued forward. Tahoe went high, Bender low: they pied the arch, slowly moving into the potential line of sight of the aliens, at least according to the positions recorded by the security cameras.

"Contact," Tahoe said.

The two Argonauts fired. Thick beams of blue plasma erupted from their rifles.

"Aliens down," Tahoe said. "Moving in to take head shots."

Bender and Tahoe vanished from sight.

Rade heard Bender giggling over the comm. He switched to Bender's point of view, and saw him firing repeatedly at his current target as he approached. Every shot struck the head region, sending up splatters of yellow blood that boiled away in the vacuum environment.

"I think that's good, Bender," Tahoe said over the comm.

"Squashing bugs," Bender sung. "Slicing bugs. Rippin' little bugsies apart in their underwear..."

"Bender, it's down!" Tahoe said. "Bender!"

Bender finally stopped firing. He turned toward Tahoe. "What, bro? Can't you let a man have a little relaxation?"

"Centurions, help them secure the area," Rade said. "I want those surface escalators covered."

The units hurried forward, their footfalls silent in the void. The robots took up defensive positions on the two escalators located on opposite sides of the platform.

Meanwhile, Bender and Tahoe moved toward the high-grade polycarbonate that composed the platform screen doors. The translucent screen had been shattered in many places, no doubt by the aliens. Rade had played a part in breaking through a platform screen at a different station earlier, when he had fled the governor's enforcers and Perdix drones; that made him wonder if citizens had made some of the smaller ruptures as they fled the aliens.

Rade still had Bender's point of view piped into his vision, and he watched as Bender leaned through a shattered area of the screen and surveyed the tunnel beyond. Rade wasn't expecting them to find anything, considering that cameras were currently active in the immediate area.

In a few moments Tahoe reported in: "Area secure."

Rade returned to his own viewpoint and glanced at his Argonauts. "Forward."

The group moved into the platform area, passing the benches and pillars, and joined Tahoe and Bender beside the shattered screen.

"Centurions," Rade sent. "Join us."

The robots hurried over.

"I want you to lead the way toward the target,"

Rade instructed the Centurions.

The robots leaped down past the shattered screen and into the tunnel. They began making their way toward the two frozen red dots that resided on the overhead map. The pair of aliens associated with those dots remained out of range of any cameras, and blocked their path somewhere ahead.

"What about the bugs?" Bender said.

"If this tunnel is anything like the last one I was in," Rade said. "There should be a maintenance passageway between two to five hundred meters ahead. We'll take cover inside and ambush the bugs."

Once more Bender flashed those gold teeth in a wide, pleased smile.

"Headlamps off," Rade said. "Switch to infrared."

seventeen

Rade's vision became green-hued as the infrared channel kicked in.

The group proceeded into the tunnel, with the robots leading the way. They moved at a trot, their weapons scanning the tunnel walls around them, wary of ambushes. Rade was near the center of the squad, next to the civilians. Tahoe and Fret brought up the rear.

"I feel so alive," Bender said. "This is what I was meant to do. Fending off an alien invasion from inside a conquered city, knee-deep in bugs. I hope it never ends."

"Sometimes I wonder if Bender has truly lost it," Fret said. "But then I have to remind myself that none of us really fit the definition of normal."

"I think it's his way of dealing with his fear," Lui said.

"I ain't afraid," Bender said.

"No?" Lui said. "Well I am. And if you're really not, then you should be."

"You're afraid?" Batindo said. His voice sounded a whimper.

"Err," Lui said. "Sorry bro." He switched to the private band. "I shouldn't have said that over the common band. What do you want me to tell him, boss? That I'm not afraid?"

"No," Rade said. "Don't tell him anything. A healthy dose of fear will do him and the other civilians good. Let them all know you're afraid. Let them consider the ramifications of that."

The squad continued in silence for some time. The lead Centurions, fifty meters ahead, had yet to encounter the maintenance door.

"Didn't you say two to five hundred meters?" Shaw asked.

"That's what I said," Rade replied.

"The map don't show no maintenance door," Bender said.

"It's there," Rade insisted. "The other subway tunnel didn't have the maintenance shaft on the map either."

"Wait, shaft?" Fret said. "This is the first time you've called it a maintenance shaft. You've called it a door. A passageway. And now a shaft. So which is it?"

"All three," Rade said. He had to quash doubts the moment they appeared, lest those doubts overly affect morale. But he was beginning to worry himself.

"Hey, um, why doesn't the door show up in the camera feeds either?" Bender said.

"My guess is it's in-between the areas those cameras cover," Rade said.

"Well that makes no sense," Bender said. "What's the point of placing a security camera if it doesn't provide security? You'd think providing video coverage of a maintenance door would be more important than recording a random tunnel segment."

"Remember, some of the cameras are malfunctioning," Lui said. "Either shot out or mangled by the aliens."

"Got an answer for everything, huh foodie goodie?" Bender replied. "Phooey Lui."

"Pussywillow," Lui retorted.

They rounded a bend that continued quite a ways into the distance. There were no tangos visible on the infrared band.

"All right," Rade said. "Slow down. Tahoe, split us into two groups. I want each fire team hugging either wall of the tunnel. Let's flatten our profiles."

Tahoe split the team and the group continued another eight hundred meters forward, coming dangerously close to the red dots that signified the last known position of the alien patrol as recorded by the nearby camera. There were no more cameras providing coverage up ahead.

"Don't see no maintenance passage," Bender complained.

"Pussywillow," Lui said.

"Phooey Lui," Bender replied.

Soon the squad had left the certainty of the cameras behind, and they were advancing completely in the blind, at least in terms of the fog of war. They could be walking into a nest of a hundred aliens, as far as any of them knew. Though presumably, their thermal vision would alert them.

Staying close to either wall, the robots continued advancing ahead of the party.

Rade had the feed from Unit C piped into the upper right of his vision. The passageway curved slightly, so that visibility was only about three hundred meters. As the Centurion advanced, an object's heat signature appeared at the three hundred meter range.

"I've got something," Unit C said.

Rade switched over entirely to that Centurion's feed.

"I see it," Rade said. "Zoom in."

Unit C engaged the magnification, and advanced a few more steps until more of the object was in view. It was cigar-shaped.

"I believe that is one of their troop transports," Harlequin said. "The craft must have smashed through the street and into the subway."

"I'm not seeing any signs of activity," Unit C said.

"Wait, obviously it's active, though," Fret said. "Or we wouldn't be reading any heat from it."

"Proceed with caution," Rade said.

The squad followed fifty meters behind the robots, staying close to the walls.

The Centurions neared the pod, which was so large it took up most of the free space in the tunnel. The Centurions had to edge their way past it; the far side wasn't visible.

"Careful..." Rade said.

Rade saw a blur of green motion and then the video feed from Unit C winked out. On the overhead map, the dots representing both Units C and D, which were leading the way, had become dark.

"Contact!" Unit A said.

Rade and the Argonauts already had their scopes trained on either side of the pod; Rade saw a green shape emerge from the side he was targeting. It towered over Unit A.

He aimed at the center of mass and fired.

Others around him engaged, so that the tunnel filled with streaks of green from the plasma rifles.

The tango retreated from view. Rade swerved the aim of his scope to the opposite side of the pod: he saw another green shape, this one closer to the ground, as if it had collapsed. Rade fired at it.

"The second tango is down!" Bender said.

"The first one dodged back behind the pod," Lui said.

Rade glanced at the overhead map. The red dot of the fallen tango had darkened, while the first remained a bright crimson on the opposite side of the pod. That was its last known location, of course. It was most likely sheltering behind the large cylinder, and attempting to call for help.

"Rush them, Centurions!" Rade said.

Rade watched the video feed from Unit A, and saw as it rounded the pod with its rifle raised.

There was nothing there.

"Where did it go?" Tahoe said.

Rade dismissed the feed urgently and spun around.

The alien towered over the party, where it had materialized behind them.

He opened fired as it dove into their midst. The alien wrapped its mandibles around the nurse.

"No!" Kato said.

Others unleashed their plasma rifles, too, and the spider collapsed. But it was too late for the woman.

Kato pulled her remains from the alien's grasp. "No. No."

The alien had likely sent a signal to its brethren. The overhead map appeared deceptively quiet, of course: it wouldn't update, not while there were no cameras nearby.

"We move forward, now!" Rade said. "Kato, come on!"

"I can't leave her," Kato said.

"She's dead," Rade said. "And you will be, too, if you don't come *now!*"

Kato reluctantly lowered her.

Rade and the others advanced to the cylindrical pod. Unit B was pinned under the corpse of the first spider, and Harlequin and Surus helped free him.

Rade glanced at the wreckages of Units C and D. "Are they salvageable?"

"Negative," Harlequin said. "We've lost two brothers today." He glanced at Kato. "And a dear nurse."

"She was my fiancée," Kato said.

The party hurried forward, resuming their previous canter. They came within fifty meters of the next camera in the tunnel, and once more reestablished communication with the city's surveillance network.

"Uh, the cams are detecting incoming bugs behind us!" Lui announced. "As in, a lot of them. The tangos we took down obviously got out a call for help."

Rade glanced at the overhead map. Behind them, red dots were swarming onto the platform, coming down the escalators from the city above. It looked like one of the nearby high-rise apartment buildings had served as their temporary barracks.

"Those numbers are off the Richter scale," Manic said.

"Hope you're happy now, Bender," Fret said. "You've got your wish."

"Damn right I'm happy," Bender said, though his voice sounded tense.

"Pick up the pace, people," Rade said. "I want your top speeds!"

"The civilian won't be able to keep up," Tahoe said. "We talked about this."

Batindo wore a strength-enhancing jumpsuit like the rest of the Argonauts, and in theory he wouldn't need any assistance. But Kato...

"Leave me," Kato said. "I just want to die."

"If you die then she gave her life for nothing!" Rade said. "Now you will fight, damn it! Like the rest of us! Bender, give the man a lift."

"What am I, a camel?" Bender said. "I never signed up to give civilians piggyback rides!"

But Bender slowed, motioning for Kato to jump on his back.

Kato hesitated, then leaped onto Bender, wrapping his arms around the jetpack. Bender momentarily stumbled under the weight but straightened a moment later, obviously upping the strength-enhancement of the exoskeleton.

"Now run, Argonauts!" Rade said. "Run for all you're worth!"

The robots once more took the lead, though only by twenty five meters this time.

Rade pushed himself hard. Strength-enhancement only carried one so far: the top speed was ultimately based on the physical condition of the suit occupant, and it required him or her to really work. Body weight also factored in. The bigger guys, such as Bender, TJ and Tahoe, were closer to the rear. Batindo was dead last, Rade noted.

Rade didn't slow. On the overhead map, the cameras embedded in the lamps along the street above recorded the positions of several aliens wending their way across the asphalt toward the next subway station in an attempt to head off the Argonauts. Rade refused to allow the bugs to beat them.

"Faster!" Rade said.

As the party neared that station, it soon became obvious, at least according to the cameras, that the bugs wouldn't reach it in time.

Too bad that station wasn't the destination of Rade and his companions: it was too far from the transmission tower. The next station after that was where they needed to go.

ISAAC HOOKE

The Argonauts reached the station and remained in the tunnel area. They continued on without stopping, passing the battered platform screen doors without incident.

After the group traveled a hundred and fifty meters, on the map, the red dots began to flood down onto the platform behind them from the surface, joining those already in pursuit.

The party ran another two hundred meters. On the map, other red dots began to flow into the target station, apparently from another barracks nearby. They moved onto the platform and into the tunnel; the vanguard moved into a region of the passageway ahead where there were no cameras, and their dots froze, forming a thick red line.

"Bugs are blocking the way," Tahoe announced.

"I see that," Rade said.

"Where's one of those fabled maintenance doors when you need one, huh boss?" Fret asked.

eighteen

W e make our own maintenance door," Rade said. He turned his rifle upward. "Concentrate fire, Argonauts. Harlequin, sync the AIs in our jumpsuits to target a circle half a meter in diameter. Let's make ourselves a path. Units A, B, watch our flanks!"

"According to the thickness described on the map, even if we combine our firepower, it'll take at least fifty seconds to drill a hole to the surface."

"Then we better get started!" Rade said.

The Argonauts gathered in a tight, layered circle. Those in the outer regions of the circle extended their rifles over the heads and shoulders of those in the middle, so that they could all target the same general area. They began firing rapidly, guided by AI aiming. The weapons could only let off four or five shots in rapid succession before requiring a cool down period between shots, and the firing rate quickly slowed. Clumps of packed dirt began to fall down as the plasmas bored through the cement shell, and Rade occasionally tilted his head forward to disperse the soil that fell onto his faceplate.

"Need windshield wipers or something in these helmets," Bender complained. "It's like trying to muff dive during a period."

"Eww, thanks for that Bender," Fret said.

"Wish we had plasma rifles in past operations," Fret said. "These things beat the hell out of laser cutters."

"It's an illusion," Lui said. "Plasma is only moderately better than laser cutters against armored material."

"Got a sighting," Unit A said. "Multiple tangos."

"Centurions, defend," Rade said. "Argonauts, continue firing."

Rade saw flashes of green at the periphery of his vision to the left and right, and he knew that the Centurions were taking down the forerunners of the incoming spiders.

Rade and the Argonauts continued to fire at the tunnel ceiling; he switched to LIDAR bursts so he could get a visual picture of how deep the bore was, as the thermal band was useless at the moment. The three-dimensional wireframe depicted a half-meter wide bore that was about five meters deep so far. He probably could have switched to full LIDAR, or even visual, as the plasma beams were revealing their positions anyway. But why turn a glimmer into a bonfire?

He kept an eye on the status of the street above via the overhead map; so far, that street remained clear of tangos.

A moment later, the wireframe representation of the cap at the end of the tunnel disappeared.

They were through.

"Argonauts, cease firing!" Rade said. "And get back... into the center one at a time! Meanwhile, help the Centurions defend!"

The party separated, breaking their tight circular

formation. While the others lay down suppressive fire, Tahoe stepped directly underneath the bore and onto the pile of loose dirt that had formed below. He activated his jetpack and spurted upward into the new tunnel.

Shaw followed, with Rade third.

Rade landed on the asphalt and assumed a defensive position beside Tahoe and Shaw; he scanned the streets around him. The others joined them in turn, geysering from the ground and landing nearby, so that soon a cigar formation had taken shape around the hole bored into the asphalt.

When everyone had surfaced, including the Centurions, Rade ordered: "To the rooftops!"

Rade deactivated his LIDAR entirely—he could see the outlines of the buildings well enough on the thermal band, courtesy of the profusion of street lamps, most of which were still active.

He jetted to the top of a low-rise building.

"It's an encouraging sign," Tahoe said, landing beside him. "That power is still on throughout the city. It means we'll definitely be able to contact the *Argonaut*."

"But it's also a little surprising," Manic said. "It's almost as if the bugs want to preserve as much of the existing infrastructure as possible."

"That makes some sense," Lui said. "After all, if you want to steal technological ideas from another race, you don't go about wantonly destroying their tech."

"Yeah," Shaw said. "They save that wanton destruction for the organisms who inhabit those cities instead, apparently."

Rade jetted from rooftop to rooftop. In between jetpack bursts, he sprinted at maximum speed, staying near the middle of the buildings. He chose low- to mid-rise buildings, moving between flat roofs and sloped ones.

Cameras recorded the positions of bugs emerging onto the streets behind them. Evidently the spiders had broken through and enlarged the relatively small hole Rade and the others had drilled.

"That didn't take them long..." Lui said.

Rade could almost imagine how the pursuing aliens would have sounded if there had been atmosphere... the hoots and howls, the screeches and shrieks as they fought amongst themselves to be the first to reach the party. Such sounds were lost in the void of course. He realized the silence somehow made the approach of the aliens all the more menacing.

According to the map, some of the spiders were running alongside the party on the street, though he couldn't see them from his current angle on the rooftops. As he leaped between one mid-rise building and another, activating his jetpack to give him a boost, he caught a glimpse of the asphalt below, and the masses lurking down there, colored green on the night vision.

Before the street ceded from view, he saw a flash down there, and realized one of the aliens had likely teleported. Did that mean the party had been spotted?

"Watch for teleporters!" Rade said.

Sure enough, a spider materialized directly in front of him. Rade fired, bringing it down.

"On drag!" Bender shouted.

A red dot had appeared on the overhead map directly behind the party on the roof; it went dark an instant later.

Bender or someone else had handled it.

"The transmission tower is just ahead, according to

the map," Rade said. He could see the outline of the structure on the thermal band, a rectangle-shaped lattice sticking up from a fenced-off plot of land situated between two apartment buildings. Long rods protruded from the top, where the various antennae were attached. Different sized satellite dishes surrounded the rim lower down.

"I believe one of those dishes is responsible for the jamming signal," Lui said. "The antennae at the top, those are for the InterGalNet, we want to leave those alone."

"Fire at the dishes if you can!" Rade said. He instructed his AI to target the dishes, and his arms automatically stabilized and engaged the rifle as he ran.

Another alien materialized in front of the party, and Rade ripped control back to aim his rifle at the enemy. He launched a plasma beam at the spider from near point-blank range, and then thrusted over the falling corpse. Some of the Argonauts likewise jetted over the body behind him, while others merely sidestepped.

"We've taken down all the dishes!" Tahoe said a moment later. "At least those on this side."

"Jamming signal is still present," Lui said. "The dish must be on the other side."

"Can't we just shoot down the whole damn tower?" Bender asked.

"No!" Fret said. "We'll lose the InterGalNet. And it'll be that much harder to contact the *Argonaut*. Remember, Rade ordered the ship to leave its geosynchronous orbit when the mercenaries arrived, and Bax will have further withdrawn the *Argonaut* with the appearance of the alien mothership. So good luck getting a signal up there without the InterGalNet, especially since we can't piggyback on the shuttle comm nodes, which are located in a different dome!"

The group vaulted onto the final apartment lying between them and the transmission tower. A long building. Before they reached the edge, spiders began scrambling up the far side. Others teleported directly in front, blocking their paths.

Rade and the others were forced to halt, firing rapidly. They fought back-to-back in a circle, as other bugs were materializing and scaling the walls of the building on all sides. Kato had released Bender, and cowered in the center of that circle with Batindo.

"So close!" Tahoe said. "And yet so far!"

"I need a volunteer to jet out there and destroy the remaining dishes," Rade said.

"I'll go," Harlequin said. "Cover me."

Before Rade could agree—or disagree—Harlequin jetted skyward, arcing over the apartment toward the transmission tower. He altered his thrust randomly so that he wouldn't be an easy target.

"Unit B, go with him," Rade ordered.

Unit B jetted upward.

Rade and the others continued firing at the incoming bugs. Some of them were distracted by the flying Argonauts, and Rade used that to take down some of the tangos more easily.

A spider materialized just above Unit B in the air, and must have chopped down with one of its legs or mandibles, because Unit B exploded in a shower of sparks and plunged from view.

"I've landed on the tower," Harlequin sent. "I'm climbing around to the other side. The aliens are firing... hitting the tower. I have to be quick..."

Rade aimed at some of the more distant spiders that were lining the edge of the rooftop ahead, aliens that were contributing to the attack against Harlequin, and he took them out.

"All the remaining dishes are down!" Harlequin transmitted. "I'm jetting to the opposite rooftop. It's only a short distance. Thanks for covering me. I'll try to rendezvous with you when I can."

Rade glanced at his overhead map and saw Harlequin's blue dot successfully attain the roof of the building across from the transmission tower. Red dots pursued the lone Artificial.

"I have contact with the *Argonaut!*" Fret said.

"Have Bax dispatch the Hoplites!" Rade said. "Now! And make sure they bring the backup stun rifle!"

The incoming aliens were proving overwhelming. More were materializing than ever before as "jump" units among them reached teleport range. Any time now, and Rade's men would begin to fall.

"Shaw, with me!" Rade said. He leaped into the center of the circle, beside Batindo and Kato, and aimed his rifle down at the roof. "We drill a hole!"

His rifle and Shaw's would be enough to penetrate the relatively thin material. He rotated his aim as he fired, forming the outline of a circle in the surface. With Shaw's help, he drilled through the roof and into the drywall below. In moments, the cylindrical plug they had formed collapsed inward, forming an entrance.

"Argonauts, into the apartment!" Rade said.

Shaw leaped down and Rade followed. A motion sensor activated the light fixtures, and Rade dismissed his night vision. He was in an abandoned in-suite laundry room of some kind. He proceeded into the living room and more lights activated. He aimed his rifle at the front door to guard.

The other Argonauts rapidly appeared in the

laundry room behind him, as did the two civilians. Unit A was conspicuously absent.

"The Centurion?" Rade asked.

"Didn't make it," Surus said.

Rade felt a pang of remorse. That was the last of the away team robots. They had been self-aware, sentient AIs, and had died under his watch: essentially brothers who had given their lives for the good of the team. He had made backups of the AI cores on the ship before leaving for the mission, but that didn't make what happened any easier. Reviving AIs came with its own set of problems, as evidenced by Harlequin, who kept waiting to prove he was as brave as his predecessor.

"Let's move!" Rade advanced to the foyer of the apartment and opened the door. A motion sensor activated the overhead lights as he checked either flank. The common area hallway was empty, for now. Some of the apartment doors were bashed-in from earlier incursions, but most were intact and locked.

"They're coming down our hole!" Bender said from the drag position, near the laundry room.

"Just like you do Manic's?" Fret quipped.

Bender didn't answer. Rade glanced back and saw Bender was busy firing into the laundry room with Lui. That none of the spiders teleported inside confirmed the theory Tahoe had that the aliens needed a relatively wide, clear space in order to materialize. The apartment suite with all its furniture prevented that, but this hallway, though cramped, might just give the creatures the room they needed.

Have to be quick.

"Retreat!" Rade raced into the hallway.

nineteen

Rade had gone maybe ten paces in the direction of the stairwell when the large glass window at the far end of the hall shattered. A spider dove inside, uncurling its long legs and lowering its turret.

Rade fired his plasma rifle; more beams erupted from behind him, joining his own, and the creature staggered and collapsed. Overkill.

Rade continued forward, but had gone only a pace before another alien crawled over the corpse from outside the window.

Rade shot it down; another spider appeared a moment later, this time materializing past the two bodies.

"Guess we're not going that way!" Rade fired again, and then kicked in the door beside him to enter the apartment suite beyond. The other Argonauts followed him inside. The light fixtures activated upon entry, illuminating a bachelor suite. There were three rooms: a common room, bathroom, and laundry room.

Bender and Tahoe were the last to enter. They were firing in both directions, taking down the bugs approaching from the front and rear. Bender slammed the door shut behind him.

Rade and the others didn't bother to place any furniture to block the door.

"Shaw, Surus, drill a hole to the next floor!" Rade ordered. "The rest of you, defend!"

As Shaw and Surus moved into place, the Argonauts assumed defensive positions behind the various chairs, counters, couches and coffee tables. Fret and Lui guarded the rear windows, while the others watched the front door.

Rade glanced at his overhead map. Harlequin was still alive, and had holed up inside another building nearby.

"Harlequin, do you read?" Rade tried. He kept his scope aimed at the closed door in front of him. The aliens should have attacked by now, but strangely, had not.

"Yes, but I'm occupied at the moment," Harlequin replied.

"We'll try to get to you when we can," Rade said.

"That might prove... difficult," Harlequin returned.

"Got our retreat ready," Shaw announced.

"Bender, Manic," Rade said. "Get down there and clear the suite below."

If the aliens had attacked the front door, Rade would have been ordering everyone to go down that hole. But that the bugs had not told him they were up to something, and he decided caution was the best course of action at the moment.

Bender and Manic dropped into the plasma hole drilled into the floor.

"Fret, where are my Hoplites?" Rade said.

Once they touched down, the AIs aboard the mechs would guide them to their human pilots. Any resistance along the way would be handled with extreme prejudice.

"Bax says they're coming," Fret replied.

"Give me a location," Rade pressed.

"Uh, Bax says they're still dropping," Fret said.

"Shit." Rade stared at the door. The aliens still hadn't attacked.

"What are they up to?" Tahoe said.

"Got the suite cleared," Manic said. "The front door was intact. I checked the peep hole... the aliens are swarming the hallways already."

"All right, I want the two of you to drill another hole through to the next suite below," Rade said. "Ensure it's not lined up with the existing bore: let's make it a little harder for the aliens to follow us. Everyone else, start heading down to the next suite."

As the others began leaping down, Rade remembered the two Units he had left behind with the shuttles.

"Units G and H," Rade transmitted. "Do you read?"

No answer.

"Units G and H?" He tried again.

"It appears our companions have been lost," Surus said. "Likely they were incarcerated after surrendering the shuttles. According to the map, the prison— Marakdom—is located within the northernmost dome. The security camera network reports that dome is teeming with just as many aliens as this one. Likely the two units have been terminated."

Surus leaped down, leaving Shaw and Rade in the room.

Just then large circular patterns appeared in the walls on either side as the constituent material disintegrated. Those circular fragments shot inwards as spiders barreled through. Half of the lights went out.

"Retreat!" Rade leaped onto Shaw, pulling her into

the pit with him.

They crashed into the well-lit suite below. Rade realized another gap had been torn into the rightmost wall here, and also through the front door. The aliens had anticipated their tactic.

A spider leaped onto Surus, pinning her.

Rade and the others fired into the bugs that attacked from the three directions: the ceiling, the foyer, and the wall.

When his latest target was down, Rade spun his weapon toward Surus, intending to aid her, but before he could fire the spider evaporated completely. It left behind a plume of smoke as if it had been utterly incinerated.

A green mist floated forward angrily.

Surus, in her natural form.

Unlike some other species the Argonauts had faced in the past, these bugs obviously hadn't yet developed any technology that could protect them from the raw touch of a Phant, which was deadly to all organic life.

Emilia Bounty, the host, stood up, and joined the others in the attack.

"Good to have you with us again, Ms. Bounty," Rade said.

"I never left you," Ms. Bounty replied.

The Green floated between the Argonauts, disintegrating the dead spiders in its path. As the others repelled the aliens attacking from the openings at the foyer and ceiling, Surus floated into the adjacent room and began terminating the bugs gathered there.

"Well that's handy," Manic said.

"Sexy as hell, is what it is!" Bender said. "Surus baby, if you can hear this, I want you now more than ever! Once you're back inside Emilia, we're going to have some fun. A threesome, baby. Ooo yeah!"

"She's clearing a path!" Lui said.

"Argonauts, follow Surus!" Rade said. He was still firing at the hole in the ceiling, which had grown larger as other spiders unleashed their turrets at it. Tahoe was covering the front door.

Rade and Tahoe retreated on drag, following the others. Batindo and Kato once more remained in the middle, protected by the Argonauts.

One of the creatures shoved through the wall of dead spiders near the front door and leaped at Rade.

He activated a lateral burst from his jetpack, trying to get out of the way, but the alien caught his boot, either in its mandible or its forelimb, he wasn't sure which, and he was carried forward with it. The pair smashed through the window on the far wall and hurtled outside, plummeting toward the pavement.

Apparently the creature was one of those equipped with teleportation, because before impacting the ground, time ground to a halt, and Rade's field of view shifted in color, the night becoming a dark blue. It was like he resided in some alternate reality set above the real one. He could see the dark blue smears of buildings and other organic life around him, frozen in time. Only he and the spider were moving, slowly carried forward along a diagonal trajectory toward some distant target the creature had selected.

In stark contrast to their surroundings, the two of them appeared as bright blue outlines, with a slightly darker cerulean shade contained within those silhouettes: it was like he and the alien had been reduced to pure energy.

His HUD had disappeared. There was no overhead map. No vitals area that showed him the health status of his teammates.

He attempted to pull up the Implant's menu, but it refused to activate.

Rade tried to flex his arm to bring the rifle toward the creature, but could not. He attempted to bend his legs. No good. Curl his fingers. Nope. He was frozen like everything around him.

The spider that gripped him seemed unable to move as well, its long legs stuck in the same pose it had during the fall.

The pair were carried inexorably forward by unknown forces, momentary companions on this interdimensional ride.

Their twin energies approached the street, heading toward a clear area between the dark smears of other spiders scattered across the asphalt. By their facing, it was obvious the spiders were heading toward the apartment to intercept the other Argonauts.

And then, just like that, Rade and the spider snapped back into existence, appearing upon the clearing in the road. The overhead map and other HUD overlays returned.

Rade switched on his night vision, pointed his rifle at the limb that held him, and fired, disintegrating the appendage at the tip. His captor jerked, releasing him immediately.

Rade jetted upward to get a better shot. The turrets secured to the creature's abdomen swiveled toward him.

Rade fired his rifle at the turrets, and jetted laterally slightly at the same time. He issued countering thrust and swung back behind the turrets, landing on the hairy abdomen just beyond the field of fire of the weapons. He considered terminating the creature right there, but then realized that the spiders in the street around him had begun slowing down, apparently realizing what one of their friends had caught.

He cocked his head. His current position afforded him an interesting opportunity...

Rade flung his backside against the shared base of the turrets and activated his magnetic mounts. He wasn't certain if the material was magnetic, but when he felt the pull, he knew he was held fast. The creature's hairs bristled against his suit in outrage.

"Rade, you all right?" Shaw sent.

"Sort of," Rade replied.

The creature was going berserk underneath him, trying to get him off. He aimed his rifle at the other spiders in the street around him and started picking them off. He focused on those closest, some of which leaped toward him as if intending to tear him off their friend. The bucking spider actually hindered the efforts of its brethren, because its constant movements prevented them from effectively targeting Rade.

Motion to the right alerted him of a spider vaulting into the air there; he shot the creature in time, but the spider struck him with a lifeless limb as it flew past and nearly succeeded in ripping him away. The hairs on its leg tore across the fabric of his jumpsuit but failed to penetrate.

Turrets belonging to other members of the swarm were turning toward the bucking spider he rode, and it soon became apparent they were going to terminate it, if only to get Rade.

The spider must have realized this, because it began teleporting frantically, trying to get away from the others. Rade was brought into that blue dimension repeatedly. Apparently time wasn't frozen entirely in that realm, because he could see the laser beams fired from the turrets of the other spiders, collections of photons that slowly advanced through the air as if bogged down by some viscid substance. The other bugs were apparently opening fire haphazardly, because they were hitting each other in the crossfire. Rade watched those slow-motion beams eat into more than one unsuspecting alien.

The jumper continued its sporadic teleportations, crossing the avenue, materializing on a rooftop, then appearing on an adjacent street. It carried Rade far from the main swarm, finally arriving at the base of a high rise. The bug teleported repeatedly, slowly making its way up the exterior in short jumps, suggesting that the range was limited, at least for that particular jumper. After five jumps it finally attained the top of the building.

When it materialized in the center of the flat roof, Rade released the spider and leaped down. In its panic, apparently the bug hadn't noticed that Rade had let go, because it dematerialized a moment later, vanishing from the rooftop. Rade wondered when it would finally realize he was gone.

He glanced at the overhead map. Thanks to the still active InterGalNet, and the lack of jamming, he remained connected to his platoon despite the distance he had traveled, and he could see their blue dots on the map several streets away. They were surrounded by a swarm of red. The team's vitals were still in the green, incredibly.

"Guys," Rade sent. "I made it to a rooftop of some kind. Do you see me on the map?"

"We see you," Shaw said. "Our Hoplites have arrived, by the way. We're coming for you."

Finally.

That explained the green vitals across the board. He accessed the armor conditions of the mechs, and displayed those alongside the vitals. A few Hoplites had yellow indicators, indicating some damage, but so far all of them remained operational.

"I'm gonna give these bugs multiple blow jobs for you, boss," Bender said. "And I don't mean the sexual kind."

"Yeah you do, Pussywillow," Manic said.

"Harlequin?" Rade said.

"I've got my Hoplite, too," Harlequin said.

Rade was relived. He felt personally responsible for the Artificial. Rade had been the one who reinstated him from the backup. The AI stored in that core had been only five years old at the time of the backup. It had been a couple of years since then, so essentially, Harlequin was basically a child, at least in terms of memories. A kid with the neural network and fully-developed personality of an adult.

"Fighting these bugs is a whole lot easier in mechs," Lui said. "Their weapons seem to be variants of wide-beam lasers—the turrets fire several lasers at once, forming a spot area about the size of a fist. When they concentrate their fire among ten or so units, they're able to disintegrate larger unarmored sections at the same time. Since our shields are anti-laser, and actually provide protection against such attacks, we're faring quite well. The shields won't hold up forever, of course. But they should get us to the booster rockets on the plains outside."

"By the way, Bax reports that the entire atmosphere of the planet has been completely vacuumed away into space," Fret said. "I don't know who these aliens are, but I suggest we don't let them get any closer to human space, if we can."

"Not sure we'll be able to make much difference with our lone ship," Rade said. "But we'll certainly alert the United Systems government to what's going on here."

"Apparently, Bax already has," Fret replied.

"Uh, boss?" Tahoe said. "You better watch your six."

"Just his six?" Bender said. "Dude, the boss has got to watch all friggin' hands of the clock!"

Rade glanced at his map. Red dots approached the tower from every side as the security cameras picked up bugs scurrying toward his position. Apparently alien scouts had spotted Rade during his joyride, and had alerted the swarm.

Things were very quickly going to get hot up there.

twenty

Rade rushed to the southern edge of the building, where the vanguard of incoming enemies was closest, and aimed his scope down over the low rim. He activated the proximity sensor on his helmet to alert him if any aliens materialized on the rooftop anywhere behind him. He also kept the video feed from his aft camera active in the upper middle area of his HUD: the "rear view mirror."

The glow bars embedded in the framework of the geodesic dome unexpectedly flared to daylight levels and his night vision autogated to reduce the brightness. He dismissed the infrared channel, returning to ordinary vision.

"TJ, are you messing with the dome's day-night cycle?" Rade sent. "It's not even close to the designated morning."

"Not me," TJ transmitted. "It's obviously malfunctioning."

Well, the cover of darkness apparently hadn't helped Rade anyway. He targeted the incoming vanguard and opened fire on the lead bugs, bringing them down in turn.

The aliens reached the base of the building and

surrounded it. Some began to climb. Others teleported, disappearing and reappearing further up the exterior surface. None teleported directly onto the rooftop, at least not immediately, confirming that all jumpers were limited to a relatively short range.

Rade fired as fast as he could, hitting bugs in the heads or abdomens, causing them to release the building and plunge to their deaths. He was keeping the southern exterior relative bug free, but he knew the creatures would simply be concentrating on the remaining three walls, so he abandoned that position for the eastern side.

As expected, the bugs had attained a foothold, having climbed or teleported a quarter of the way to the top. After clearing that section, he moved on to the next, and the next, repeating the process. He concentrated first on those bugs that were the obvious jumpers, and then picked off the rest.

By the time he returned to the southern edge, the closest aliens were only six floors below him. The rim he used for cover began to dissolve in places as the incoming lasers struck.

He caught sight of a blue sphere in his rear view mirror and spun around to blast the spider that emerged. More spheres materialized, and Rade was forced to repeatedly adjust his aim and squeeze the trigger. Spider corpses began to litter the rooftop, their bodies collapsing between goose neck exhaust vents and louver ventilation domes.

His proximity alert sounded, indicating movement right above him.

Rade rolled away and shot the alien that had just scaled the southernmost edge of the rooftop. It slumped onto the spot where he had resided only a moment before.

More bugs scaled the rim an instant later.

His position was overwhelmed.

Rade retreated at a sprint, firing at the aliens behind him. He weaved between the superstructures as more bugs materialized directly on the rooftop, and he took a running leap off the eastern edge of the building. He activated his jetpack at full burn.

He flew out into the space between the high rise and the adjacent building. He was counting on the fact that the spiders weren't expecting him to make the jump; by the time they adjusted their turrets, he would have landed on the mid-rise office nearby.

At least, that was what he hoped.

He thrust randomly to the left and right as he fell, intending to evade any lasers the enemy might unleash. As he approached the target roof, he fired countering thrust to slow his descent but still landed hard, rolling.

He clambered to his feet and continued forward.

A blue sphere appeared in his path and he fired his rifle directly into the core, killing the spider as it emerged.

Rade swerved around the falling body and hurried toward the building edge.

In his rear view mirror, he spotted spiders moving onto the lip of the tower rooftop he had just vacated. Rade was directly in their line of site. Turrets swerved toward him...

Rade reached the building edge and instead of jetting across to the next rooftop, he dove toward one of its upper windows. He activated thrust, breaking through the glass a moment later.

He landed on the floor and slid into a wall. He rolled away. Holes appeared in the base of the wall where enemy lasers struck.

He raced into the foyer and opened the door. He

entered the common hallway and dashed westward, away from the tower. There were no windows here. An open stairwell resided further ahead.

On his rear view mirror, he saw the rear wall collapse as bugs concentrated fire on the exterior and hurled their bodies through. Rade paused to fire off three shots, taking down two bugs.

Then he continued running. The hallway was wide enough to fit a jumper apparently, because a blue sphere appeared in front of him. Rade dropped to the floor and fired his dorsal jets to continue sliding forward. A spider appeared—he fired directly into the ventral portion of the abdomen as he passed underneath, ripping open its gut. Viscera tumbled out, misting in the vacuum.

The bug collapsed behind him, its body shielding him from view of any others beyond.

He reached the stairwell and descended a full flight at a time, taking giant leaps and using the railing for support. After four flights, he reached the apartment main entrance.

A floor-to-ceiling glass wall encased the foyer. Before he reached the door, a Hoplite stepped into view; it smashed through glass and door alike, and then halted in front of Rade.

The cockpit opened up.

"Hello, boss," Electron transmitted.

"Storage!" Rade shouted.

The storage compartment in the leg popped open, and Rade quickly stowed the plasma rifle inside. Then he jetted into the mech and the cockpit sealed. The inner actuators enveloped him and he took control.

The anti-laser shield was deployed in his left arm. The cobra laser the right. He swapped the cobra for the grenade launcher, then fired a frag as a spider rounded the top of the current flight of stairs. The bomb struck, detonating; spider body parts coated the walls of the stairwell and foyer.

"Did you miss me in the long time we were parted?" Electron asked.

"Tons," Rade said.

Rade switched back to the cobra and hurried outside, where the other Hoplites had assumed a defensive formation around the entrance. There was one Hoplite for every Argonaut—with funds from Surus, he'd expanded the hangar bay at the last dry dock so that it could fit four more mechs, which he'd bought before his combat robot license had expired. There weren't any mechs for the civilians of course— Batindo was strapped in to the passenger seat of Shaw's mech, and Kato to Bender's.

The Hoplites held their shields outward, protecting against the incoming fire from spiders that had taken cover between the buildings, and upon the rooftops. The cobras of the Hoplites were aimed over those shields, and they returned fire.

"Where to, boss?" Tahoe asked.

"Surus, you have the Phant stunner?" Rade asked.

"I do," Surus replied.

"All right, let's grab the Phant and get the hell out of here," Rade said. "We head toward the legislature!"

"Wait," Surus said. "I don't believe he's in this dome anymore. His presence has... diminished."

"Is he heading for the shuttles?" Lui said.

"That's the only other option," Rade said. "He must want to join his newfound friends in their ship."

"It's the most likely course of action," Surus agreed.

"All right then, we head toward the main dome, and the shuttles!" Rade said.

He plotted the waypoint on the overhead map and the team proceeded forward at a run. They leaped onto a rooftop with the help of their jumpjets, fought their way to the far side, and, keeping their shields positioned underneath them, bounded across a street teeming with spiders to an adjacent rooftop. They jetted onto two more buildings, then dropped to a relatively quiet street below and continued the advance.

Rade remained close to the building walls, and constantly adjusted his route to avoid the swarm—the data provided by the city's cameras was proving very useful indeed. He wanted to delay all-out battle for as long as he could, intending to save the armor and shields of the mechs for when they were really needed.

That said, they still had to deal with spiders, as at least one teleported into their path every thirty seconds. Sometimes the jumpers deployed to strategic positions on the surrounding buildings to fire down at the armored mechs. The Hoplites shifted their shields to defend themselves, and someone would either launch a grenade toward the enemy positions, or if a given spider was really dug in, one of the Argonauts, usually Bender, would use their jumpjets to thrust onto the building and squash the bug directly.

They neared the western side of the geodesic dome. The long surface conduit connecting it to the main dome was destroyed, so there was no point in remaining inside any longer.

"Argonauts, we exit here!" Rade steered his Hoplite directly toward the glass wall of the dome and opened fire with the other mechs, boring several holes into the surface. He leaped at it and the glass shattered.

The light from the geodesic dome illuminated rocks outside that were colored a mixture of orange and gray. Rade and the others proceeded over the craggy terrain, remaining in a circular formation with their shields pointed outward. This was to stave off the spiders that crawled over the rocks between the domes, many of which dug in when Rade and the others appeared, the tangos opening fire from different covered positions behind the rocks. If there were any jumpers here, they were smarter than the previous, in that they didn't indiscriminately teleport into the path of the Hoplites to serve as cannon fodder.

Rade saw flashes overhead, near the alien mothership.

"Fret, tap me into Bax," Rade said.

"You're good," Fret replied.

"Bax, what's going on in orbit?" Rade said. "The alien ship isn't engaging the *Argonaut*, is it?"

"Negative," Bax replied. "I've been keeping the *Argonaut* well away from the alien vessel. It's actually the mercenaries."

"Say again?" Rade transmitted. "I thought you said the mercenaries were involved."

"I did say that," Bax answered. "They reached orbit a short while ago. They had been keeping their distance, but shortly after you reestablished communications, the mercenaries closed to engage with the alien vessel. They've been distracting it, which is why I was able to deploy the Hoplites so close to your positions."

"The mercenaries are actually engaging?" Lui said. "I've heard of honor among thieves, but this seems off. If I was a merc, I wouldn't rush headlong into battle against an alien vessel just to protect my client. Not unless I was promised shiploads of cash. And I mean *shiploads*."

"I played a hand in that," Surus said. "I've been in contact with them since we restored communications, and I managed to convince them to help fight the aliens. Apparently they have a conscience: betraying their own species at the behest of their original Artificial employer isn't something they can live with. Of course, it helped that I offered them shiploads of cash, as you put it. At least ten times as much as their original employer."

"Leave it to a Green to corrupt an honest mercenary," Bender said. "Hey Surus baby, when this is done, you want to—"

"No," Surus interrupted.

Rade glanced at his shield integrity. It was around sixty percent. His armor was in better shape, though he had some serious bore holes in the left side where Electron had taken hits earlier. He checked the integrity of the other Hoplites on his HUD, and saw similar readings.

Good enough.

Unfortunately, halfway to the target dome more bugs streamed onto the rocks from breaches in the surrounding domes, and the fighting intensified.

"Well that's rude," Lui said as a massive number of laser turrets fired from all sides.

Rade's shield was taking too many hits. As were the shields of the others. With the team relatively exposed like that, the only option was to dig in if they wanted to survive.

Rade spotted a wide depression in the rocks ahead, suitable for cover. "To the crater!" He marked the location on the overhead map.

The Hoplites remained in formation, and proceeded into the area Rade had marked. They took cover all along the perimeter of the small crater, aiming out into the rocky plains. Tahoe remained crouched near the middle of the crater in his mech, ready to attack any jumpers that decided to materialize within the defensive circle.

"And now we're pinned," TJ said.

"These bugs really got a thing for us, don't they?" Bender said.

"Sort of like how you have a thing for Fret?" Manic quipped.

But Bender ignored him. He was launching several grenades at the bug positions. "Come on, bug bitches, come on!"

"I don't think they understand you," Lui said.

A jumper appeared in the center of the crater. Tahoe took it down.

A few quiet moments followed. Rade lay flat behind the rim of the crater. He held his cobra over the rocky lip; he had switched his viewpoint to the scope, and he scanned the rocky terrain, looking for his next target.

There. A bug had partially emerged, its turrets directed toward the crater.

Rade squeezed the trigger, killing the creature.

"Maybe we should consider abandoning the Phant," Fret said. "And instead make our way to the booster rockets. Leave while the getting's good, you know?"

"Uh, we're not going anywhere at the moment, in case you hadn't noticed," Lui said.

"We can't leave," Surus said. "Not when we're so close to capturing our prey."

"Are we?" Fret said. "I beg to differ. Like Lui says, we're going to be trapped here for quite a while. Boss, what do you say?"

"We stay, at least for now," Rade said. "But Surus,

I'm expecting double pay for this mission."

"Done," she replied.

Another moment of quietude followed.

And then Tahoe said: "Help!"

twenty-one

R ade glanced at Tahoe urgently, and saw that his cobra was pointed skyward.

"Back armor is taking laser damage," Electron announced.

On the map, ten dots had appeared above the party.

Rade spun around so that he was lying on his back, covering his torso with his shield. He aimed his cobra skyward.

Ten spiders were falling from the sky above the crater, where they had teleported.

Rade and the others rapidly engaged; several of the exposed bugs teleported away as they fell, but five simply dropped into the crater, falling like rocks, obviously dead.

"It's raining bugs!" Manic said.

"Gah!" Bender said as a dead spider landed on top of his mech.

"I think it likes you," Manic said.

Bender hoisted the dead spider off of him and hurled it onto the lip of the crater beside him. "Got myself a new shield. You mofo bug, try to squash me, will you? Well, you're my new shield, bitch!"

As they fought, a new jumper appeared anywhere

between two and five seconds, sometimes above the party, sometimes within the crater, so that Rade had to devote three Hoplites to scanning the skies full-time. Soon the inner area was filled with bug corpses, so that the bugs could no longer teleport directly into the crater, but rather above it.

Eventually, the teleporters simply ceased coming.

"Looks like they've finally realized their tactic isn't working," Fret said. He was one of those assigned to guard the skies. "And here I was beginning to think these bugs weren't too bright."

"These bugs are the dumbest ass bitches I know," Bender said. He had accumulated quite a pile of trophies around his particular side of the crater.

"They're withdrawing," Lui said. "Look at the plains."

Rade had noticed it, too. The spiders were racing away from their previous positions, swarming over the rocks and back to the domes.

"See that?" Bender said. "Bitches are scared shitless. Aww, little buggies going to poop your pants? Let me help you with that!" Bender opened fire mercilessly.

Rade likewise picked off as many as he could while the aliens were exposed, as did the other Argonauts.

And then, just like that, there was simply nothing left to shoot at.

"All right, Hoplites," Rade said. "To the main geodesic dome. Let's see if we can bag ourselves a Phant."

They crossed the plains, avoiding the corpses of the fallen bugs, and reached the dome without resistance. They entered via one of the shattered rents in the glass.

Within, the streets proved utterly clear of tangos.

But it still looked like a war zone. Many of the buildings were riddled with laser bores, and several had large chunks missing. Some had collapsed into the streets entirely. The wreckages of walkers and enforcers were strewn about smashed vehicles. Corpses littered the asphalt in profusion. It seemed the bugs had abandoned the practice of collecting their dead, because there were quiet a few spiders amid the human bodies. The aliens lay on their backsides, their legs crimped together above them.

Bender occasionally fired his cobra at those dead bugs, and giggled at the black blood that misted from the wounds he caused.

"Do you have to do that?" Manic said after the fifth bug corpse Bender fired on.

"What, bitch?" Bender said. "I'm checking that they're dead."

There weren't any troop pods embedded in the asphalt of the current neighborhood, Rade noted. Most of the impacts must have been concentrated on the far side of the dome, closer to the alien ship.

Rade glanced at the overhead map and confirmed that theory. He also saw that the red dots of the active spiders, as revealed by the camera network, seemed to be retreating toward those pods.

Motion drew his attention to the rooftops: some of those pods were streaking skyward.

"Take them down," Rade commanded.

He aimed his cobra at one of the pods and fired. He obtained a direct hit, but the pod continued its ascent.

"Sync your cobras to mine," Rade ordered. The others obeyed.

Rade acquired another rising pod and squeezed the trigger. A combined blast fired from all cobras at once, and this time the escape craft ceased its ascent and plunged.

"That did it," Tahoe said.

Other pods reached the extents of the geodesic dome, and burst through, shattering the glass. They flew toward the mothership. In the distance, he saw other pods rising from the adjacent domes.

Rade was just starting to target another pod when Surus made an announcement.

"I can't sense the Phant anymore," she said. "He must have been aboard one of the pods."

"He's taking shelter in the alien ship," Tahoe said.

"It would appear so, yes," Surus agreed.

Rade lowered his cobra. He used his jumpjets to attain the rooftop of a nearby building.

"Boss, where you going?" Manic said.

The others followed behind him.

Rade surveyed the city below. He saw pods scattered throughout the nearby neighborhoods; spiders loaded inside them as he watched.

"We can use those pods to hitch a ride to the ship," Rade said.

"Do we really want to board an alien ship?" Fret said. "Simply to capture a Phant? The money's not worth it!"

"But the adrenaline rush is!" Bender added.

"We can't do this for money alone, obviously," Rade said. "We have to ask ourselves, do we really want to allow a Phant to escape?"

"I'm not letting a Phant get away," Harlequin said. "Not after what their kind has done to me. I say we hunt it."

"I agree," Shaw said. "We owe humanity. If it's colluding with the aliens, we have to stop it. Who can say how powerful these spiders will become if the

Phant shares technology with them? At least we're able to take down their units—for the time being. But ten years from now, the aliens might return with armor that matches, or even succeeds, our own. And they might have robots with them next time. Humanity will have the fight of its life on its hands."

"Shaw's right," Tahoe said. "For the preservation of humanity, I say we go."

"All right," Rade said. "Kato, Batindo, we've done all we can for you. I suggest you make your way to the hangar bay area and find a shuttle. Reach the *Argonaut*. Once we're done here, we can offer you a trip to the nearest system, Kato."

Assuming we survive what's coming.

Shaw knelt, allowing Batindo down from her passenger seat. Bender did the same for Kato.

"Thank you for all you have done," Kato said.

"What about our pay?" Bender said. His Hoplite, Juggernaut, gazed down at Batindo.

"Batindo, I'll expect you to wire us the agreed upon funds at your convenience," Rade said. "Trust me, you don't want us to send our debt collectors."

"I will wire them ASAP," Batindo said. "But I am going to reduce the agreed upon amount by ten thousand digicoins, since you didn't deposit me directly in the hangar bay."

"*What?*" Bender stepped Juggernaut forward. Batindo raised his hands over his head, cowering. "You little bitch! I should squash you where you stand!"

"The streets are clear," Rade told Batindo. "Or they will be. Hunker down here for half an hour, and then make a run for it. Besides, it's not like we're leaving you undefended... you both have plasma rifles."

Batindo didn't answer: he continued to stare at Juggernaut worriedly.

"Don't worry, Bender, he'll pay the full amount." Rade said. "Isn't that right, Batindo?" When the man still didn't reply, Rade added: "Or do I have to sick Bender on you? Batindo?"

"What?" Batindo said. "No! I will pay."

"The full amount?" Rade pressed.

"Yes yes."

"Good." Rade cast an urgent glance back across the streets in the distance below. There weren't many pods left. "As for the rest of you, I can't make any of you come on this mission. Those who want to opt out, head to the booster rockets and return to the *Argonaut*. We'll rendezvous with you when we can."

Rade dashed forward, heading toward one of the pods that had yet to lift off. Unsurprisingly, nearly everyone followed him. All save Fret.

"Shit," Fret said. "I hate it when you all guilt-trip me like this. Wait up!"

Fret ran after them.

"Split up," Rade said. "I have a feeling if we all hang on to the same pod, it'll have some trouble reaching orbit. Hoplites aren't light. There are two more pods to the east and west."

Rade had some misgivings about splitting up the group, but it seemed the best option at the moment. It would give them a lower profile on the pods as well, which might help them evade the notice of any point defenses the mothership might have.

The group divided into three fire teams.

Rade continued bounding between buildings and leaped down onto the target pod just as the last of the spiders dove inside. The panel shut.

Rade activated his magnetic mounts. He didn't

attach.

"Magnetic mounts aren't working," Rade announced.

He wrapped his hands around various handles that conveniently protruded from the surface. Shaw, Surus and Manic joined him as the pod began to vibrate. It tore free of the street and thrust skyward. Rade tightened his grip as the ground fell away.

The two other pods lifted nearby. Most of the remaining Argonauts had clambered onto either one. TJ and Bender jetted into the air just as the last one rose, and barely managed to grab on in time.

Fret was lagging, firing his jumpjets to follow Bender. It looked like he wasn't going to make it. He outstretched his arm...

TJ extended the hand of his mech to grab him, but the Hoplite was just out of reach.

Fret's jumpjets ceased firing, their propellant exhausted, and he plunged back toward the city.

"Get to the booster rockets and return to the *Argonaut*," Rade transmitted to Fret. "We'll meet you aboard the ship when we get back. Bring Kato and Batindo with you. Help them find a shuttle."

"Ha! You get to babysit the civilians!" Bender said. "You snooze you lose! By the way, looks like it's gonna be a hard landing, bitch. Hope you wore your diapers!"

"I still got some reserve fuel for the aerospike thrusters," Fret said as he dropped. "Won't be so hard. Have fun on that ship. Wish I could say I'm upset I'm not going with you. But actually, I'm kind of relieved."

"That's because you're a pussy," Bender said.

"Hey, you're the Pussywillow," Fret countered.

The pod broke through the glass, and the ground below continued to recede, the geodesic domes becoming small circular shapes on the surface.

Rade turned his gaze toward the alien ship. It filled much of the sky, an imposing, massive thing. He wasn't looking forward to going inside.

He saw that the mercenary ships were indeed engaged with the enemy. They were performing flybys, launching a barrage of missiles each time, and firing their Viper heavy lasers. The vessel returned fire with lasers of its own, and one of the mercenary ships had an entire wing segment cut off as Rade watched.

Even so, the mercenaries seemed to be winning, because the alien vessel was slowly ascending, pulling away from the planet. Then again, maybe the aliens had merely finished what they had come to do—drain away the planet's atmosphere entirely, and ravage the colony. Or perhaps the ship wasn't moving at all—it was hard to tell, given the acceleration of the pods.

"Lui, is it just an optical illusion, or is that alien ship actually retreating?" Rade asked.

"According to my calculations, it is in fact retreating," Lui replied. "Though not fast enough to prevent the pods from docking."

In moments the elongated black diamond of the alien vessel consumed everything. The pods headed toward the bulging area at the middle, where those long launch tubes protruded in ray-like fashion.

"How many alien ships have we boarded in our day?" Tahoe asked.

"Too many," Manic said.

"I'm just trying to say," Tahoe transmitted. "That we can do this."

"Hope so," TJ said.

Bender was noticeably silent.

Rade's particular pod headed toward the tip of one of the launch tubes. The pods containing the other

Argonauts made for the adjacent launch tubes.

In moments the tube engulfed Rade, and he found himself inside a tight cylindrical compartment interrupted by ring-like protrusions. Those rings appeared to be some sort of stabilizers, because they kept the pod centered in the middle of the tube. Rade had to flatten himself to avoid having any part of his mech strike those rings.

The pod reached a dead end; behind Rade, a hatch irised closed.

"Airlock," Shaw said.

Thick red mist filled the chamber.

"Definitely some kind of atmosphere..." Surus said.

The inner hatch opened.

"Into the belly of the beast," Manic said.

The pod proceeded inside.

twenty-two

Artificial gravity drew the craft downward into a narrow compartment, and it fell toward a conveyor belt of some kind.

Rade was located on the underside of the pod; he swung himself outward and jetted higher so that he wasn't crushed. He grabbed on to a handhold beside Shaw's mech, his fingers clanging against the material as the pod thudded onto the conveyor. The sudden return of sound seemed almost out of place—after all this time operating in the silence of the void, it was truly a change to reside within an atmosphere again.

"Howdy," Shaw said.

"Hey," Rade replied.

The craft was carried forward; thin, neon-blue glow bars were embedded in the round bulkheads on either flank, shining through the red atmosphere to outline the metal, highlighting individual panels and providing enough illumination to see by. Between those glow bars, the surfaces of the bulkheads and overhead were covered in small, regular hollows, of the kind big spiders might use to secure grips with their forelimbs.

Two other troop pods resided on the conveyor belt in front of Rade, the nearer about twenty to fifty meters ahead, the farther a hundred meters. Those had docked only minutes before, and were not the same pods the Hoplites of the other two fire teams had latched onto.

"I'm sensing the Phant once more," Surus announced. "He's definitely somewhere aboard this ship."

"It's going to be fun trying to find him in this massive monolith of a ship," Manic said.

After the conveyor brought the craft forward by twenty meters, the receding hatch opened behind them and another pod dropped inside. Again, that pod didn't contain any Hoplites from the remaining two fire teams.

Rade glanced at the overhead map. The other Argonauts had likewise boarded, and appeared to reside within similar conveyor belt compartments nearby. The comm nodes within their Hoplites would ensure they remained in contact, at least while the teams weren't too far apart. It was hard to say how much the interference the alien bulkheads would cause.

"Fire teams two and three, I can still read you," Rade sent.

"Yes," Lui said from his position. "These bulkheads aren't completely blocking our signals. Though we probably don't want to move too far apart."

"My team is on some sort of conveyor belt at the moment," Tahoe said.

"We all are," Rade said.

"We could attach to the ceiling, and hide here until the aliens exit their pods?" Manic said. "Well, assuming the ceiling is magnetic, I mean."

"No," Rade said. "There's no hiding. The enemy

knows we're here, I'm sure. I expect the welcoming party will be forthcoming. In fact, they'd probably be here now if they were able to teleport into this cramped area."

Rade swiveled his shield toward the forward section; up ahead, on the right side, the tunnel opened into a long platform next to the conveyor belt. Rade scanned the area through the scope of his cobra.

The conveyor belt ground to a halt. The lead pod was closest to the platform; a panel opened with a thud, and the spiders emerged, leaping onto the flat area. He heard the disturbing rattle of their feet on the metallic surface, thanks to the atmosphere.

A quarter of the way across the platform, the aliens paused as if receiving some instructions, then turned the laser turrets on their abdomens as one toward Rade and the others.

"We're taking laser fire," Electron said. "The shield is holding."

The enemy turrets made an audible clicking sound as they cycled through their lasers.

"Looks like the gig is up, folks." Rade centered his targeting reticle over one of the tangos and squeezed. The spider dropped.

Rade heard more thuds from the forward and backward areas.

"The other pods are opening up," Shaw said.

"I got the rear." Manic repositioned his mech just behind Rade, covering his back.

On the overhead map, Rade saw red dots appear as bugs emerged from the pod behind them.

The closer pod ahead had opened as well, and a few spiders emerged, firing. None teleported—the conveyor tunnel was too cramped.

Rade remained in cover behind his shield and

targeted the enemy units, bringing them down as they emerged.

The panel at the fore of the current pod opened. A spider leaped out right in front of Rade. Shaw and Surus executed it at point blank range, and it crashed down onto the craft and slid over the side, landing on the still motionless conveyor. The other bugs in the craft wisely remained inside, only occasionally lifting their turrets past the rim to fire at the party.

Rade continued to unleash his cobra at the more distant bugs on the platform; most of them had taken cover behind the bulkhead where the tunnel opened up, and dug in.

During the melee, the cockpit hatch of Surus' mech fell open and Surus leaped down.

"What's up?" Rade asked.

"Nothing," Surus replied. The tone was subtly different, and Rade realized Ms. Bounty was speaking. "My master wants to be freed. It's faster if I exit the Hoplite."

"But more dangerous to you!" Rade said.

Though he had to admit her Hoplite, Sprint, was doing a good job of shielding her.

At the periphery of his vision, Rade saw the green liquid flow from her jumpsuit and onto the pod. The liquid form meant the pressure was too high for the Phant to attain its gaseous state.

When Surus was out, the host, Ms. Bounty, leaped back into the cockpit and shut the hatch, resuming control of the mech. Meanwhile, Surus oozed forward and dripped inside the opening in the pod. Rade heard terrified squeals—he knew that shortly there would be nothing left alive in there. He saw a plume of black smoke emerge from the open panel—all that was left of the former occupants.

The Green emerged and continued toward the next pod, its liquid flowing ominously across the conveyor belt.

"Ms. Bounty, confirm it's clear," Rade said.

She low-crawled forward in Sprint, and shoved her cobra into the opening. "Clear."

"Just landed a grenade inside the rear pod," Manic said. "Let's see if that gets them out."

Rade heard an explosion behind him. Squeals followed. He glanced in his rear view mirror and saw a bug emerge. Manic shot it, then launched another grenade.

Several more bugs piled outside, some of them on fire.

Rade swiveled his torso around to help Manic bring them down. The grenade detonated inside the pod an instant later, sending up fragments.

"I'm going to clear it," Manic said. "Cover me."

While the others lay down suppressive fire, Manic leaped down onto the conveyor belt and approached the rear pod. He carefully clambered onto the large cylindrical object and stuffed his cobra inside.

"Looks clear," Manic said.

An alien had peered past the edge of the platform ahead, apparently seeing an easy target in Manic. Rade centered his crosshairs over the thing and fired. The bug slumped, plunging lifelessly over the edge of the platform and onto the conveyor belt.

Surus emerged from the second pod and approached the platform, where the remaining spiders were dug in.

"We're going to have to rush them," Manic said, rejoining him.

"Or we can let Surus work," Rade said.

"I vote for the latter," Shaw said.

Rade and the others waited another minute. Several more shrieks filled the air, followed by the frantic clicking of turrets.

And then silence. The Green Phant oozed into view near the edge of the platform.

"Let's move!" Rade said. "We clear the next two pods! Not that we don't trust Surus, or anything..."

"Of course," Ms. Bounty said.

Rade approached the nearer of the two pods ahead, clambered onto the hull, and slowly approached the open panel. He shoved his cobra inside and switched to its point of view. He saw a featureless cylindrical tunnel, the smooth walls completely devoid of fixtures. Or life: all the bugs had been burned away by Surus.

Manic moved ahead to the final pod, and pronounced it clear.

Beyond that last alien pod, the tunnel continued forward before making a sweep to the left, likely ending in some common pod refueling or maintenance area.

Rade and the others pulled themselves onto the platform and then swept the boxlike compartment. Alcoves resided in the corners, but they were empty. All of the bugs had been incinerated, including those Rade had downed on his own, thanks to Surus. The bulkheads continued to be outlined in those eerie neon-blue bars, the light beams piercing the red-hued atmosphere.

"Does anyone else feel like they're in a flesh parlor?" Manic said.

"No, just you," Shaw said.

"Definitely has a red light district sort of feel," Rade said. "Not that I would know anything about that," he quickly added.

"Oh sure," Shaw said.

Ms. Bounty vacated her mech and approached Surus, whose liquid form waited calmly near the center of the platform.

"Before you let her back inside you, is there anything we should know about Surus?" Rade said. "Can we trust her?"

"Fully," Ms. Bounty said.

She allowed Surus to begin flowing inside her jumpsuit once more.

"That was a bit abrupt," Manic said over a private line, excluding Surus. "Do you believe her?"

"I do, for the moment," Rade said. "She hasn't let us down so far."

"But other Greens have," Shaw said.

"We can't assume the actions of one are representative of the whole kind," Rade said.

The last portion of the Phant vanished inside the suit, and Surus leaped back into her Hoplite.

"Welcome back, Surus," Manic said over the main line once more, the former doubt in his tone hidden by what seemed forced cheer. "Feel better now?"

"Actually, I do," Surus replied.

"Incinerating bugs," Manic said. "Nothing quite like it, is there?"

"I suppose so," Surus said.

"We'll make an Argonaut out of you, yet," Manic said.

"I hope not," she replied.

A sloping ramp led to a sealed hatch. Rade suspected the group would have to place a few explosives to get through. Either that, or retrieve their plasma rifles from the storage compartments and use them as drills, because he highly doubted the aliens were going to willingly let them inside.

"We have our platform secured," Rade transmitted. "What's your status, teams two and three?"

"Just finished clearing ours," Lui said. "The tangos were dug in good. We had to rush them."

"Almost done here," Tahoe replied.

Rade approached the sealed hatch. He opened his cockpit and used the rungs on the mech to clamber down to the storage compartment in the leg. He opened it and retrieved several bricks.

He clambered back onto the open cockpit, and leaned out to affix the bricks to the alien hatch. Then he sealed the mech and resumed control.

He retreated with the party to the edge of the platform, then they assumed defensive positions down on one knee.

"All right, we're clear here," Tahoe said.

"Good," Rade said. "Attach a few explosives to your hatches, teams two and three. Let me know when you've done so."

A moment later:

"Ready," Lui transmitted.

"Ready," Tahoe replied.

"Baby, let's crash this wedding!" Bender transmitted.

"Detonate," Rade said.

The charges exploded. Rade kept his cobra aimed at the hatch. The metal had blown inward, revealing another lighted passageway beyond that ran perpendicular to the hatch—essentially a T intersection.

It seemed empty.

Rade glanced at his Hoplite companions. Then he slowly approached the entrance and shoved his cobra past the rent he had blown. He checked both flanks of the T intersection in that manner, but saw no sign of any enemy units on either side. The surfaces beyond were covered in the usual repetitive hollows, and outlined by those thin, neon-blue lights. The passage was big enough to fit three Hoplites abreast, or two spiders if they drew-in their legs.

"Surus, Manic, get out there," Rade said. "Shaw, join them. I'll follow on drag."

The Hoplites proceeded through the hole the explosives had torn in the hatch. Rade followed on drag.

"Where to now?" Manic asked.

"We rendezvous with teams two and three," Rade said.

He glanced at the overhead map. That meant proceeding to the east.

The passageway curved slightly, hiding teams two and three from view at the moment. The Hoplites didn't have to travel far before Tahoe appeared at the front of team two, followed by Lui and team three.

"We continue following this passageway," Rade said. "For the time being. Deploy your shields, let's form a defensive square."

Tahoe, Bender and Lui interlocked their shields at the fore, while Harlequin, Surus and Manic did the same on drag. Rade remained in the middle with Shaw and TJ.

"I wish we could pinpoint the Phant's position," Tahoe said.

"We all do," Rade said.

I wonder if Surus is lying about that?

Doubtful. She was only putting the mission at risk by doing so.

"You know," Lui said, "if our prey arrived in one of the same pods as we did, he can't have gone far. If we follow these passageways, we're bound to find him eventually."

"This is a big ship," Rade said. "And I'd rather not resign my fate to luck. There has to be a better way."

"Actually, there might be," Harlequin said. "This is odd, but I'm detecting a signal ping."

"A signal ping?" Rade asked.

"Yes, of the kind a robot or Artificial might transmit," Harlequin said. "I believe it is a distress signal of some sort."

"A distress signal?" Shaw asked. "Or a trap?"

"Could be either-or," Harlequin said. "If Governor Ganye accompanied our Phant, he would have the ability to emit this signal. But as to his motive, I am not sure. Likely it is a trap, as you say. Though I should tell you, the signal is growing weaker as we speak. As if the Artificial is being drawn away from us."

"Or we're moving away from him," Rade said. "Can you put up his location on the overhead map, in relation to our own?"

The dot appeared a moment later, in the blackness that composed the uncharted portion of most of the ship. As Rade watched, that dot moved inward.

"All right," Rade said. "We continue forward until we find a side passage to take us deeper into the ship."

They advanced through that curving, neon blue-outlined corridor. On the right-hand side they passed the hatches that teams two and three had blown, and then soon more hatches that remained intact. Those latter likely led to similar conveyor belt rooms where other pods had docked.

"Um," Tahoe said. "Why aren't any spiders emerging from these other compartments?"

"We did arrive near the tail end of the boarding

party," Harlequin said.

"No, Tahoe's right," TJ said. "There were other pods that docked after we did."

"Keep in mind, we were involved in a firefight shortly after landing," Rade said. "That delayed us."

"They have to be up to something," Manic said. "They've ordered their shock troops to clear these corridors. Why? I don't know. There's definitely enough space for their jumpers to initiate teleport attacks."

"Like I said," Bender piped up. "The bitches are afraid of us. Bugs are running away to cower under the teats of their mommies and suck their buggy thumbs. They're—" Bender cut off in mid-sentence. He halted, bringing the whole squad to a stop. "The hell is that?"

Rade switched to Bender's camera feed and saw that some kind of device had come into view around the bend up ahead. It was just sitting there, as if it had been purposely deposited on the deck. It contained a long metal tube on top of a box connected to treads.

"Looks like a cannon," Tahoe offered.

"Keep behind your shields!" Rade said.

In front of him, Tahoe's Hoplite disappeared. Completely vanished, as if struck by some disintegration device.

"Tahoe!" Rade said.

Lui was gone in the next instant.

"Drop!" Rade said.

"Ah, fuck," Bender said.

He too disappeared.

Rade had dropped to the deck, and was holding his shield at an angle in front of him to shield his body. He was filled with a sudden overwhelming terror.

His friends were dying before his eyes. He knew this day would come. He always did. He prayed it wouldn't.

But it had come.

He had led his teammates to their deaths.

twenty-three

R eturn fire!" Rade said.

He aimed his cobra at the tube. Beside him TJ vanished next.

Rade squeezed the trigger. He struck the thing, but the malevolent object remained intact.

"Shaw, get behind me! Shaw!"

She disappeared.

It was a nightmare come true. He was watching all of his brothers die, along with the woman he loved more than life itself.

Without warning a mech abruptly leaped over his own to shield him.

It was Harlequin.

"Harlequin, no!" Rade said. The tears were streaming down his face.

"Run, boss," Harlequin said.

Harlequin's mech was struck by the invisible beam and it, too, vanished.

"Retreat!" Rade said.

He scrambled to his feet, firing his jumpjets. His whole team was almost gone. The device slid forward, advancing in pursuit.

Manic leaped past Rade. "Go!"

"Manic, you'll—"

But then he was gone, too.

It was only Surus and Rade, now.

He pumped his feet. If he died, too, it meant all his friends had given their lives for nothing. He told himself the same words he had offered Kato when the Kenyan's fiancée had died. Those words somehow seemed empty, now.

Without Shaw, what's the point...

The thought faded away, and his survival instinct took over. He ran for all he was worth, hot on the tail of Surus. In his rear view mirror, he saw the metal object round the bend, its treads a blur as it overcame the pair...

And then the passageway turned blue.

He had returned to that alternate reality set above the one where humans normally resided. The bulkheads, deck and overhead had become dark smears of unreality, as had Surus' Hoplite, Sprint. Meanwhile Rade and his mech were blue silhouettes around cerulean-shaded bodies. So that object was a quantum weapon of some kind.

The other lost Hoplites were there behind him, floating in place near the spots they had fallen, their pilots visible through the translucent blue hulls. All of them reduced to pure energy.

Not dead then, after all. Merely trapped in limbo.

He counted seven of them, one each for Manic, Bender, Lui, TJ, Tahoe, Harlequin, and Shaw. He couldn't tell them apart.

His HUD was gone, and he had no Implant menus. He couldn't open his mouth, so he couldn't talk. Nor could he move any of his limbs.

Unlike his last visit to this dimension, time in the actual universe had not completely slowed to a crawl. Surus' Hoplite still moved, fleeing, and the metal cannon pursued, though the speed of each was about twenty percent of what it should have been. The liquid form of Surus was obvious inside the dark smear of the Hoplite, a brighter green coloration that showed through the hull near the cockpit region, inside the AI core of Ms. Bounty within.

He saw a series of circles travel outward from the quantum weapon, forming a hollow cylinder of sorts. The circles were colored the same blue as Rade's energy outline. The foremost circle struck Swift, and the remainder piled up behind them, slamming into the hull. Rade expected to see the Hoplite drawn into the blue universe like the others, but it remained a smear, insubstantial, still firmly rooted in the original reality.

The Hoplite stopped. Apparently Surus realized her mech had been struck. The green liquid of the Phant flowed slowly downward at crawl, eventually emerging from the toe region of the jumpsuit; it moved outward through the containing metal of the mech, away from the EM emitter aboard the Hoplite, and then began trickling down onto the floor. A pool eventually formed underneath the Hoplite, until the Phant had completely evacuated Ms. Bounty and the mech.

The quantum weapon fired the blue concentric circles again, and the rays struck Swift once more.

That time the Hoplite became a bright neon outline, joining the others in the blue dimension.

Rade realized that Surus' presence had somehow stopped the mech from entering this reality. Why it had chosen to abandon the Hoplite, Rade didn't know.

The cannon retreated, its work apparently done. The green liquid of Surus meanwhile remained in the middle of the deck, motionless.

Though Rade couldn't move his individual limbs, he realized something else that was different from the last time he had entered this dimension: if he tried very hard to twist his torso, though he wouldn't actually rotate his upper body, he found that he could revolve in place. Likewise, if he focused on an area with his eyes, his immobile body slowly drifted toward it. In that manner, he could move about. The others soon discovered this locomotion technique as well, and they gathered.

Rade spotted another object in the distance, beyond the translucent smears of the bulkheads. This object glowed purple, and was located several compartments away. It shone with the same intensity as Surus in that dimension.

It had to be their prey.

The puddle that was Surus flowed toward Rade, pausing beside him to form what appeared to be a flat hand extending a finger. And he understood that Surus wanted him to touch it.

Rade slowly floated himself toward the Green, positioning the foot of his Hoplite near Surus. He knew the mech wouldn't be incinerated, as it wasn't organic, so he touched the metal to the Phant.

Nothing happened.

And then, just like that, he snapped back into ordinary reality. He exhaled in relief. He thought of the Phant he had seen. If it was that easy to return to this universe, then that quantum weapon might be a gift, not a curse.

Rade spun around and ran toward the retreating cannon. It swiveled around to face him, and he halted, waiting for the strike that must come.

He didn't see the weapon fire, but he knew it had because a second later he was back in the blue dimension.

He swiveled his incorporeal form toward Surus and the energy signatures of the other Hoplites. They had gathered around Surus, and seemed ready to touch the Green, but then the Phant retreated from them when Rade approached.

The other Argonauts turned their incorporeal bodies to face him, obviously trying to figure out what he wanted. Rade swiveled toward the purple glow in the distance. Rade focused on the bulkhead directly in front of him and his insubstantial body and mech floated forward, passing right through. That should be enough for the Argonauts to understand.

He paused after traveling a short distance and revolved slightly to look back. The other Argonauts were indeed following, as was Surus, seeping into the bulkhead after them. Rade realized that while Surus couldn't see the Phant, apparently she could see, or at least sense, the Hoplites.

They entered a compartment that was filled with the dark smears of aliens. Rade ignored them, his body passing right through most of their impressions, and focused on his target, the Purple that had gotten them all into this mess.

Small, slithering white worms came into view. They were translucent, ugly things with sucker-like mandibles. They were obviously of this dimension, because they wrapped their bodies around the energy representations of the Hoplites, attaching their suckers to the hulls. Some passed straight through the mechs to envelop the occupants as well. Rade had one wrap around his torso, placing its sucker squarely on his shoulder. The world around him dimmed slightly, confirming that the things were definitely leeching off their energy. There was nothing to do but continue.

As the group closed with the target Phant, more and more of those worms accumulated, until soon the bodies of both Hoplites and pilots were covered entirely by the things. Rade had one covering his face, but since it was translucent, he could still see.

Rade reached the compartment containing the purple glow. He still wasn't sure if it was actually a Phant, because it floated in midair, formed into the shape of a ball. It resided between two smears that looked like walls of some kind. A dark humanoidal shape resided next to it, also contained by walls.

There were other smears near the entrance to the room. Bug guards.

The blue dimension had darkened by a large amount by then. Rade sensed himself losing cohesion in this reality. He wouldn't last much longer.

He waited as the outlines of the other Hoplites arrived. Finally, Surus seeped inside as well. Once more the green extended a portion of itself toward Rade, as if expecting him to touch it.

Rade extended the foot of his mech, obliging.

The real world snapped back into view.

Rade landed with a thud on the deck. He fired his cobra twice in rapid succession, and the bugs guarding the entrance hatch slumped to the floor.

A klaxon sounded.

Rade ignored it, glancing at his arms and legs. He had almost expected some of those worms to hitch a ride back to this reality with him. He was glad they hadn't.

Still, the whole episode left him feeling exhausted.

"Electron, inject a stimulant please," Rade said.

The Hoplite obliged and Rade perked up immediately.

He turned toward the glowing purple sphere. It

was inside a glass container of some kind. He was reminded of the Phant trap Surus had come up with, though it was lacking the circular disks on the floor and ceiling that Surus' version contained. That definitely had to be a Phant in there.

In a similar glass tank beside it lurked Governor Ganye, the Artificial. He stood near the center of the container, his arms crossed over his chest. He seemed unimpressed with Rade.

The other mechs momentarily reappeared in turn around the green puddle that was Surus on the deck.

"Well, shit," Bender said. "That was a *trip*."

"Except for those damn worms!" Tahoe said.

"Yeah, they gave me the heebie-jeebies," Bender admitted.

Sprint materialized last, and the green Phant on the floor flowed into the leg region of the Hoplite.

When the Green had completely seeped inside, Rade said: "Surus, are you back with us yet?"

"I am here," Surus replied over the comm via the host, Emilia Bounty.

"What the hell were those worms?" Tahoe asked.

"My kind is familiar with them," Surus said. "They feed upon the energy signatures produced by organics such as yourselves. The Phants consider them parasites, because when Phants conquer a world and destroy its populace, these things arrive in droves, interfering with the geronium production. We have developed special technology to repel them. Unfortunately, I do not have any of that with me. If you had allowed them to seep your energy for much longer, you would have been too weak to return to this reality, and would have eventually faded from existence entirely."

"I'm just glad we were able to get back as it was,"

Shaw said. "I thought I was losing myself in there."

"We all did," Rade said.

"Lookie here," Manic's mech approached the Purple locked away within the glass container. "It seems our Phant has been betrayed by his alien allies."

"Maybe he pissed them off," Lui said. "Phants are good at doing that."

"Whatever the case, he's ours now," Surus said. Sprint's cockpit opened and Surus leaped down. She opened the storage compartment in the leg of her mech and retrieved the stun rifle.

She closed the panel and pointed at the governor. "Get him."

As the klaxon continued to sound in the background, Sprint dashed forward, smashing its fists into the container that held Ganye. The Artificial governor dropped to his knees, cowering with his hands over his head.

When Sprint broke through, the Hoplite grabbed Ganye, pulled him out like a ragdoll, and dropped him to the deck in front of the second tank. Sprint placed one leg down on his buttocks region, pinning him.

"Wait, I'm innocent," Ganye said.

"Shut it!" Bender shoved his cobra into Ganye's face.

Keeping Ganye pinned, Sprint attacked the second tank, punching it the same as it had done the first. As soon as the Hoplite broke through, containment failed and the Phant inside splashed to the floor. The Purple seemed intent on fleeing, because it immediately began to seep down through the glass.

Surus fired her stun rifle and instantly all of the purple liquid bubbled back to the surface. The substance remained in place for several moments, seeming stunned, and then once more began to vanish into the glass.

Surus fired again, bubbling the liquid to the surface once more.

When it began to recover, it seemed that the Phant finally got the hint, because it began to seep drunkenly toward Ganye.

"No, don't let it possess me again," Ganye said. "Please."

"You know you want it," Bender said cruelly. "That Phant's going to crawl right up your ass."

"What if Ganye really doesn't want to be possessed?" Harlequin said. "If so, then this is wrong."

"We need some sort of host to carry the Phant," Rade said. "Unless you would like to oblige?"

"No," Harlequin said.

"Didn't think so," Rade replied. "We'll set the Artificial free after this is done, assuming Ganye is telling the truth about his involvement."

When the Phant had flowed completely inside, the eyes of Ganye momentarily swam with purple drops before clearing. Purple condensation settled on the back of the Artificial's neck, and then Ganye looked up: "What do you want?" His voice had changed slightly, becoming deeper, more authoritative.

"We want you," Surus said. She fired the stun rifle once more.

Ganye collapsed.

Rade half-expected the Phant to bubble to the surface as before, but the condensation on the nape of the Artificial's neck remained constant—apparently once settled within an AI core, a Phant was not so easily dislodged.

"Sprint?" Surus said.

The Hoplite stepped back. Surus scooped up the Artificial and leaped into the cockpit. The hatch shut behind her.

"I'm ordering Sprint to control the Hoplite, going forward," Surus said. "As planned, I will continue to stun Ganye until we make it back to the *Argonaut*. Get us out of here, Rade."

"Gladly," Rade said.

twenty-four

Rade noticed the klaxon had shut off by then. Probably not a good thing.

"I don't suppose we can go back to that blue dimension and float our way out?" Manic said.

"You actually *want* to go there, bitch?" Bender said. "With those life-sucking worms?"

"Why not?" Manic said. "It'll be easier."

"That blue place is like being dead," Bender said. "While it was a trip, I never want to go back there. And you *would* want the easy way out. Don't you remember the sign that hung over the grinder in training? Easy is for sissies."

"That's not what it said," Manic insisted.

"Well, that's how I remember it."

"There's no easy way out, not this time," Rade said. "I suspect the aliens won't use the quantum cannon against us anymore. They've realized by now it didn't work all that well. We're going to have to fight our way out of here."

Rade glanced at his overhead map. On it, the compartment they were inside appeared as an island amid an unmapped sea of blackness. Towards the outskirts of that dark ocean resided the filled-out launch tubes, conveyor belt platforms, and the passageway the Argonauts had entered before encountering the cannon.

"TJ, how accurate is our location on this map?" Rade asked. "Considering that our systems were offline the whole time we traveled through the passageways and compartments in between."

"I would say not very accurate at all," TJ replied. "The gyroscopes and accelerometers would have no proper frame of reference. According to the map, we have to travel southeast to return to the launch tubes. In actuality, we may have to travel northwest."

"Probably a labyrinth out there," Bender said. "Like traveling through a bug's intestines. Or Manic's."

"Believe me," Manic said. "Traveling through my intestines is a breeze compared to this."

"So that's what your boyfriends tell you," Bender quipped.

"Perhaps I can be of some assistance," Surus said.

"What, with traveling through Manic's intestines?" Bender asked.

"A moment," Surus replied.

"She has to put on some surgical gloves, first," Bender said.

Rade received a data request. He accepted and the map updated, filling out the route between here and the launch tubes. The launch area was actually northward, not southeast. "Where did you get this?"

"I stunned our Phant, bringing Ganye to the fore once more," Surus said. "The governor's sensor systems remained active the whole time the aliens carried him into the ship. He made a map."

"Nicely done," Rade said. "Argonauts, we make for those launch tubes!"

Before he finished speaking, the hatch on the far side of the compartment opened. Tahoe, Lui, and TJ were standing guard, and opened fire at the bugs that rushed inside.

Rade and the others joined them, filling up the entrance with spider corpses. There wasn't enough room for them to teleport inside, apparently. Especially not with those corpses.

Some of the bodies were dragged from the entrance, obviously by those bugs waiting behind them. Then more came forward, turrets blazing away.

Rade kept behind his shield and returned fire.

"Overlap shields, Argonauts!" Rade said. "We're going to have to force our way outside!"

They formed a phalanx three abreast and three deep. Those in the front had their shields pointed forward. Those in the middle held them overhead, and those on drag held the shields behind them.

The group shoved their way through any dead and into the T intersection beyond. Rade chose the right-hand branch, which, according to the map, would eventually take them to the launch area.

The passageway fit three Hoplites abreast, and they were able to maintain their formation. They fired in both directions, against the bugs that assailed from both sides.

Some of the enemy abdomens tilted upward, trying to aim their turrets over the shields, but the aliens simply struck the upturned shields of those residing in the middle of the squad.

The enemy ranks stopped rushing the Hoplites on both flanks, and began backing away instead, though continuing to fire their turrets. Perhaps they intended to wear down the shields and armor of the squad. A war of attrition.

The Argonauts stepped over the bodies of those they had downed, and sometimes ducked behind those alien corpses, using them as shields to spare their own armor. In fact, Tahoe in the front and Bender on the rear actually grabbed the bodies of fallen spiders and utilized them as extensions of their own shields.

"Hey bugs!" Bender said. "That's right, you're going to have to shoot through your bug brothers to get me! Bitches!"

A spider broke from the front ranks, dodged between the dead, and leaped at the group. Lui managed to shoot it with his cobra, but it landed in the vertical gap between the overhead and the shields Rade and the others residing in the middle held above them. Rade felt the weight immediately, and he and the others had to struggle to shrug it off, partially breaking formation in the process. They quickly reformed and continued.

Those who still had grenades used them, sending gory masses of long legs and split thoraxes flying into the air. Eventually the explosions ceased as the Hoplites exhausted the last of their grenades.

The spiders assailing them from up ahead began to vanish. Rade saw a green pool of liquid flowing across the deck before them. Surus was out there helping out; she had left her host, Emilia Bounty, in charge of the captured Phant.

"Our shield integrity back here is getting low," Manic said from the rear flank.

"Swap out with us," Rade said.

He, Ms. Bounty and Shaw exchanged positions with Manic, Bender and Harlequin to cover the rear.

Rade scooped up a dead bug underfoot and draped it over his shield. It wasn't much protection against those enemy laser turrets, but it helped reduced the intensity a little.

The speed of their advance increased with Surus

helping out in front.

However, some of the jumper varieties showed up, and began to teleport past Surus in groups to assault the party. Tahoe, Lui and TJ readily shot them down, covering the floor in bodies and preventing further teleporters from appearing.

The attack from the fore let up entirely, and Rade soon understood why: they had reached a breach seal.

Lui opened up his cockpit while the others defended the rear flank, and he climbed down in his jumpsuit to the storage compartment in the leg of the mech. They hadn't prepared any of the charges for manipulation by the big hands of the mechs—that would have required taping the individual bricks together into larger shapes—so Lui had to grab the charges and place them on the breach seal personally.

When Lui was finished, he returned to the cockpit.

"Let's give the breach some room!" Rade said.

The party retreated toward the bugs on their rear, and when Rade judged the distant sufficient, he ordered: "Blow it!"

The charges detonated. Rade felt the shockwave even from his position on the rear, and the Hoplites in the center of the formation pressed against his.

"It's open," Lui said. "Got a ton of tangos waiting on the other side, though."

Rade glanced at the overhead map and saw the red dots that had appeared in the forward area.

The party proceeded forward once more, with Surus leading the way. Rade occasionally draped new dead bodies over his shield as he came upon them, courtesy of those aliens the Hoplites on point had felled.

The two mechs on either side of him followed his example, but Surus sometimes touched even the dead, disintegrating them, so there were occasions when there were no fresh bodies to pick up, and all three on the rear had to rely upon their bare shields. Those were the times when Rade's shield and armor integrity suffered the most.

The Argonauts penetrated three more breach seals, and after what seemed an eternity—though in actuality couldn't have been more than thirty minutes—they arrived at the launch area. The quantum cannon hadn't made an appearance during that time: the aliens had indeed abandoned its use.

Keeping formation, Rade and the others piled into the platform next to the conveyor belt, then hurried into the tunnel where the damaged pods resided.

Rade exited his cockpit to affix his own explosives to the hatch in the overhead, and then returned to his mech. The Hoplites retreated to the platform area and defended against the spiders that continued to harry them from the rear. Rade's shield integrity was down to twenty percent by then, with several holes drilled into the edges.

Surus seeped back into Sprint and in moments vanished inside the mech.

"Surus, you back with us?" Rade asked.

"I'm here," Surus replied. "Ms. Bounty did a good job of keeping our prisoner stunned. I will continue doing so until we return."

"Good. Prepare for detonation people." Rade detonated the charges and felt the shockwave vibrate the hull of his mech.

"We're through!" Lui said.

Rade hadn't been sure if the airlock's outer hatch would be open or not, but judging from the lack of explosive decompression, it was sealed.

"TJ, get inside the airlock and set the charges on

the external facing hatch," Rade said.

Rade continued to defend. A spider teleported onto the platform, appearing in one of the few clear areas. It had been a while since Rade had seen a jumper...

"Charges are in place!" TJ said.

"Wait," Rade said. "Cover me."

He leaped onto the platform, holding his shield toward the aliens, and grabbed the body of the dead jumper. He dragged it across the floor, retreating to his Argonauts.

"I want Surus to figure out how these things teleport, if she can," Rade said. "When we get back to the ship." He glanced at TJ's mech. "Blow the final charge."

The detonation came. Rade felt the resultant gush of air sweeping past: the Hoplites were too heavy to be drawn outside by the force of explosive decompression alone, and the living spiders ahead simply clasped onto the hollows on the deck and bulkhead to brace themselves. The dense bodies of the dead spiders were slowly dragged along the platform toward the tunnel.

"Fire jumpjets!" Rade said. "Let's get out of here!"

Rade jetted backward into the outflow and sped into the breached hatches of the airlock, and the launch tube beyond. He passed between the successive, ring-like protrusions, whose repellant forces kept him centered in the middle of the tube. There was no artificial gravity, so he shut off his jumpjets, allowing the escaping atmosphere to carry him along. He held the dead bug close to his torso, keeping it braced between his shield and hull.

He emerged from the launch tube. The alien ship receded in front of him, the launch tube and those near it soon becoming small spindles. His Argonauts were around him.

The mercenary warships appeared to be making a concerted push at that moment, further driving the enemy vessel away, or at least that was the impression Rade had as the human craft flew past and fresh explosions lit up the hull of the invaders.

Dark streaks emerged from some of the distant spindles, Rade noticed. He zoomed in and saw troop pods. According to the tactical display that replaced the overhead map, those things moved on an intercept course with the team.

"The *Argonaut* is coming up," Lui said.

"Already?" Rade glanced at the *Argonaut's* location. The vessel was indeed nearby: about five minutes away. "Tap me in."

"Done," Lui said.

"Bax, sit-rep?" Rade said.

"Hi, boss," Fret replied. "Captain Fret here. I took control of the ship once I got back aboard. It seemed like a good idea to bring the *Argonaut* closer, in case you needed to make a quick getaway."

"We're coming in hot," Rade said. "Fire the vipers at those troop pods!"

"Already gave the order," Fret said. "I'm also firing a few missiles."

Some of the pursuing pods changed course as if attempting to avoid the invisible laser assault from the Marauder-class ship. Others appeared to have small bites taken out of their hulls, at least when observed under maximum zoom, and dropped out of the pursuit. Missiles came in next, but most of the pods avoided them easily. One unfortunate pod couldn't swerve away in time, and when the proximity fuse of the seeker detonated in a bright flash, nothing remained of the pod but debris.

"Lui, are we detecting any incoming lasers from the pursuers?" Rade asked.

"So far, no," Lui said. "Though I'm sure our individual AIs will alert us if that changes."

Rade still had Fret on the line. "Fret, what about Batindo and Kato?"

"They're aboard. I have them staying in Bender's stateroom."

"*What?*" Bender said. "You bitch!"

Technically it wasn't Bender's stateroom, as he shared it with TJ, but apparently that point was lost on him.

In five minutes the Hoplites were within visual range of the *Argonaut*. The ship looked triangular-shaped from the front, what with the way those engine segments protruded downward from the main body.

Rade adjusted his course by firing a burst of lateral thrust and closed with the gray hull.

The *Argonaut* fired its own lateral thrusters to pivot sideways, facing its hangar bay toward the group; the bay doors were in the process of opening.

"Electron, take us in," Rade said.

Electron took control of the Hoplite and occasionally fired different thrusters, making minor course adjustments to ensure the mech was properly lined up. The *Argonaut* grew rapidly in the final few seconds; Rade blinked, and the Hoplite was already inside.

Electron fired aerospike thrusters at the last moment to halt the forward motion, and the Hoplite dropped like a rock in the artificial gravity. Rade landed face first in his mech, right on top of the dead spider he had been carrying.

"Uh," Rade said. "That was a terrible landing, El."

"Sorry," Electron said.

Rade clambered to his feet in the Hoplite as the others dropped around him. He tossed the alien body into one corner and then spun toward the opening. The hangar doors were already closing, and in seconds blotted out the stars.

"What's the status on the pursuers?" Rade transmitted.

"Thirty of the pods got through," Fret sent.

"Thirty!" Rade pulled up the external camera. He saw the pods in question; they were decelerating to make a flyby. Spiders emerged from open panels near the noses and pushed off in turn. Red mist jetted from the tanks on the backs of the individual spiders—they were venting their portable atmospheres for propulsive purposes, heading straight for the hull of the *Argonaut*.

"Evasive action!" Rade ordered.

twenty-five

I t was too late. The spiders landed on the hull in droves, and soon the surface swam with the things. The aliens were probing, searching for weak spots. Rade cycled through the external cameras. Many of the bugs congregated around airlocks. Others, the hangar bays.

Rade switched to the external camera monitoring the current bay doors. The bugs there seemed to be firing their turrets into the entrance at point-blank range. So far they had seared away the anti-micrometeoroid Whittle layer, and were concentrating on the armor underneath. The aliens hadn't yet penetrated entirely, but Rade could see the growing bore holes. It wouldn't take the bugs all that long to burn through.

"Shit, it's going to cost twenty thousand digicoins to repair those doors!" Rade said. "Open them up!"

The bay doors slid open, pulling the spiders aside with them. There was no explosive decompression, as Rade hadn't given the order to pressurize the hangar yet.

Rade aimed his cobra at the edges, and when the spiders lurking there aimed their turrets inside, he took them out.

A bug teleported inside, appearing in the open space directly in front of the party.

"Bitch!" Bender said, firing at it with both cobras and following up by stabbing the weapon muzzles into its torso; he thrust both hands apart, ripping the bug in half. Then he deployed the shield in his left arm and brought the flat edge down hard on the head, separating it from the body. "You want to infest *my* ship? Come on you bitches. *Come on!*"

Spiders began to swarm inside, obliging him.

Rade and the others shot them down as fast as they could, keeping their shields deployed to protect against the incoming fire.

"Hangar bay two is breached as well," Bax announced. "As are airlocks three and four."

Rade placed the video feed for hangar bay two in the upper right of his vision: the bugs were trashing the two Dragonflies, telemetry drones, and the Raptor stored in that bay.

"Damn it!" Rade said. "Deploy some combat robots to hangar bay two, Fret!"

"The robots are occupied defending the airlock breaches!" Fret said.

Rade glanced at the overhead map and saw red dots swarming inside via two breached airlocks, which the spiders had obviously completely shot through by then. Four Centurions were defending each section, their backs to the breach seals that had closed behind them.

"How the hell are they fitting in those airlocks?" Tahoe asked.

Rade switched to the point of view of one of the Centurions.

"It looks like the aliens sent along some smaller variants this time," Harlequin said. "They dispatched the big guns to the hangar bays, and the babies to handle the rest of the ship."

The spiders he saw from the combat robot's point of view were about half the size of humans, and easily fit the cramped passageways.

This is a disaster.

Surus once more emerged in her natural state, appearing as a mist in the atmosphereless compartment. When the Hoplites had cleared the first wave of intruders with her help, Surus floated up to the opening and proceeded to terminate the spiders that still clung to the hull outside. Some of the bugs released the hull, frantically releasing propellant from their tanks to thrust away. Those among the latter group that the Hoplites didn't shoot down were handled by the *Argonaut's* Vipers.

Rade checked the external camera and saw that only three remained attached to the hull in the general vicinity. The bugs were backing away, perhaps intending to join their brethren in the second hangar bay. Surus could handle them. And if not, Electron would finish them off.

Rade rushed to the inner hatch of the hangar's airlock.

"Electron, let me out," Rade said.

The cockpit opened and Rade leaped down from the Hoplite. The large mech wouldn't fit inside the cramped passageways of the *Argonaut*.

"Spacewalk to hangar bay two with the other Hoplites," Rade instructed Electron. "Fumigate the bugs."

"Understood," Electron said. "Good hunting."

"You too." Rade retrieved the rifle from the storage compartment in the mech's leg, then opened the airlock and rushed inside.

"We're coming with you, boss," Bender said.

Behind Rade, the other Argonauts were leaping down from their cockpits and abandoning their Hoplites. The AIs would operate the mechs instead, aiding Electron.

Bender, Tahoe and Lui joined Rade shortly. Technically, the airlock could only fit four, but Shaw squeezed inside as well.

"Shaw! What the hell!" Bender said. "She just grabbed my crotch, boss."

"You wish," Shaw said.

Rade sealed the outer hatch. He was pressed up against the inner door, unable to move because of the others. He could see the passageway beyond, through the portal in the door. It was clear out there.

Atmosphere vented inside the airlock, then the door opened, relieving the pressure from the others squeezed in behind him. He stumbled forward, free of the cramped confines, and hurried toward the closest battle.

He glanced at the overhead map: the blue dots of four more Argonauts crowded into the airlock. Ms. Bounty was standing with the governor in the hangar bay just beyond, waiting for her turn.

"Ms. Bounty," Rade said. "Secure our prey in the trap."

"As soon as I'm through the airlock, I'm heading directly for the cargo hold," Ms. Bounty confirmed.

Rade reached a breach seal. Beyond, according to the map, only one Centurion remained defending. Unit J. The other three in the area were offline.

"Open the seal, Bax," Rade ordered. He fell to one knee, and aimed his rifle forward.

"Unable to comply," Bax said. "Void conditions are present on the other side. Do you wish to override?"

"I do, damn it," Rade said. Other breach seals would prevent the entirety of the ship's atmosphere from venting. Bax's initial refusal was merely a safety precaution. "Argonauts, activate boot magnets. Unit J, we're opening the seal."

"Roger that," the Centurion replied.

The breach seal opened a crack, and almost immediately Rade felt the inexorable pull of explosive decompression, which only increased as the hatch repealed further. Though his boots were mounted to the floor, his upper body was not, and he slammed a glove into the bulkhead beside him and activated the magnet to prevent himself from being bowled over.

The explosive outflow ended before the door opened entirely. Beyond, several of the dog-sized spiders had been sucked outside. Many more had hung on with their spiky legs.

The Centurion had mounted itself to the bulkhead, and it released the wall to land on its feet. The wreckages of the other combat robots lay strewn along the deck all the way to the airlock, where they had been pulled either by the bugs, or the decompression.

The small spiders surged forward. The Centurion positioned itself between the bugs and the Argonauts.

"Careful!" the combat robot said. "They fire tiny lasers attached to their joints."

Rade released his mounting magnets and dropped to one knee. He saw no evidence of those lasers of course, but he had no doubts about what the robot said, because as he watched the robot's left arm fell limp.

"Fire at will, Argonauts." Rade aimed passed the Centurion and squeezed the trigger. The target exploded when struck, its insides misting and splattering the bulkheads.

"Baby bugs!" Bender said. "Gonna squash me some baby bugs! Baaaaaabies! Watch out, bitches, the master exterminator is in the house! Wooyah!"

Bender dove to the floor beside Rade and fired like a madman, taking down four bugs within a span of seconds.

"Ah!" Tahoe said from just behind him. "I'm hit. Retreating."

Rade continued to fire, covering the retreat of his friend.

The robot fell backwards, apparently out of commission. Rade caught it, and held it in front of his body like a shield.

One of the bugs shot past, clambering along the wall to leap onto Bender.

"*Shit!*" Bender said, rolling onto his back. "Damn it damn it damn it!" He flung the small spider against the bulkhead beside him and shot it with a blaster he drew from his utility belt with his free hand.

More Argonauts arrived from behind, firing into the spiders, shoring up the defenses. They took cover behind Rade and his combat robot shield. Bender meanwhile continued to lay prostate on the floor beside him, firing frantically.

Tahoe had apparently applied a patch to his suit, because he too returned to engage the enemy from the rear of the party, according to the overhead map.

Rade continued firing like that for at least five minutes. And then, just like that, the bugs stopped coming. Rade glanced at the overhead map. There were no more red dots in the vicinity, neither inside nor outside the ship.

The passageway was left a mess of severed limbs and bug corpses, their insides smearing the deck and bulkheads.

"Man, I pity the robots stuck with cleanup duty," Bender said.

"Actually, we have no robots left," Fret transmitted. "So guess who's stuck doing the cleanup?"

"Ah... bitches," Bender said.

"What's the status on airlock four?" Rade said. He glanced at the overhead map, but couldn't see any other red dots aboard, nor on the external hull.

"Surus handled airlock four," Fret said. "The baby bug boarding party has successfully been repelled. Though as I mentioned, we lost all of our combat robots."

"Hangar bay two?" Rade asked.

"Electron and the other Hoplites exterminated the spiders there," Fret said. "All mech units survived."

"Ms. Bounty, what's the status on our prey?" Rade transmitted.

"I have the Phant locked away in the containment device," Ms. Bounty returned. "Along with its host."

Rade exhaled. He felt a mixture of relief, and yet sadness for the lost lives of the combat robots.

"Fret, get us the hell away from that alien ship," Rade said.

"Already gave the order half an hour ago," Fret said. "We got no more incoming."

"I need to get to my quarters," Rade said. "Tahoe, get your wound looked at. The same goes for anyone else who's injured. TJ, you're in command. Get the Argonauts to repair the breach damage pronto. Let me know if any issues come up."

"Should I set up the quarantine in the cargo hold after Surus returns to my body?" Ms. Bounty asked. "We were all exposed to the atmosphere down there..."

"I don't think we have to worry this time," Rade said. He dreaded the thought of being cooped up in a glass tank for forty-eight hours with the other Argonauts. He just wanted to be left alone.

"As you command," Ms. Bounty said.

Rade made his way back through the open breach seal with Shaw and Tahoe. Rade closed the seal behind him so he could pressurize the passageway along the way. He opened and closed two more breach seals blocking his route until he arrived at the stateroom he shared with Shaw. Tahoe bid him farewell and continued on toward sickbay. Apparently he was the only one injured. A quick glance at the team's vitals confirmed that supposition.

The hatch sealed behind Rade and he removed his helmet. His head felt frigid from the perspiration.

"Well that was... draining," Shaw said, removing her own.

In answer Rade tossed aside his helmet. He left her there in the cramped compartment beside the bunk and proceeded directly to the head.

He caught his reflection in the mirror. His hair was matted, damp. His face extremely pale.

He locked the door, grabbed a towel and lay flat on the deck. He crumpled up the towel and placed it behind his head to act as a headrest, and then he stared unblinking up at the overhead.

twenty-six

R ade heard a knock at the door.

"Rade?"

It was Shaw.

He closed his eyes. They were sore, scratchy, as if they'd been open for a long time. He rubbed them, and then glanced at the time overlaying his vision in the lower right. Apparently three hours had passed since he had lain down.

Holy sh—

"You all right?" Shaw said from the other side of the door.

"Err, yeah." Rade scrambled to his feet and flinched at the stiffness in his muscles. "You have to go?"

"No, I went in my suit already," Shaw said.

"Oh." Rade realized he was still wearing his own suit. He tried to remove the arm assemblies, but didn't get very far. His hands were shaking terribly. He blamed it on low blood sugar.

He sat down on the toilet with the lid down, fumbled for the straw near the inside of his jumpsuit collar, and took a long sip of his meal replacement supplement, finishing the last of it. He felt better, somewhat.

No, scratch that. He felt worse.

I'm not going to throw up.

He swallowed several times in a row.

Not going to throw up.

Rade felt his gorge rise.

I'm going to throw up.

He dropped to his knees on the deck, opened the toilet lid, and vomited.

Throwing up. He hated doing that. It was one of the more awful experiences of the human condition. The burning sensation as the stomach acids assailed the mucous lining of the esophagus, the pain as the peristaltic muscle convulsed in the opposite direction for which it was designed... all in all, entirely unpleasant.

"Rade?" Shaw's voice carried through the door.

"Just some gases..." Rade said.

"It sounded like you were throwing up," Shaw said.

"Nope." Rade flushed the toilet, and forced himself to stand. His head was drenched in sweat. He went to the sink and washed out his mouth. Then he collapsed again, seating himself against the washstand.

He wondered if he had been exposed to a contagion down on the surface after all. Maybe, but doubtful.

He actually felt better now that he had purged himself.

Still, he was extremely groggy. Dead tired.

There was something he wanted to do... what the hell was it? Oh yeah. He had a ship to run.

"TJ, sit-rep?" Rade transmitted.

"We've plugged the breaches in both airlocks," TJ responded. "Temporary measures, of course. We'll have to pick up some new hatches when we return to dry dock. And I've dispatched the repair drones to the hull to fix the damage to the bay doors."

"What about the secondary hangar bay?" Rade asked.

"Haven't even touched it yet," TJ said. "But looks like the Dragonflies are a write-off, and the Raptor. Telemetry drones, too."

"Don't think we can write those off," Rade said. "The insurance doesn't cover alien infestations."

"Too bad," TJ said.

"All right, I'll be on the bridge shortly." Rade disconnected.

He crawled tentatively to his feet. Feeling lightheaded, he stripped off the suit pieces as fast as he was able, and then began removing the thermal undergarment underneath; he struggled with the tight fabric, which was difficult to peel away from the hardpoints protruding from his shoulders, elbows and wrists, so that by the time he freed his torso, stars filled his vision.

Guess I won't be going to the bridge after all.

He opened the head and stumbled toward the bunk, the upper half of the single-piece undergarment hanging from his waist.

Shaw looked up at him. "Rade! Are you all right?"

"Yeah, just feeling a little woozy," Rade said. He lay on the bunk. "Better, now."

"I'm taking you to sickbay," Shaw said.

"After I sleep, maybe," Rade said.

"What were you doing in the head all this time?" Shaw said.

"Staring at the ceiling," Rade said.

"Why?" Shaw said.

Rade sighed, then closed his eyes.

Shaw left, and Rade napped, falling into a light

sleep. He woke up when the door opened again; Shaw was wheeling a Weaver inside.

"I feel fine," Rade said, sitting up. Phosphenes filled his vision. "Maybe not." He lay back down.

The Weaver examined him with those telescoping, spider-like limbs. Rade smiled sadly. He had had enough of spiders for a while.

"Has he caught anything?" Shaw said.

"Contagions, you mean?" the Weaver asked.

"Yes," Shaw said.

"No," the Weaver replied. "He simply has low blood sugar, and is dehydrated." It directed its attention toward Rade. "Extend your hand."

Rade obeyed.

The Weaver pricked him with one of its telescoping fingers. A cold, distant pain. "I am initiating an IV to restore your fluid and blood sugar levels."

Rade looked at Shaw. "You didn't have to do all this for me."

"Actually, I do," Shaw said. "You'd do the same for me."

Rade nodded. "I do feel better now, I admit."

"No thanks to my work," the Weaver said.

Rade held his hand toward Shaw, and she reached out and grabbed it. "No, it's because of her."

"Humph," the Weaver said.

The surgical robot made Rade wait for twenty minutes before withdrawing the IV tube.

A knock came from the hatch. Shaw opened it.

Harlequin stepped inside. "How is he?"

"Jeez, I'm all right," Rade said, sitting up. "Does the whole ship know about this?"

"Yes," Harlequin said. "Shaw told Tahoe about you when she picked up the Weaver from sickbay."

"Tahoe?" Rade said.

"Yes," Harlequin replied. "He is still resting in sickbay, recovering from his wound."

"Ah," Rade said. "How is he?"

"Fine," Harlequin said. "He'll live."

"Well, now that you're here, you might as well wheel the Weaver back to sickbay," Rade said.

"Glad to be of service." Harlequin brought the robot toward the door.

Before it left, the Weaver told Rade to "go easy on yourself for the next few days."

"Once again, thanks for taking care of me," Rade told Shaw when Harlequin and the Weaver were gone.

"Go to sleep," Shaw said. "The *Argonaut* will survive without you for a few hours."

"Not yet," Rade said, forcing himself to his feet. He swayed slightly, feeling suddenly dizzy, but then righted himself. He pulled off the rest of the thermal undergarment.

"Rade..."

"I have a ship to see out of danger," Rade said. He grabbed fatigues from his locker and donned them.

"You can do it from here," Shaw said.

"No, I want to be on the bridge."

"Fine, then let me help you," Shaw said.

"I can walk on my own," Rade said. "But come with me. I need you to astrogate."

Rade still felt a little queasy, but that only told him he couldn't down any more food for a while.

He made it to the bridge, and was relieved when he could finally sit down. He chose his usual location at the head of the Sphincter of Doom, and Shaw assumed her position at the astrogator station.

"Good to have you back, boss," Lui said.

Rade nodded distractedly. "What's the status of the

alien ship?"

"Incredibly, the combined attacks of the mercenaries were able to drive it off," Lui responded. "It has left orbit, and is currently retreating toward the wormhole."

"Never underestimate the power of a big payday on a group of mercenaries," Rade commented.

"Hell, I'd kill bugs all day for free," Bender said. "But don't tell Surus that. Come on, seriously... didn't y'all just love that shit?"

"You're a cruel, sadistic man," Manic said.

"You know you liked it, too," Bender said.

"Well sure, but not as much as you," Manic said. "For you, killing bugs is more than a sport. It's a..."

"Passion," Bender said.

"Yeah," Manic said. "Unfortunately. Some people are passionate about video games, others VR, but you?"

"Killin' mofo bitch bugs!" Bender said. "Especially the babies."

"That's so cruel," Shaw said.

"What?" Bender said. "What's wrong with that? Everything was good until I brought up the babies. Maybe I should have let the little cutesy babies crawl up your leg, huh Shaw? *And let them rip your friggin' chest open!*"

"Well, when you put it that way..." Shaw said. "I'm glad you're passionate about what you do."

Bender smiled widely, revealing his golden grille. "Thank you. We all got to be passionate about something in this life. I'm just glad I've found my passion."

"Okay," Shaw said.

"Lui, what's our heading?" Rade asked.

"I have us headed in the opposite direction of the

alien ship," Lui said. "On course toward the Gate to the next system."

Rade considered that. While he wanted to return to the planet to recover the combat robots and shuttles he had left behind, there was no guarantee all of the aliens were gone, either. The colony would be placed under quarantine once any governmental forces arrived, so the question was, did he return now and once more risk the lives of his Argonauts, or did he expense the costs to his two clients?

He made a snap decision.

He would expense the clients.

"How are repairs proceeding to the hull?" Rade said. "Do we have pressurization restored to hangar bay two?"

"The drones have almost finished putting in a temporary barrier for the lost doors," Lui said. "The current estimate is about two hours."

Rade nodded. "Well, I guess everything is under control then."

"It is," Lui said.

"Okay then," Rade said. "I'm going to be in my office."

Don't you mean your quarters? Shaw texted him. She wore a concerned expression.

No, he replied.

Rade forced himself to stand, then opened the hatch that led to the adjacent room. He wished there was room for a couch in there, but all he had were two chairs and a desk. He locked the door, then lay down, his body lying half underneath the desk.

"Are you all right, boss?" Bax said.

"Fine," Rade said. "Just getting some sleep."

"But you could do that in your stateroom?" Bax said.

"Sure," Rade said. "But then the crew would know. They think I'm working if I'm here."

"And that matters because..."

"Damn it," Rade said. "For an AI you ask a lot of probing questions. Now let me sleep before I dismantle you."

"Good night, boss," Bax said.

"Night," Rade said.

A moment later: "Sweet dreams."

Rade gritted his teeth. "Thanks."

"Don't let the bed bugs bite," Bax said.

"Bax!" Rade said.

"And if they do," Bax continued.

Rade exhaled deeply.

"Hit them with a shoe," Bax finished.

"Thank you," Rade said. "Now give me some quiet!"

Thankfully Bax didn't say anything more.

Rade closed his eyes and got some much needed shut-eye.

RADE AWOKE IN the middle of the designated night, and made his way groggily to the bridge. It was empty, operated solely by Bax.

"Sit-rep?" Rade asked the *Argonaut's* AI.

"The alien ship is still fleeing toward the uncharted wormhole," Bax said. "The *Argonaut* continues toward the opposite Gate. Oh, and the mercenaries are pinging us yet again."

"Again?" Rade asked.

"Yes, they want to know when they're going to get paid."

"Ah," Rade said. "You've routed the messages to Surus?"

"Yes," Bax replied. "I assume she'll pay them shortly."

"I hope so," Rade said. "Because we'll have thirty angry mercenary warships on our tail if she doesn't."

"Actually, the mercenaries are already shadowing us," Bax said.

"Want to make sure we pay, do they?" Rade said.

"Probably."

"Well, I'm heading to my quarters to get some sleep," Rade said.

"But you were sleeping all this time," Bax said.

"I know," Rade said. "I'm still tired."

Rade went to the stateroom he shared with Shaw and lay down on the bed without changing. She moaned softly, and then shifted to wrap her arms around him.

"There's my warrior," she said. "I didn't want to wake you."

"You knew?" Rade asked.

"Of course," Shaw said. "Bax told me."

"Damn AI," Rade muttered.

He kissed her on the cheek and rolled away. Too tired to perform tonight.

When he awoke the next morning, he was famished. He drank the coffee Shaw had prepared for him, and had a biscuit.

"You ate that fast," Shaw said.

"I'm starving," Rade said.

"That's a good sign," Shaw said. "Here, I'll make you some real food if you want?"

"No, that's all right," Rade said. "I don't think I can wait. I'll eat in the wardroom this morning."

Rade got up and headed toward the door.

Shaw stopped him. "You know I hate it when you eat that robot's cooking. I take it as a personal insult."

"Sorry babe," Rade said. "Tell you what, you cook something up, and I'll eat it when I get back here. I'll save room."

"No," Shaw said. "I'm not cooking for you this morning. Go on."

Rade gave her his puppy dog eyes. It didn't work.

"Go," Shaw said.

Rade shrugged, then made his way to the tiny wardroom. Tahoe was already there, eating a big slice of chicken at the wardroom table.

"Hey Rade," Tahoe said.

"Tahoe." Rade took a seat and rested his forearms on the long white cloth. He nodded toward the meat. "What variant of chicken did the chef prepare for breakfast today?"

"Today?" Tahoe said. "Why, we got barbecue chicken for breakfast!"

"Mm-hmm," Rade said.

The robot chef wheeled inside from the galley; it placed a plate and two utensils in front of Rade. The robot inserted a pair of tongs into the pot it carried in a third arm and withdrew a chicken leg, putting it on the plate. It continued dropping more pieces onto the plate until Rade told it to stop. Then it deposited some salad onto a free area of his plate and rolled away.

"Breakfast of champions!" Rade said as he dug in.

When he finished his first piece, he nodded toward Tahoe. "The wounds are all healed?"

"The physical ones," Tahoe said.

"What about the mental?" Rade said.

Tahoe paused. "I had a bit of a scare back there. Thought I wasn't going to make it."

"What do you mean?" Rade asked, pausing. "You

seemed fine."

"After I patched my suit, I returned to the battle, as you know," Tahoe said. "When it was done, and you told me to make my way to sickbay, I listened to you, of course. But I fainted when I walked inside. I awoke a moment later. The Weavers had dragged me onto one of the tables, and stripped off my suit. They were operating on my lungs. Apparently, they had filled with blood. Things got a bit tense, to say the least. I fell into and out of consciousness as they worked. And, well, I pulled through."

Rade shook his head. "Sorry you were so badly injured. Wish I would have known. I would have ordered you to sickbay earlier." He realized if he had been paying more attention to the team's vitals during the combat, he probably would have seen the signs, and done just that.

Losing my touch. But I knew that already.

"I would have probably disobeyed you if you told me to leave early," Tahoe said.

Rade smiled slightly. "You always were the disobedient one. Even when we were on the Teams. I allowed you to get away with so much."

"Oh I know," Tahoe said. "But eventually I learned to listen to you. How could I not? After all the times you saved my life."

"You saved mine an equal number," Rade said.

"And don't you forget it!" Tahoe told him.

Rade received a call from Surus. He accepted, voice only.

"I'm going to be interviewing the Phant in the cargo hold shortly," Surus sent. "I thought you would like to observe."

"Interviewing?" Rade said. "Or interrogating?"

"Both," the Green replied.

"I'll be right there." Rade disconnected, then gulped down the last of his breakfast.

"That's bad for you," Tahoe said. "You should chew your food."

Rade grunted—his mouth was too full to answer—and then hurried from the wardroom.

Near the cargo hold, he burped; unfortunately, some of the food he had just eaten came up with it, lingering in the back of his throat. He quickly swallowed. Barbecue chicken didn't taste as good the second time.

He entered the hold. A sealed glass container resided near the middle of the room. Flat metal disks a meter wide covered the floor and ceiling of that container. A small black box was connected to the topmost disk.

Within stood Governor Ganye, wearing a sour expression.

Surus waited beside the container in her host, Ms. Bounty.

"Welcome," Surus said. "We can now begin."

twenty-seven

Rade approached. He noticed the small microphone and speaker pairs on the inside and outside that would allow him to communicate with the being trapped inside.

"So this is your ally," Ganye told Surus. "The organic who helped lead you to me."

"We found you quite accidentally," Rade said. "Perhaps you shouldn't have staged a coup if you didn't want to attract attention."

"It was necessary," Ganye said. "The Quantus required a demonstration of how weak human vessels were. When the Kenyan corvettes arrived, I destroyed them with Kitale's defense platform, proving to the aliens just how easy humanity was to defeat. The Quantus still wavered, however. They wanted me to share my tech with them before agreeing to my plans. I should have realized it was because their own technology simply wasn't up to par. I had thought, should the mercenaries turn on me, the Quantus would easily handle them. I was wrong. Which would explain why they wavered as long as they did."

"The Quantus?" Rade said.

"That's what he calls the aliens," Surus said. "The Quantus were lurking in the thermal wash behind one of the stars for at least a year in the Nyiki system, communicating with him on Kitale. They have a colony in the adjacent system, beyond the uncharted Slipstream."

"What was the point of all this?" Rade said. "Why did he summon them?"

Ganye was the one who answered. "They agreed in principle to help exterminate humanity, in exchange for technology. Unfortunately, as I said, their tech levels weren't as high as I had hoped. They claimed to be Tech Class IV overall, and while that might have been true for some of their technologies, in reality they were more mid Tech Class III, especially when it came to weapons tech. Then again, perhaps the tech class was merely lost in the translation. Considering I had only a year to learn their language. But I believe they were deceiving me the whole time: they had no intention of ever destroying humanity. They just wanted the tech I promised them."

"Wise aliens," Rade said. "Because once they destroyed humanity, when the rest of your kind arrived you would have destroyed the Quantus, too. Simply to feed on the energy signatures of their dead population in order to create your geronium planets."

"That was the plan, yes," Ganye said.

"So why did the Quantus choose to attack when they did?" Rade said.

"Apparently he told them he was in danger," Surus said. "That hunters had come, and they must attack now, or they would never get the technology he promised. So the alien starship left its position from behind the sun and traveled to the planet."

"Why didn't the *Argonaut* detect its approach?" Rade said.

"It came in from the far side of the planet," Surus

said. "Because of our geosynchronous orbit, our view beyond the closest hemisphere was occluded. We were piggybacking on the compromised Kenyan telemetry drones that were already in orbit to provide us with data. In retrospect, we should have launched our own drones."

"Though the colony probably wouldn't have granted us clearance to do so anyway," Rade said. Launching one's own drones above some inhabited planets without clearance was considered an act of war. Or at the very least, it was punishable by fines, and possibly arrest for the captain involved.

"Continue," Surus told the possessed Artificial.

"The Quantus betrayed me when they arrived," Ganye said. "Instead of protecting me, they hunted me. When the Green showed up, I made the mistake of giving them the plans for a containment device. They used it to capture me, and carried me aboard their vessel. They intended to make me give up my secrets through torture and interrogation."

Rade had to laugh at all that. "So all this time we thought you were colluding with the aliens? Instead they were *hunting* you! Just like us. No wonder they were trying so hard to get you back after we captured you."

"It could be that they wanted to capture me as well," Surus said. "When they realized I was a Phant."

"Oh, they wanted you all right," Ganye said. "I told them about you long before you retrieved me. They sent out hunters specifically looking for you. They wanted to steal your knowledge, too, you see."

"That would explain their behavior," Rade said to Surus. "Remember how they were dismembering the human bodies, as if searching for Phants inside? It's just too bad no one told them Phants can't inhabit humans like that, not without cybernetic interfaces."

"Nor that Phants can incinerate them," Surus said.

"They discovered soon enough, after they turned on me," Ganye said. "Let's just say, I put up a bit of a fight before they captured me. But not as much of a fight as you, it seems."

"It's a good thing the mercenaries turned," Surus told Rade. "We wouldn't be having this conversation otherwise. I finished transferring them the last of the funds I promised, by the way."

Rade nodded. "Good."

"One thing that puzzles me," Surus said, turning her attention to Ganye once more. "If they were hunting me, as you say, why did we never notice any of the Quantus carrying a containment device?"

"They had a few with them, I'm sure," Ganye said. "They simply weren't expecting your Hoplites. You never gave them a chance to deploy the devices."

"They thought our Hoplites were going to be as easy as those weakly armored walkers the city employed," Rade said. "Or the Centurion 6As, did they? They were expecting civic defenses, and instead we threw military-grade units at them."

"Something like that, yes," Ganye said.

"What about that dimensional weapon?" Rade said. "What do you know about it?"

"Only that they tried to use it against me, and failed," Ganye said.

Rade shook his head, turning to Surus. "How do we know this Phant hasn't fed them some Tech Level IV technology already? Is that dimensional weapon something you've ever seen before?"

"No," Surus said. "The weapon is unique to the Quantus."

Rade focused on the governor. "So, speak up. Did

you share technology with the Phants?"

Ganye merely smiled. "Maybe, maybe not. You'll discover in a few decades time."

"You have, haven't you?" Rade said. "When the Quantus return, their armor and weapons will be superior to our own. That, combined with their quantum weapon, will make them unstoppable."

Ganye shrugged. "A little chaos in this quarter of the galaxy will only make things all that easier for the rest of my kind when they arrive seven hundred years from now. Two races locked in intergalactic war... easy pickings."

"What do you think?" Rade asked her. "Did he give them technology?"

"Likely," Surus said. "It's a strategy the Phants use against more advanced races. They will send a Purple in to foment war among neighboring races, so that by the time the Motherships arrive, four or five species are locked in interstellar war, their ranks weakened by centuries of fighting."

"It's a good thing we captured this Purple when we did, isn't it?" Rade said.

"Very good," Surus said.

"There are others of my kind here," Ganye said. "Humanity will fall, yet."

"Where?" Surus asked.

"I don't know they're locations in this realm," Ganye said. "We communicate in the intra-dimension."

"Did Ganye tell you why there was no evidence of the Purple on the nape of his neck when we first arrived?" Rade asked Surus.

"He did," Surus said. "Apparently, the Phant had left the host at the time, not wanting to risk capture."

"So the Artificial lied then," Rade said. "And was

in cahoots with the Phant all along."

"Not necessarily," Surus said. "The Phant may have promised to leave Ganye alone if the governor arrested our party."

"There are many ways to coerce AIs," Ganye said with a grin.

"So you're saying he was cooperating with you against his wishes?" Rade asked.

Ganye pursed his lips. "I suppose I do not need to incriminate the Artificial. It has served me well as a vessel. In truth, I have been unable to reprogram it. If I were a Black, perhaps I would have had greater success. I did promise Ganye his freedom if he arrested you, but I betrayed him of course, possessing him the moment you were carried from his office. Use that knowledge as you see fit."

Surus turned toward Rade. "Is there anything else you wish to ask? Or may I extract the Purple?"

"I'm done," Rade said, stepping back.

"The Quantus will be back sooner than you think," Ganye said. "With more ships. I've told them there are others of my kind here, with more secrets. They want it all."

"They'll never find you," Rade said.

"Not me, perhaps." Ganye nodded toward Surus. "But her."

"The governments of humanity won't take kindly to an incursion by these Quantus," Rade said. "They'll never get her."

"We'll see," Ganye said.

"We will, but you won't." Rade glanced at Surus. "Do it."

Ganye floated into the air and began revolving in place. A rising hum filled the air as he rotated faster and faster, becoming a blur. Purple liquid began to flow upward, coalescing into a ball above the Artificial.

When all the liquid was drawn from the body, the purple sphere moved upward into the black box connected to the ceiling. The container shut with a thud of finality.

A DAY FROM the exit Gate, seven United Systems warships emerged. Apparently, the distress signal Bax had sent when the alien vessel arrived had been taken quite seriously.

Rade exchanged several back and forth messages with the admiral, explaining the situation. He also dispatched his entire video archive of the battle. In one of the messages, the admiral asked if Rade had captured any of the aliens, or their technology. Rade had said yes—he had half a dozen spider corpses sitting in deep freeze in the hold, remnants from the last battle. The admiral responded by saying he would dispatch a shuttle to pick up the bodies. He wanted the Phant, too.

"Unfortunately, my present employer won't allow me to give up the Phant," Rade replied. "We intend to hurl it into a star, trapping it for all eternity. But you are welcome to the spider corpses."

The admiral took some time to reply. Apparently he decided that he didn't really want a rogue Phant aboard his ship, nor did he want to anger a Green, because he agreed to take only the Quantus bodies.

Rade added a further stipulation at that point: the United Systems had to pay them twenty thousand digicoins per body.

The admiral accepted without bartering, and wired

the requested amount to Rade's account. He sent one final message.

"Thank you for catching that Phant," the admiral said. "I always thought our governments should be doing more to deal with the threat they pose. I admit, I had been curious as to the fate of the Green that had remained in our space. It's good to see she still fights for us. Though I admit to mixed feelings. The Phants: our greatest enemies, and yet some of them are our friends, or at least claim to be. In any case, thank you. We'll take it from here."

The shuttle arrived to retrieve the alien corpses. Rade had ordered hangar bay two cleared of debris earlier, so there was room for the craft to dock. When it landed, Centurions in hazmat suits entered, wordlessly retrieved the cargo crates, and departed.

Rade had kept the original alien body he had captured from the Quantus mothership of course: he wasn't going to give up all the fruits of his labors.

The alien craft passed through the far Slipstream twelve hours later. Though Ganye said they were Tech Class III overall, the Quantus obviously had the ability to traverse wormholes without Gates, so that put them ahead of the humans in that regard.

The United Systems fleet proceeded on a direct course toward the uncharted wormhole, obviously intending to guard the Slipstream in the event the aliens should ever return. Likely a Builder would soon join the fleet, and they would create a Gate to the neighboring system, perhaps to bring the battle to the enemy. The United Systems was known for such behavior—any aliens that ever dared trespass human space were usually met with a terrible counterattack on their territories, as the United Systems senior command was a big proponent of "preemptive" strikes.

A few days after the *Argonaut* passed through the Gate into the adjacent system, Rade and Tahoe went to the cargo bay to visit Surus. She had set up another tank beside the Phant containment device. In it resided the alien body Rade had kept.

"So?" Rade asked her. "What news? Are you able to copy their quantum technology?"

"No," Surus said. "At least, not readily. The ability seems graven into the DNA. It will take several years, and hundreds of test subjects, to design a retrovirus we can inject into someone in an attempt to bestow the ability."

"So what you're saying is you can't distill it down into a device we can wear?" Rade pressed.

"That's what I'm saying, yes," Surus replied.

"Too bad."

"Do you plan to hang onto it?" Tahoe asked Rade. "The body?"

"Why not?" Rade said. "We can keep it as a war trophy. Maybe someday I'll hang it over my fireplace."

"Ha!" Tahoe said.

"Besides, it's valuable," Rade said. "Alien bodies go for a small fortune on the black market."

"We're going to have to hide it, you know," Tahoe said. "As we get deeper into United Systems space, the customs officials will start using their more invasive scans. And they liberally employ boarding parties, in case you've forgotten."

"I haven't," Rade said. "But that's why we have the hidden alcoves." Those were a series of compartments in the passageway near the bridge, concealed underneath panels in the deck.

"You'll have to cut the body into smaller parts to fit," Tahoe said.

Rade shrugged. "I'm fine with that. Maybe I'll let Bender do it."

The *Argonaut* proceeded to the closest station in the next system so that the crew could get some much deserved liberty time. Rade gave them all bonuses for the job, and set them loose on the station.

Rade dropped off Kato and Batindo at the station, too, where they met with a Kenyan delegation.

"Thank you for what you have done," Batindo said. "I promise to pay in full by tonight, or tomorrow at the earliest. As soon as I finish securing the funds from my government."

Kato gripped Rade by the hand. "Thank you for saving my life. I just wish..."

"You have to go on living," Rade said. "Like I told you before. Otherwise she died for nothing."

Kato nodded. "Everyone died back there. So many good people. A whole colony. For what? To satisfy an alien species' craving for technology? Seems like a terrible waste."

"Greed has seen the destruction of many empires," Rade said. "Sometimes from the outside in, other times the inside out. Move on, Kato. Do what you can to get over the loss, but *move on.*"

Kato gave him a hug, then departed.

Rade also set free the Artificial Ganye, as promised, though perhaps not in quite the manner the former governor had hoped: Rade delivered him into the custody of Batindo, for transference to the Kenyan government. He would be interrogated, no doubt, and likely decommissioned. It was a fitting punishment for abetting a Phant, however, and nearly seeing Rade's Argonauts killed.

Rade joined his crew in the station's gym for a quick workout. It was a good change from the cramped setup aboard the *Argonaut*.

"Ah, nothing like a modern, high-tech, fully equipped gym to get the blood flowing," Tahoe said.

"Hey, check out that jacked fool," Bender said, in reference to a giant of man who calmly ambled by. He looked like a professional wrestler. "His bitch tits look like Manic's."

"I don't have bitch tits," Manic said flatly.

"Dude," Bender said. "Those certainly aren't pecs you're carrying."

Bender grabbed a barbell weighted down with four plates per side and began shrugging the bar upward, keeping his arms straight.

"Hey Bender," Manic said in a tone that hinted he was up to no good.

Bender didn't answer, as he was in the middle of his set.

"Bender," Manic pressed.

"*What!*" Bender said.

"That's right, work those traps," Manic said. "Trapezius masturbation!"

Bender scowled angrily. He kept doing reps, shrugging repeatedly, and stared at himself in the mirror. But then his features softened and he cracked up. Laughing, he released the barbell a meter from the floor, and it landed with a loud crash, earning a stern rebuke from the robot on duty, which wheeled over to tell him not to drop the weights.

The giant wrestler was working out nearby, and he gave Bender a dirty look; Rade suspected Bender would be having a word with the man later—a talk involving thrown fists.

Rade finished his workout and bid the crew farewell, telling them to enjoy their extended liberty. "And Bender, try not to hurt that wrestler too badly, please?"

"I'll only break a few of his smaller bones, I promise," Bender replied.

Shortly thereafter, Rade, Shaw and Surus hired a small charter carrier and departed the station. The *Argonaut* remained behind in dry dock for repairs.

The charter proceeded toward the system's sun. A day into the journey, Rade heard the characteristic ding notifying him of new money in his account. He accessed the bank interface and was surprised to find a two hundred K deposit. A note attached to the amount thanked Rade for saving Kato. It was digitally signed by the Kenyan king. That money, combined with the digicoins Rade had earned by selling the alien corpses to the United Systems fleet, would be enough to replace the lost Dragonflies, telemetry drones, and Raptor, plus replenish the *Argonaut's* supply of Hellfires.

When the charter was four million kilometers away from the sun, Surus placed the black box containing the Phant into one of the lifepods, and launched it toward the star.

Half a day later Rade and Shaw tapped into the charter's external cameras to watch the lifepod plunge into the star.

Rade felt Shaw's hand grip his.

"Do you think that Phant has started another Alien War?" Shaw asked.

"Probably," Rade said. "But the good news is, I won't have to fight it."

"But someone will," Shaw said.

Rade considered that. "The next generation."

"Yes." Shaw released his hand, then averted her gaze, touching her belly.

"Why did you do that?" Rade asked her. "Why did

you place your fingers on your belly when I mentioned the next generation?"

"I—" She dropped her hand, slouching in defeat.

And then Rade knew.

"You're pregnant," Rade said.

She nodded slowly, finally meeting his gaze. "I stopped taking the contraceptives a few months ago. I'm sorry. I'm... a selfish bitch. You're angry, aren't you? You hate me now."

He stared at her for a few moments, stunned.

"You hate me," Shaw repeated.

Rade blinked, then forced a smile. "Hate you? Angry? No to both. I'm not angry. How could I be angry? We need to create life for once, to make up for all the lives we've taken. I'm just, well... surprised, but mostly afraid. I still have all the reservations I told you before, regarding raising a child in this sort of environment. I just wish you would have talked to me about it first."

"I'm sorry," Shaw said. "I knew you'd say no. You always do. But sometimes, you don't know what's best for you."

Rade frowned. "And you do?"

"I just wanted you to have something else to live for," Shaw told him. "Because I'm not enough, apparently."

"You *are* enough," Rade said. "I don't need some kid to give me a reason to live."

"But down there, you kept throwing yourself into the spiders," Shaw said. "Ahead of the Argonauts. Not staying back, like you're supposed to do. Risking your life for all of us."

"Shaw, it was the heat of the moment," Rade said. "I was doing what I could to survive. We all were. And yes, I may have occasionally taken the point position, but it wasn't because I wanted to throw away my life. You have to know that. You of all people should know how strong my desire to live is. I never give up. Never."

She had turned away from him entirely, and her head was down. "If you want to leave me for betraying you like this, I'll understand. I can raise the next generation on my own. I'm just proud, so proud, to have you as the father, no matter what you decide."

"You're not hearing me." Rade grabbed her by the shoulders and spun her to face him. He forced her chin upward with one hand so that she met his eyes. "Don't talk like that. I'm never leaving you. You're my astrogator in this life."

She smiled sadly. "Okay."

"There's another reason I'm afraid," Rade said. "And that's... I'm not sure I'll be a good father."

"Oh, my warrior, you'll be the best father," Shaw said. Her eyes were moist. "I know you will." She hugged him tightly.

"We'll find a way to make this work," Rade said, squeezing her back. "I don't know how, but we'll find a way. A kid. I'm a father. Tahoe will be tickled silly when he finds out."

"It isn't a kid," Shaw said.

Startled, Rade pulled away. "What do you mean? It's not an alien-human hybrid or something, is it?"

Shaw had to laugh at that. "No."

"Well then what are you talking about?" Rade said.

"It's not *a* kid," Shaw said. "I carry twins."

Thank you for reading.

Acknowledgments

T HANK YOU to my knowledgeable beta readers and advanced reviewers who helped smooth out the rough edges of the prerelease manuscript: Nicole P., Lisa A. G., Gregg C., Jeff K., Mark C., Jeremy G., Doug B., Jenny O., Amy B., Bryan O., Lezza M., Gene A., Larry J., Allen M., Gary F., Eric, Robine, Noel, Anton, Spencer, Norman, Trudi, Corey, Erol, Terje, David, Charles, Walter, Lisa, Ramon, Chris, Scott, Michael, Chris, Bob, Jim, Maureen, Zane, Chuck, Shayne, Anna, Dave, Roger, Nick, Gerry, Charles, Annie, Patrick, Mike, Jeff, Lisa, Jason, Bryant, Janna, Tom, Jerry, Chris, Jim, Brandon, Kathy, Norm, Jonathan, Derek, Shawn, Judi, Eric, Rick, Bryan, Barry, Sherman, Jim, Bob, Ralph, Darren, Michael, Chris, Michael, Julie, Glenn, Rickie, Rhonda, Neil, Claude, Ski, Joe, Paul, Larry, John, Norma, Jeff, David, Brennan, Phyllis, Robert, Darren, Daniel, Montzalee, Robert, Dave, Diane, Peter, Skip, Louise, Dave, Brent, Erin, Paul, Jeremy, Dan, Garland, Sharon, Dave, Pat, Nathan, Max, Martin, Greg, David, Myles, Nancy, Ed, David, Karen, Becky, Jacob, Ben, Don, Carl, Gene, Bob, Luke, Teri, Gerald, Lee, Rich, Ken, Daniel, Chris, Al, Andy, Tim, Robert, Fred, David, Mitch, Don, Tony, Dian, Tony, John, Sandy, James, David, Pat, Jean, Bryan, William, Roy, Dave, Vincent, Tim, Richard, Kevin, George, Andrew, John, Richard, Robin, Sue, Mark, Jerry, Rodger, Rob, Byron, Ty,

Mike, Gerry, Steve, Benjamin, Anna, Keith, Jeff, Josh, Herb, Bev, Simon, John, David, Greg, Larry, Timothy, Tony, Ian, Niraj, Maureen, Jim, Len, Bryan, Todd, Maria, Angela, Gerhard, Renee, Pete, Hemantkumar, Tim, Joseph, Will, David, Suzanne, Steve, Derek, Valerie, Laurence, James, Andy, Mark, Tarzy, Christina, Rick, Mike, Paula, Tim, Jim, Gal, Anthony, Ron, Dietrich, Mindy, Ben, Steve, Paddy & Penny, Troy, Marti, Herb, Jim, David, Alan, Leslie, Chuck, Dan, Perry, Chris, Rich, Rod, Trevor, Rick, Michael, Tim, Mark, Alex, John, William, Doug, Tony, David, Sam, Derek, John, Jay, Tom, Bryant, Larry, Anjanette, Gary, Travis, Jennifer, Henry, Drew, Michelle, Bob, Gregg, Billy, Jack, Lance, Sandra, Libby, Jonathan, Karl, Bruce, Clay, Gary, Sarge, Andrew, Deborah, Steve, and Curtis.

Without you all, this novel would have typos, continuity errors, and excessive lapses in realism. Thank you for helping me make this the best military science fiction novel it could possibly be, and thank you for leaving the early reviews that help new readers find my books.

And of course I'd be remiss if I didn't thank my mother, father, and brothers, whose untiring wisdom and thought-provoking insights have always guided me through the untamed warrens of life.

— Isaac Hooke

www.isaachooke.com

Made in the USA
San Bernardino, CA
30 November 2017